Maddox g  opened his mo[u]

macho and sexist, several rounds of automatic gunfire hit the front of the building, burning through the flimsy wood like a knife through butter. The mirror behind the bar shattered under the barrage, showering her and Tweeter with glass.

She shoved out of Tweeter's arms then pulled him to the floor. Satisfied he hadn't been hit, she belly-crawled from behind the bar, ignoring everything but the need to get to the back room to retrieve the H&Ks she'd left there along with her backpack and all the ammo.

"Keely," Tweeter yelled, his hand just slipping off her booted foot.

"I've got her," Maddox shouted. "Start laying down some fire out the front and block the fucking door!"

Continuing her fast crawl, she threw a frowning glance over her shoulder. "Has my mom met you?" He shook his head, confusion evident in his eyes. "Don't ever use the f-bomb around her. She'll make you pay."

Maddox snorted. Same sound she'd heard earlier. He'd been—still was—laughing at her. *Ass.*

"You think that's funny? Just wait until you owe her a small fortune," Keely muttered.

He put a large hand on her hips, shoving gently. "Move it. What have you got in the back room? An arsenal?"

"How'd you guess?" She ignored his sarcastic tone and threw a glare over her shoulder. "Move the hand. Tweetie is looking—and he won't like it."

REVIEWS FOR *EYE OF THE STORM*

Recommended Read!

"*Eye of the Storm* will hold you captivated with its passion, suspense, and humor, and leave you wanting the next book immediately. I know it did me. A keeper that begs to be reread often…"

—*Jo at A Joyfully Reviewed*

5 Diamonds

"Prepare yourself for one fantastic read."

—*Shannon at Got Erotic Romance.*

5 Nymphs

"*Eye of the Storm* is the first in the *Security Specialist International* series and a fantastic action packed suspense that had me wanting to race to the end."

—*Minx at Literary Nymphs Reviews Only*

"I can't wait to read the next book in this series!"

—*Lisa at The Romance Studio*

★★★★ ½

—*Just Erotic Romance*

"With memorable moments of humor and a mystery to solve, this was an engrossing read."

—*Chris at Night Owl Reviews*

EYE OF THE STORM

A SECURITY SPECIALISTS INTERNATIONAL BOOK

MONETTE MICHAELS

Eye of the Storm
A Security Specialists International Book
Monette Michaels

ISBN-13: 978-1467978750
ISBN-10: 1467978752

E-Book, Published by Liquid Silver Books, imprint of Atlantic Bridge Publishing, 2010.

Editor: Terri Schaefer
Cover Artist: April Martinez

This is a work of fiction. The characters, incidents and dialogues in this book are of the author's imagination and are not to be construed as real. Any resemblance to actual events or persons, living or dead, is completely coincidental.

ACKNOWLEDGEMENTS

To Sherry, the best crit partner a girl could have.

To Terri, my editor. What can I say? You rock.

And, last, but not least, to April,
your cover art is the best.

CHAPTER ONE

Iguazu River, Argentina, the Triple Frontier

Keely Walsh stopped to rest. Even with the shade from the rain forest canopy, the heat was oppressive. Tipping back her broad-brimmed hat, she wiped the sweat out of her eyes, then took a deep drink of water from the canteen she carried. So far, according to her portable GPS, she'd traveled two klicks from her landing site. If her coordinates were correct, and they always were, she should see the village in less than another kilometer. Right now all she could see were trees, low-growing foliage, and more trees.

After she'd landed the chopper in a small, elevated clearing, she'd followed a faint path leading down and away from the landing site. She surmised the path had been cleared a day or so ago, then just as quickly overgrown. It led in the general direction of the village. She'd seen marijuana growing in the clearing, so it made sense the locals would need a path to get to their cash crop.

Shrugging her backpack off, she let it slip to the ground. She knelt and pulled out the white cotton shirt she'd worn on the plane, then put it on over her tank top. It was way too hot and humid for any covering, but she couldn't have her brother go nuts if he saw the bruises on her shoulders and upper chest. Time enough for explanations later, after they were safe in the hotel suite she'd booked in the Iguazu National Park before securing transportation and her weapons. She sighed, imagining how good the air conditioning would feel after this steam-bath hike. The hotel had a pool and a pool bar. She could almost taste a large Pepsi with ice as she dangled her legs in the cool water.

God, she hated heat, humidity, insects and snakes, all of which jungles had in abundance. Only for her favorite brother, Stuart "Tweeter" Walsh, would she do this—plus there had been no one else. Her father, Marine Corps Colonel Kennard Walsh, was on a training mission. The call to her other four brothers had not produced the instant response needed. The twins, Loren and Paul, were on a SEAL mission and the other two, Devin and Andy, were Marines searching Afghanistan's caves for terrorists. By the time their emergency leave was approved, Tweeter would be dead. And she couldn't trust anyone else but her mother Molly—and her Dad would kill her if she involved her mama in this mess.

She was it—the only person who could warn her brother about the trap. She couldn't stay safely in Massachusetts while Tweeter was in danger. He'd protected her over the years, and she could do no less for him.

She let the shirt tails hang over her baggy khakis. She slid the knife she'd bought from a wizened little man named Bazon in Puerto Iguazu into its sheath, then clipped it and the holster holding the Bren Ten she'd purchased onto the belt at the small of her back. Nothing like a Bren to make your point. She'd taken the finding of the rare gun as a sign that her mission would be a success. There'd only been fifteen hundred made and the odds were astronomical against her finding the gun she was most comfortable handling. Her dad had taught her to shoot with a Bren. It was highly accurate and had hitting power. She checked the magazine and found it fully loaded with all ten .45 caliber rounds. She locked the hammer back to the "condition one" setting; a flick of the safety and she would be good to go for single shot or automatic fire.

Satisfied she was as ready as she could be, she headed once more in the direction of the village where Tweeter, along with his Security Specialist International team, were allegedly meeting an informant.

SSI was a security firm specializing in international troubleshooting for private corporations and governments who would rather not use their own intelligence personnel. Ren and Trey Maddox, both ex-special forces, had established their headquarters and training facility in Sanctuary, Idaho, a SSI-owned town at the edge of the Nez Perce National Forest. SSI's current mission had been arranged through the U.S. Department of Defense and the National Clandestine Service or NCS; the classified report she'd come across while working on a project for the government had outlined the mission as an information-gathering on a reputed al Qaeda organization operating out of the Argentinian section of the Triple Frontier.

What it really was? A specially designed trap for Ren Maddox and anyone who accompanied him.

If the trap hadn't been sprung by the time she

made it to the meeting place, they'd hoof it out and head for the helicopter she'd also rented from Bazon. In the Triple Frontier, it was easy to find weapons and drugs—and to rent military-equipped helicopters. She hadn't asked the old man where he'd gotten the Kamov KA-60, kitted out with belly guns and air-to-ground missiles. She never looked gift battle-ready helicopters in the mouth.

Bazon even had ordnance for the belly guns. For double the rental price, she'd had him load the ordnance, checking his work as he did it. She might not be able to lift the ammunition, but she knew how it should be loaded.

She'd been surprised when the man hadn't tried to gyp her. When she'd asked him about it, he'd given her a mostly toothless smile and said, "For you, *pequena muchacha de oro*, it is a pleasure." Then Bazon had winked at her, and his flirtatious manner had her choking back laughter. The Argentinian had to be old enough to be her grandfather.

It probably hadn't hurt that she'd paid him five thousand USD in traveler's checks. Say what you want about the economy and international relations, the almighty dollar was still the currency of choice in the world's hellholes.

Now, if the trap had been sprung—well, she'd cross that bridge when she got to it.

To this point, her trek had been merely hot and sweaty, but not dangerous. She'd seen no one other than monkeys, toucans, butterflies and other inhabitants of this particular subtropical rainforest. Nothing, not even the local four-legged predators, had bothered her. She was more worried about chancing across the two-legged variety before she reached the village. As her father had drilled into her and the boys, "always expect perimeter guards when approaching a danger zone". Since her father had survived some of the hairiest conflicts on the planet and taught thousands of other Marines to pull through in some of the worst places in the world, he knew of what he spoke.

Keely's gaze now moved continuously, watching for anything out of place. She attempted to differentiate the background noises, hoping she'd sense a change when peril approached. The jungle fauna were nature's version of an early-warning system.

When danger did appear, it was on the path. Or, more explicitly, lying across it. She stopped, her steel-toed hiking boots just inches away from a trip wire strung across the path. Was the trap for those stupid enough to steal the villagers' marijuana crop? Or, had it been placed there more recently by the mercs hired to take out the SSI team?

She knelt and examined the wire. She snorted. It went nowhere and was attached to nothing. A red herring. Somewhere around here was the real trap.

She lifted her head and swept the area around the path and a few feet ahead. Ahh, there it was. A disturbed area, no new vegetation had grown, so the digging was recent. After the wary traveler stepped over the more obvious wire, the poor unsuspecting sap would then step onto a pressure plate and die before he or she even finished congratulating themselves on a narrow escape.

Keely couldn't leave the trap for some hapless villager or for her and the guys to stumble over on the return trip to the chopper. Looking around, she spied a pile of rocks. Stepping off the path, she carefully picked her way toward the outcropping, which looked to be the remnants of a small building. She edged around the rubble, picked up a rock, then lobbed it with an underhanded toss. It hit the plate just as she ducked for cover. The explosion was loud, startling birds and other animals into heading for shelter higher in the rain forest canopy. The sound of detritus hitting the broken-down hovel told her it had been a fragmentation mine.

Crouching back under the cover of some low-growing palms, she waited. After the explosion, the sound of silence was pregnant with tension. It was as if the animals of the forest remained silent just as she did, waiting to see who would respond to the mine's destruction.

She just hoped whoever investigated would look, see no body parts, and leave. She wasn't up for killing anyone else this trip just to get to the village. She could kill if she had to—and had recently done so in self-defense—but it had cost her a piece of her soul. Her stomach clenched, acid roiling at the memory. Taking deep breaths, she conquered her nausea, then shoved the images of two men with broken necks, lying in a dirty warehouse in Boston, to a dark corner of her mind.

At the start of this hastily thrown-together trip to South America, she'd thought she could get to the SSI team and let them handle any dirty work. Arming herself was one thing, using her weapons was entirely another. She shook her head in disgust at her naïveté. Obviously, she hadn't thought far enough in advance. The sound of pounding feet on the hard, red dirt prevented her from replaying the past. It was the present that counted, the mission to save her brother and his friends.

She peeked through the palm fronds and noted that the two approaching men didn't use the marked path at all. She'd follow their example when she headed out once again, not wanting to hit any other mines or hidden traps.

Breathing shallowly and slowly, she calmed her rapid heart rate enough so the sound of it pounding in her ears would subside. She needed to hear what the men said.

The two walked around the small crater created by the explosion. One even scratched his head in a "what the fuck happened" gesture. She choked back a laugh. They might look confused, but she wouldn't count on it. Even clueless people could shoot to kill.

Her Spanish was more than good enough to follow their conversation and what they said was revealing. They were some of the mercs hired by Reyo Trujo to kill the SSI team. And from what they said, the trap had *not* been sprung—they were waiting on someone. Possibly Trujo?

If her intel proved accurate, there was a team of at least twenty mercs in this jungle version of Purgatory. If she eliminated these two, then there would only be eighteen or so.

Should she take these two out? And if she did, how

soon would they be missed? Did they check in face-to-face? Over communication devices like the military used? She looked between the palm fronds and saw nothing in their ears or on their vests. Maybe they used walkie-talkies? She didn't see anything like those, either. Face-to-face, then. Odds were in her favor that by the time their buddies missed them, she'd have the guys heading out. Disabling these two would improve the odds later if there were a firefight.

Shooting them was out of the question. First, because it would be cold-blooded murder and second, there would be too much noise. The sound of gunfire carried miles at this altitude.

Could she overpower them and tie them up? She assessed the two men. On the plus side, they were short and wiry. On the negative side, they were mercs and probably had some military training.

She laughed silently. She also had military training. Growing up, she'd survived fights with five older brothers and all their friends. Then there were the attacks by predatory men and other assorted bad guys her brothers knew nothing about. The odds were better than good she could come out on top. But still, it would be better to take them one at a time.

And if she had to kill in self-defense, she always had

her knife—the silent option.

She unbuttoned the shirt she'd just put on and stuffed it into her pack. Her tank top displayed a healthy amount of cleavage and some really nasty bruises and teeth marks. Maybe she could lure them over with sex and sympathy? She snorted. It was much more likely they'd see her as an easy victim with whom to wile away their afternoon. Either way, she was bait for the trap.

She let out a low moan and remained behind the pile of rubble. They could come to her.

"¿Quién está allí?" one of the men called out. Slowly, he headed in her general direction. She moaned again and he corrected his trajectory. He gestured to the other man to stay and guard.

"That's good, boys," she muttered, "investigate one at a time."

The man left behind nodded to his friend, his gaze quartering the area, maybe looking for a trap. She grinned. He was looking in all the wrong places.

His buddy walked toward her, also keeping an eye out.

She had to give them credit—they were cautious—but it wouldn't help them.

When the man spotted her, he froze in his tracks and let his gun's barrel drop toward the ground. *Big mistake, amigo.* A wide, leering smile broke out on his swarthy face. Bastard probably thought he'd died and gone to nookie heaven. Men—and Latino men especially—loved her pale cream-colored skin, her strawberry blonde curly hair, the full breasts on her petite frame. Suckers never looked to see it was all window dressing. Never noticed the muscles under all the female attributes or the calculating and sometimes lethal look in her eye.

The man opened his mouth to say something—to her or his friend—she didn't know or care. Smiling as if she were happy to see him, she moved toward him quickly, thrusting the heel of her hand up his nose, breaking it. He moaned and tried to turn away. Before he could attempt to shout to his friend or even defend himself, she chopped his windpipe sharply with the side of her hand and then grabbed his shoulders to steady him for a knee to his balls. As he bent over, bleeding, choking and gasping, she steadied him once more and thrust her knee forcefully into his diaphragm twice, effectively cutting off his ability to gain enough breath to make any loud noises for some time. Dirty fighting, but effective—and it all had taken less than fifteen seconds.

He fell to the ground like a stone, clutching his

manhood and struggling to breathe. She pulled a set of flex-cuffs from her pocket, secured his hands behind his back and used his belt to bind his ankles. Pulling his shirt from his trousers, she used her knife and cut off a strip to gag him. He could breathe through his nose—just—so he wasn't in any danger of suffocating any time soon.

Keely then moved back under cover and waited for his friend to come find him. If the men had any communication devices, now would be the time for the other guy to use one. He didn't. Instead he called out, *"Pablo, ¿qué se está encendiendo?"* Too bad Pablo couldn't tell him what was going on.

Checking the area around him once more, Pablo's buddy headed her way. His finger was on the trigger of the semi-automatic weapon. Not good. She'd have to disable him before he could shoot. She pulled her knife and waited to take her best throw. If she failed, she'd resort to her handgun.

When the mercenary was ten feet away, she rose and threw the knife, hitting him in the arm. The knife stuck in his arm, just above his elbow. His finger slipped from the trigger as he grabbed to pull the knife out. She made her move and took him down just as she had Pablo. While he gasped for breath, she restrained him in the same manner as she had his friend. She retrieved her blade from his arm and cut his shirt for a compression bandage and a gag, then wiped the knife off on some grass and sheathed it.

She studied the two men who flopped on the ground like beached whales. She was in no immediate danger from them, but it was always possible if left apart that one might be flexible enough to escape the restraints and get away to warn the other mercs. She couldn't chance it.

Taking a page out of her father's "subduing the enemy" lecture, she tugged the two men closer together. God, they were heavier than they looked. She wiped the sweat dripping down her face with the hem of her tank top exposing her stomach and the lower curves of her breasts. Pablo stilled his frantic movements, his leering gaze fixed on her exposed skin.

"Pervert," she muttered. She pulled out her last set of flex-cuffs and secured the men to each other, back-to-back by their bound hands. Both men made noises around their gags. She was pretty sure her ancestors and her were receiving a tongue-lashing in Spanish. She patted each of them on the head. "Save your breath, *amigos.* You might just live long enough for someone to rescue you."

She retrieved her pack, pulled out some duct tape and wrapped their lower legs together and secured the cloth gags by covering them with the multi-purpose tape. They weren't going anywhere. They were close enough to the main path some villager would see them sooner or later and let them go. She wasn't going to worry about it. Old Pablo would have raped her in an instant, then turned her over to his friend. She'd seen it in his cold black eyes.

Stripping them of their extra ammunition, she put it in her backpack. After shrugging her shirt back on, she picked up her pack and put it on, shouldered one of the downed men's weapons and kept the other in her hand, ready to fire. Tweeter and the guys might need the extra weapons and ammunition if they had to fight their way back to the chopper.

Checking out the submachine guns, she said, "Hmm, H&K MP5. Very nice, boys. And clean. My dad always did say 'Keely, take care of your weapon and it will take care of you.' Too bad you had to run across me on one of my mean days."

The men glared at her, making noises in the backs of their throat. She turned away from them and resumed her trek to the village, paralleling the path but staying off it. Looking back, she made sure the men couldn't be seen too easily from the path. They couldn't. The undergrowth was too thick.

Using more caution than before, she stealthily approached the village. The meeting the SSI team was to attend was to be held at the local version of a cantina.

She stopped on the outskirts of the village, although calling it a village was generous. There were three small palapas, typical rain forest huts woven out of palm leaves, and one larger, sturdier building, the bottom half of which was constructed of local wood with a roof of tightly woven leaves.

If she were a betting woman, she'd put her money on the larger building being the bar. It had a generator running outside of it, meaning there could be cold beverages inside. The thought of anything cold and wet right now sounded orgasmic. She swiped a sweaty curl that had escaped her hat out of her eyes.

Sidling around the edge of the village, still under the cover of the forest, she moved until she was immediately behind the cantina. She'd seen no one. No villagers. No mercs. That worried her. Had those two bozos been wrong? Had the trap been sprung while the two had a siesta? Where were the sentries? Or were the bad guys all holed up somewhere, waiting on *el jefe*?

She crossed a small clearing and crept toward a hole

serving as a window on the side of the building. The noise of the nearby generator would cover any sounds she might make. Letting out a breath, she peeked over the sill of the opening.

Her shoulders sunk in relief. Tweeter was in there. Alive. Safe—for now.

She also spotted Renfrew Maddox. A frisson of awareness shot down her spine at seeing him in the flesh. He was huge, even sitting down. His face was all angles, his jaw stubbled with a day or more of growth. His dark hair was longer than it had been in the military photo she'd seen in the DoD file she'd downloaded. His eyes were grey-blue like those of an Arctic wolf—and like the wolf he looked to be a predator. He reminded her of the men in her family—all male, all macho—and all deadly grace.

The other SSI operative was the Russian, no, he was Ukrainian, Vanko Petriv. His icy blond good looks and slightly smaller stature when compared to Maddox and her brother was deceptive—and she imagined a lot of his opponents had underestimated him to their detriment. The file she had on him described his training as an assassin. He'd often gone under deep cover for Interpol to ferret out Russian *mafiya* terrorizing European enterprises.

She scanned the room again to see who else was present. That was all of them—other than the bartender.

God, Maddox had balls. She shook her head. That or he was stump-stupid, only bringing three men to an intel meeting supposedly on al Qaeda operations in the Triple Frontier. But Maddox had been a highly decorated SEAL and Petriv had his lethal reputation through Interpol. Plus, her brother wasn't exactly helpless either. While he had a doctorate and never served in the military, he had the advantage of being trained by their dad and beat on by four older brothers. She smiled. She called Tweeter an alpha-geek, a nerd with muscles. So, maybe it only took three SSI operatives to deal with a meet. And, of course, they hadn't known their intel gathering mission was a death trap designed specifically for Maddox.

Ghosting along the side of the building toward the back, she stopped before inching around the corner. Good thing, too. An armed man came out of the dense rain forest foliage, striding toward the rear entrance of the bar in an "I'm-the-king-of-the-jungle" manner.

He must have seen her movement because he quickly headed her way. When he saw her fully, his jaw dropped open. He recovered instantly. This guy was more by-the-book, not as lecherous or easily distracted by a woman as Pablo. He raised his weapon and opened his mouth to yell at or challenge her. His demeanor was fierce, mean—and deadly. He was twice her size. He looked buff and strong. No time to take him out hand-to-hand, if she even could.

Her assessment of the situation had taken less than two seconds. In even less time, she pulled her knife and in one fluid movement, threw it. She caught him in the throat, cutting off anything he might have yelled. She hurried to meet him as he stumbled around. The man didn't know it yet but he was dead. Still, he grabbed at the knife with both hands, his gun falling to the ground. His expression was shocked as he stared at her. He grew weak quickly. His mouth opened and closed like a guppy seeking air. His eyes dimmed as life drained out of him.

Pushing aside pity, she stiff-armed him with her left arm, then pulled the knife from his throat with her right hand. Blood gushed from the wound, but it was not arterial. He would take a while to die and suffer horrific pain. She had to finish him off and warn her brother about the imminent attack. This man had been the advance man. She had no doubt in her mind they'd have to fight their way out now. She'd beaten the main attack, maybe by minutes.

Taking a deep breath, she murmured a silent prayer before slicing him across his carotid, using a backhanded motion. She danced away from the arterial spray as the man fell to the ground. His lifeless eyes turned to the sky.

Keely turned her head and gagged. Pulling her canteen from her pack, she drank, swallowing the sickness threatening to rise in her throat once more. She wiped the knife on a tussock of grass by the building before sheathing it.

How much time did they have? She stared into the dense green foliage. She saw nothing. The sounds of the rain forest were loud, seemed normal, so no one approached yet. Her gut told her they might have ten, maybe fifteen minutes.

She picked up the dead man's gun from where he'd dropped it, another H&K. She drew the line at wading through the blood pooling around the man's body to retrieve his extra ammo. Turning, she approached the rear of the cantina, listing in her head what needed to be done. Clear the backroom. Secure it against intruders. Disable the bartender. She was on what she suspected to be a short clock, so she'd better get to it. Aftermath for the bloody kill could come later—much later, at the hotel.

Sticking her head around the doorframe, she found no one in the crammed-to-the-rafters back room. It wasn't big and there were no places to hide. She entered, then shut the door and slid a metal bar used to lock it through an iron loop. That should slow down anyone trying to sneak in the back. Just in case, she quietly shifted a couple of cases of empty beer bottles in front of the door. Breaking bottles would make a lot of noise, warning them.

Now for the barkeep. She turned, then opened the door between the back room and the bar area. She thanked God someone kept the door hinges oiled. It barely made a sound. Looking around the corner, she located the room's four inhabitants. The bartender was behind the bar, and her brother, Maddox and Petriv were still at a table by the front door.

The bartender fidgeted, his body swaying from foot to foot, his gaze shifting to the doorway where she hid in the shadows. *Sorry, Charlie. Your buddy ain't coming to tell you what to do.*

As the bartender, his back to her now, began making what looked like a Mojito—lime, yummy— she ghosted into the room and came up behind him. She placed the flat blade of her less-than-pristine knife along the man's carotid.

"Don't move, *senor*. I might slip and cut you," she said, her voice loud enough to draw her brother and his team's attention. "Don't bother to finish the Mojito. We're not staying for drinks. Although I'd kill for a to-go Pepsi."

"Imp! What the fuck are you doing here?" Her brother's question was in the form of a roar. "And whose fucking blood is that?"

She glanced down and noted the blood spatter on her white shirt. Well, hell, she bet she had blood all over her face. *Eeuw*. She breathed slowly to dampen her renewed queasiness. No time to be sick, things would go tango uniform soon enough.

"No time for explanations. Someone needs to cover the door and windows. Company's coming." Using her knife as incentive, she forced the bartender to move with her—or chance getting his throat cut.

"Keely Ann Walsh!" Her brother stomped toward the bar. His face, a mask of calm, but his eyes held a powerful mixture of emotions—fear, concern, anger— all aimed at her. "Talk. Now."

Maddox followed her brother. Petriv moved to the side of the open doorway. At least someone was taking her seriously. "I was looking for you—to warn you." Her hand trembled; she really needed some sugar and fast. She wasn't kidding about killing for a Pepsi. She recognized now her nausea, her weakness was because she had low blood sugar, not an uncommon occurrence for her in hot, humid environments. The bartender jerked away from the blade. She pulled him back, emphasizing her point by pricking him with the point of her knife. "Not a good idea, *senor.*"

"About the company. Got that. Goddamit, are you hurt?" She recognized that tone. He wanted answers and he'd keep them there all the damn day until he got them.

She sighed. "It's not my blood, okay? Had a run-in with a merc out back."

Cursing in gutter Spanish, the bartender attempted to pull away again. She drew a line on the barkeep's flushed neck with the dull edge of her knife, leaving a trail of his friend's blood in the sweaty folds of fat. "Your friend is dead, *senor.* Please don't do anything stupid. I've done more than enough killing in the last two days."

The bartender spit to the side. "I have no friend, *senorita.* I am sorry, I also have no Pepsi. I have Coca-cola." His English had a Brooklyn-tinge to it.

The bartender tensed. Stupid, stupid. He was thinking, planning. She could almost see the wheels spinning in his head, powered by little Chihuahuas. She'd let it play out, see how dumb the man really was. Plus, the resulting lesson would show Tweeter's friends she could handle herself. They'd soon have to trust her to fight alongside them.

"Coke? That'll do." She withdrew the knife, giving the bartender an opening to make his move. "Get me one. Carefully."

Tweeter cursed under his breath. So did Maddox and Petriv, in assorted languages, each of them very vulgar. She shot them a warning glance. This was her fight, her lesson. Her brother glared at her and pointed his gun at the bartender's head. She shook her head and glared back. Overprotective brothers had been the bane of her existence. Maddox and Petriv she'd excuse for having their guns trained on the bartender, they didn't know any better. But Tweeter should. *Sheesh.*

Petriv moved away from the door to get another angle on the bartender's head. Maddox stood alongside her brother. The SSI owner's nostrils flared. His lips thinned. His piercing gaze watched every move she and the bartender made. Her conclusion? He was way pissed, but still ready to make a move to save her poor little female butt. She almost snorted. He'd learn she could save her own hind end—and soon. The bartender really was that stupid and would try to take her.

"A Coke for the *senorita. Un segundo.*" The man turned to smile at her. His face showed his shock. She got that a lot from men she'd held at knifepoint. The bartender's grin widened. Sucker thought he could take little ole her. *Not going to happen, dumbass.*

She sensed movement from her brother and Renfrew Maddox. She didn't shift her gaze away from the bartender as he reached toward an under-bar refrigerator. "Let the man get me my Coke, guys."

Maddox made a noise that sounded suspiciously like a growl.

"Keely—" The warning in her brother's voice would normally make her cringe, but she was too busy concentrating on the barkeep's movements. All weakness was temporarily gone, due to a timely surge of adrenaline. She fondled her knife, keeping it ready.

Instead of bending down to get a cold soda, the man turned, his head and body just enough below the bar top to mess up the other three's shots. He used his arm to knock her knife hand up and away. Expecting something like this, she kept a firm grip on her weapon. She thrust the heel of her left hand up and broke his nose. Too bad for *el fatso*—she had two hands and was equally adept with both.

There was still some fight in the man. Howling, he lunged for her. Using his forward momentum, she blocked the hand reaching for her knife with her forearm and kneed him in the balls. Then to add insult to injury, she used the old trusty knee to the diaphragm. Her dad and brothers had taught her to fight dirty. While the big strong man thought he could contain the little slip of a female, she had him on the ground, crying like a little girl.

By the time Tweetie and Maddox came around the bar, she'd flipped the very unhappy barkeep and had a booted foot in the small of his back, holding him down, her knifepoint at the nape of his neck.

"You got any flex-cuffs? I used mine on the way here. My source in Puerto Iguazu only had three sets. I was just thrilled the guy had ordnance for the Kamov that'll haul our butts out of here."

Her brother's lips thinned and flags of white appeared around them. His was furious, but containing it well. After all, he *was* the most even-tempered of her brothers. He tossed her a set of cuffs from his belt, which she caught with her left hand. Pressing down on the bartender's left kidney with the heel of her hiking boot, she sheathed her knife and cuffed the man's hands behind his back, then flipped him over. His moan told her she might have broken a rib or two. She blamed it on the adrenaline.

Now that the immediate danger was past, she was shaking from the combination of too much adrenaline and too little sugar. Stepping over the downed man, she peered in the refrigerator under the bar and indeed found cold, six-ounce bottles of Coke. Pulling out two of the small bottles, she closed the door. Popping the top off one on the edge of the counter, she held up a finger toward her brother who had relaxed enough to open his mouth to speak, then downed one bottle. God, she needed that. She could already feel the sugar and caffeine blasting into her bloodstream.

Maddox stood next to Tweeter, glancing from her to the man on the ground and back, a look of stunned disbelief on his chiseled face. Petriv joined the other two; his lips quirked. The stone-cold assassin was fighting a smile. Who knew he'd have a sense of humor? His file hadn't mentioned it. Intelligence files usually mentioned everything right down to the size of a man's dick. Petriv's was seven inches, slightly above average from all her reading; Maddox's, eight. She managed to avoid looking at their crotches to see if her intel had been correct.

Petriv caught her eye and winked at her. She

inclined her head graciously. The Ukrainian threw back his head and laughed. Maddox shot Petriv an angry glare. Ooh, he didn't like his associate flirting with her, huh? Tweetie had told her his boss had no use for women and had established a "no-single-women-on-Sanctuary rule." Only operatives' wives, long-term, live-in girlfriends and fiancées were allowed to live on the property. The DoD and CIA files on Maddox labeled him as a loner; he'd had only two long-term relationships in his life, one for twelve months and another for nine, and neither of those women had lived with him 24/7. Knowing the male of the species fairly well—with a dad and five brothers how could she not?—he probably didn't avoid sexual conquests; he wasn't a monk, he just had no use for permanent relationships.

She placed the empty bottle on the bar with a thunk and opened the second. This one she intended to savor. "Uh, someone really needs to watch the door." She broke what had become an uncomfortable silence. She hated being the cynosure of everyone's eyes. "You were led into a trap, guys. I took care of the back door. The sound of breaking beer bottles means they're coming in that way."

"Keely, what the fuck…"

"Tweeter, you can't say that word. I'll tell Mom." Their mother, Molly Walsh, disliked the f-word, but with a house full of military men, she fought a losing battle. Her response was to demand payment—a quarter for every f-bomb. Her mother sported some very nice jewelry because the Walsh men and their friends uttered a lot of f-words.

Keely frowned at her brother to underline her point, then turned to the man at his side and held out her hand. "Mr. Maddox? In case you hadn't guessed, I'm his little sister. I worked on a project for NSA through the auspices of my employer MIT until about twenty hours ago. While working for them, I came across this anomaly in the COMINT, uh, the communications intelligence I processed—which I will explain later if y'all really want to know the deets. Bottom line, this is a trap. There is no al Qaeda cell in this hole in the jungle. They're all across the river in Paraguay, if you really want to know. *This* is a trap set by Reyo Trujo, who seems to have a humongous hard-on for you, through the machinations of a highly placed traitor in the Department of Defense." Then she smiled sweetly and pulled out a granola bar from her pocket, unwrapped it and took a bite. Caffeine and sugar only went so far in combating low blood sugar—and she'd need all the energy she could muster for the fight to come.

Maddox looked at her hands as if they might rear up and bite him. Again a sound somewhere between a rumble and a snarl came from deep in his chest. His icy grey-blue eyes warmed and turned a deep, smoky slate blue. His gaze traveled over her as if trying to classify her species—or figuring where to take a bite out of her first. She shivered. Now, she knew firsthand what a soft furry bunny felt like when a wolf had it in its sights. The man was an honorable, dominant, alpha male with predatory tendencies, much like her dad and brothers. This was a good news-bad news thing. Good in that she knew how to deal with the alpha personality; bad in that such honorable alphas wanted to cocoon her in bubble wrap and put her somewhere safe.

She didn't get "put" easily.

"Keely." Tweeter's voice had gone low and soft. Too soft. He was pissed—and really, really scared. "How did you get here?"

When in doubt about handling men getting on their protective high-horses, her mom told her to answer their questions literally, in great detail and at length. Such responses had a way of distracting the overprotective male.

"I flew commercial until Puerto Iguazu—and

let me tell you there are no straight-through flights anywhere in this part of the world."

Someone snorted. She turned. Had the sound, much like stifled laughter, come from Maddox? Nah, his face was stone cold, the expression of a man who ate nails for breakfast. She must have imagined the sound. He caught her look and raised an arrogant dark brow. She glared at him, then turned back to her brother.

"Then I rented a chopper—"

"The Kamov," Petriv offered. He winked at her. Again. A trained assassin with a sense of the ridiculous. How fun. "A good bird."

She shot him a sunny smile. "Yes—you were listening. Good, 'cause we need to get out of here." She chased the granola with the second Coke, then stepped over the wiggling bartender and headed around the bar.

None of the three men moved. She stood, hands on her hips. "Did y'all hear me? Bad guys. Twenty of them or maybe more—well, come to think of it, seventeen or maybe more … I'm not counting the bartender—are coming to kill you."

Her brother grabbed her arms and shook her. She winced. "Tweets, you don't know your strength. You're hurting me."

He hovered over her, attempting to use his foot or

so advantage in height to intimidate her. He should have learned by now it didn't work on her, but he always tried.

"Don't give me that crap," he said, exasperation in his voice. "I'm hardly touching you. Are you sure none of this is your blood?" His forehead creased with concern as his gaze traveled her torso and a finger traced the blood spatter down the front of her shirt.

She slapped his hand away, then leaned her forehead on his chest and sighed. Unwanted tears welled in her eyes. She refused to let them fall. That was a wussy-assed thing to do, and there was no time to be weak. She was safe and her brother was safe. She'd made it in time.

He held her more tightly against him. "I hate to ask—but why are there now only seventeen or so mercs left?" He took her hat off and leaned his chin on top of her disheveled, sweaty curls, his fingers soothing her scalp as he untangled the mess now falling to the center of her back.

One of the other two men gasped. Typical male response to her hair. She hated her hair. Most days, it was a nuisance. It was thick and heavy, and in hot humid weather, it curled and frizzed like crazy. But all her brothers, her dad and, most importantly, her mama begged her not to cut it.

"Why seventeen, Keely Ann Walsh?" He rocked her within the circle of his arms as he used to do when she skinned her knees as a little girl.

"Because I had to, um, disable two on the way here and then kill the guy out back. I was on a short clock, like Dad always says. I couldn't let anyone or anything stop me from getting here. Okay?" She wasn't happy that her last word had ended on a shrill note. She took a breath and let it out slowly. If she had a mantra, she'd be chanting it.

"Okay, calm down, Imp." He smoothed her hair, a losing battle since it always did what it wanted to anyway. "Did you see any of the other mercs?"

"Nope, but I think the guy who I killed out back was coming to let the bartender know the attack was imminent. The two guys on the trail said something about waiting on someone. I figured Trujo wanted to be in on the kill."

Maddox grunted, drawing her attention. As he opened his mouth to say something, probably something macho and sexist, several rounds of automatic gunfire hit the front of the building, burning through the flimsy wood like a knife through butter. The mirror behind the bar shattered under the barrage, showering her and Tweeter with glass.

She shoved out of Tweeter's arms then pulled him to the floor. Satisfied he hadn't been hit, she belly-crawled from behind the bar, ignoring everything but the need to get to the back room to retrieve the H&Ks she'd left there along with her backpack and all the ammo.

"Keely," Tweeter yelled, his hand just slipping off her booted foot.

"I've got her," Maddox shouted. "Start laying down some fire out the front and block the fucking door!"

Continuing her fast crawl, she threw a frowning glance over her shoulder. "Has my mom met you?" He shook his head, confusion evident in his eyes. "Don't ever use the f-bomb around her. She'll make you pay."

Maddox snorted. Same sound she'd heard earlier. He'd been—still was—laughing at her. *Ass.*

"You think that's funny? Just wait until you owe her a small fortune," Keely muttered.

He put a large hand on her hips, shoving gently. "Move it. What have you got in the back room? An arsenal?"

"How'd you guess?" She ignored his sarcastic tone and threw a glare over her shoulder. "Move the hand. Tweetie is looking—and he won't like it."

He slowly pulled his hand away, caressing her rear

end. "Tweetie?"

They were in the middle of a fight for their lives and he wanted to share personal family info? Fine. She could multi-task. "I couldn't say Tweeter when I was little. Want to know when my brothers first short-sheeted my bed?"

He grinned and shook his head. "Maybe later."

He choked back another laugh at her muttered, "Ass." She dragged the backpack to her and pulled out ammo, tossing him a couple of magazines and then one of the H&Ks.

His mouth quirked. "Hand me the extra H&K for the guys. They'll need the extra firepower." He stuck his hand out.

She shoved the weapon at him, which he took and crawled into the other room. He'd left his weapon so he was obviously coming back. Lucky her.

Out of habit, she checked it over for him. Say what you would about hired guns, they did take care of their weapons. The H&K was clean and good to go.

After shoving some boxes of canned foods around, she built a place for them to hide behind. She put bags of flour in front of the boxes. Might stop some bullets from getting through. Then she dropped behind the makeshift barricade and checked her weapon again.

Maddox crawled back into the room and gave her preparations a surprised and approving look. She answered the unasked question in his eyes. "Too many years of following my brothers around and playing war games." She shoved his gun toward him. "I checked it. Thirty-round mags and I set it for bursts."

"Trained by a Marine, I see." He checked over the weapon himself.

She wasn't insulted. He'd be dumb if he hadn't. "My dad—and a couple of SEALs. My oldest two brothers are Navy." She wished they were here now. It sounded like WWIII in the front. She anticipated an attack on the back any time.

Before Maddox could make a comment, something thudded against the back door. Two more thuds and the bad guys figured they couldn't knock it down, so they shot at it. Splinters flew as the door was riddled with bullets.

Keely lay on her stomach and poked the muzzle of her weapon through a firing hole she'd created. Maddox was next to her, his body heat and male scent engulfing her. She felt more threatened by his closeness than by the murderous goons attempting to breach the back door. She wiggled away, opening up her personal space, but he followed, his body now touched her from hip to ankle. *Damn.* He was ready to cover her body with his to protect her. He'd learn eventually—she always carried her weight. She didn't need a man to cover her ass.

He looked at her. "Short bursts. Go for the head. They might have body armor." He followed his words with an example, aiming head high through the door. A body fell through the decimated door. A perfect head shot.

She shouted to be heard over the return fire. "I know. Don't baby me. I can hit what I aim for. You could ask my brother, but he and Petriv sound busy."

The merc force had thrown the main firepower to the front. Maybe they thought the SSI men would be distracted and forget there was a back door. That would be stupid thinking on the mercs' part. She let off a short burst of gunfire at the next man who stuck his head around the shredded door. The man fell forward on top of his buddy, the top of his head missing.

Keely touched Maddox's muscled, hairy forearm. His arm tensed under her fingers. His eyes burned blue like the heart of a gas flame as he turned to look at her. She frowned—distracted by the flames in his eyes. He wasn't angry, but she wasn't sure what he was feeling. She shook off the effect of his intent look. "Um, FYI, the three I took out had no armor. It's too frick-fracking hot for Kevlar."

Maddox laughed, a full-out sound that reached into her gut and turned her insides to mush. O-o-kay, the guy could lighten up—though now might not be the right time.

While the battle raged at the front of the building, the gunfire had temporarily halted at their position. The enemy had to reassess their strategy. Two of theirs were down and they hadn't even fully breached the rear of the cantina. The lull would not last forever. Already, Keely's neck itched like crazy. It would be soon.

"Way too hot." He lifted her chin with a calloused finger. This time she was the one to tense. She had the little-prey-feeling again. She licked suddenly dry lips, wishing for another Coke. His gaze turned frigid, the color of Arctic ice. "No one gets through."

In other words, don't be a girl about killing. If he only knew— "Gotcha." She attempted to smile, but failed. "Don't worry, Mr. Maddox."

"It's Ren." He tweaked her chin. "Say it."

The cessation of fire at their position still held, but it couldn't be much longer before someone tested the door again. *Humor the man, Keely.* "Ren."

His eyes warmed. She licked her lips again. His

eyes darkened to the deep grey-blue color peculiarly his before he turned away to concentrate on the rear entrance. Yet, she sensed he knew every breath she took, every movement she made, even if it was minor.

"Uh, I won't let y'all down." She bit her lower lip. "I just wish I could've warned you before you left Idaho. Some guy named Quinn said I just missed Tweetie."

"You made good time. We just got here two hours ago."

She fixed her gaze on the door and away from him. He was a distraction—and she was usually hard to distract. She focused on her weapon, her finger ready to pull the trigger. "You had to sneak in. I came direct. Makes a difference." She took a deep breath. "They're regrouping—it shouldn't be long now."

"Yeah. Nervous?"

She caught his sideways glance. He was concerned. He probably wished her anywhere but here. His type would always protect the little helpless woman. She wished she could convince him she could handle her end of the fight. Well, he'd learn soon enough. "A little. I hate killing. But I'll do what I have to do."

"But you shouldn't the fuck have to." His tone was angry tinged with regret.

"I tried to get some of my brothers freed up, but

they would have been too late."

His look told her she should've tried harder. She was tempted to stick her tongue out at him, but just then his head whipped around to face forward as two men burst into the room through the decimated wood door. Their guns blazed amidst the crash of bottles as the cases spilled open. The two were immediately followed by others. *Guess the strategy was to hit them all at once.*

In her shooting zone, Keely was barely aware of anything around her. She shot in short bursts, aiming for heads and legs. When it became evident that they did not, in fact, have body armor, she adjusted and went for heart shots, even if she missed the heart, torso shots at this caliber had stopping power. Her mathematical mind figured angles and trajectories, anticipated movements and coordinated with her muscle movement and eye-to-hand coordination. Her sniper training courtesy of one of her dad's buddies stood her well. She wasted no ammunition. Each man she aimed at, she hit. When they went down, they stayed down.

She emptied a magazine and swiftly and efficiently ejected it and inserted another.

Ren's muttered "goddamn—a warrior sprite" had

her glancing his way. But he was concentrating on shooting and not her. She must have imagined his words.

They fell into a rhythm, each taking out every other man through the narrow door. When one reloaded, the other took up the slack. It was as if they could read each other's minds.

Finally, the attackers stopped coming. Bodies lay strewn across the floor of the small back room. Smoke hung in the air. Silence fell over the bullet-riddled building. Tweeter and Petriv spoke in low rumbles in the other room. But Keely's tension increased rather than decreased with the cessation of the attack.

"Fudge ripple, that's not good. It was too easy." She looked at Ren. His eyes were narrowed as he examined her. "I don't like this. Maybe my intel wasn't complete. There were too many of them—so there could be a lot more out there."

"They could've changed the plan after you set out." Ren's tone was low, rumbling, meant to soothe her. "Don't worry about it, sprite."

She hadn't imagined him calling her that earlier. Before she could call him on the carpet— "Something's coming."

"What?" Ren turned toward her, crowding into her

personal space even more. "What do you…"

A grenade thrown through the doorway tumbled into the room.

Ren's "fuck" barely registered. Keely was closer. Tossing her weapon to the side, she went for the explosive. As she rolled across the floor toward another set of boxes, she grabbed the live grenade, then lobbed it side-handed out the rear door. She kept rolling and made it behind some boxes of frijoles before the explosion rocked the back of the building.

She rolled onto her stomach and pulled her Bren from the holster at her back. She flicked off the safety and held it two-handed just in case someone was alive to follow through.

"Keely, what the fuck was that?" Her brother's frightened bellow was loud and cut through the ringing in her ears. She could make out Petriv swearing in some highly colorful Russian.

A quick glance told her Ren was okay—but visibly furious. "Don't you ever fucking do that again!" He glared at her instead of paying attention to the new hole in the wall.

She shrugged and fired over his head at a man attempting to come through the smoldering opening. The dead man drooped over the jagged remnants of the wall, half in and half out of the room.

After another furious glance at her, Ren double-tapped the intruder to make sure he was dead.

Why the heck was he mad at her? She'd kept them from being blown into hamburger and then saved his life? She deserved an "atta-girl."

Silence reigned once more over the small, battered building. Her itchy feeling was gone, thank the Lord. She laid her weary head on her forearms, but kept her handgun in her right hand, just in case her spider sense was wrong.

"Keely!" Tweeter's worried voice came from the front room once more.

"I'm fine, Tweetie. How many did you get on your side?"

"Vanko and I got us a confirmed ten motherfuckers."

She ignored her brother's profanity, allowing for the situation. "My three on the way here plus your ten plus we have eleven, no, make that twelve on the floor and hanging over the hole in the wall. That's twenty-five. We might have taken out one or two with the grenade out the back door…"

"What fucking grenade?" Tweeter yelled. "Where did you get a fucking grenade?'

"The live grenade your fool sister picked up and

threw out the back door." Ren's jaw clenched and unclenched. He belly crawled toward her.

"Tattletale." She stuck out her tongue.

His eyes narrowed as he moved toward her. "Brat."

Ignoring him, she turned and crawled into the bar area with Ren so close behind her she could feel his hot breath on the bare skin of her legs above her hiking boots. She met her brother just inside the doorway as he crab-walked toward her. He looked her over, then sighed.

"I think that's the same blood you already had." He closed his eyes and shook his head. "Imp, don't do that shit. Let us do it."

"It" being the throwing of live grenades, she supposed. "*It* was closer to me—and I know how to handle a live grenade, ya know." And why was she getting defensive?

"Yeah, Mom never let Dad live that training session down, did she?" He grinned at her. A shaky finger stroked her cheek.

"Nope, she didn't." She sat up and pulled her knees to her chest, her arms hanging loosely over her bent knees, her gun still in her right hand. "There could be more mercs waiting in the jungle—or the survivors of this team could be regrouping. I say we get out of here before they can come at us with bigger guns or something. Plus, we have the belly guns on the helo and all that armor-plating Russians love to layer on their aircraft. I'll feel better once we're up and can shoot down on them."

Petriv's shout of laughter had her smiling. Someone appreciated her. She grinned at the Ukrainian.

Knee-walking, Ren came up against her back. His knee nudged her bottom and his body almost covered hers from behind. He grabbed her arms, keeping her from moving away from his heat and scent. What was his problem now? She was just sitting here.

"Ren?" Tweeter frowned. "You're crowding my baby sister. Back off."

CHAPTER TWO

Ren's jaw tensed as he glared at Keely's brother. Tweeter had the good sense to back off.

Was everyone nuts but him? Keely Walsh was a small, delicately built female. Hell, a stiff breeze could probably knock her over. She had adequate shooting abilities—okay, more than adequate—and had handled the bartender very neatly. And she'd warned them about the trap and brought extra weapons and ammo. But she was not in charge. This was his op and he would take control now, which included protecting the woman from herself if he had to. It was obvious her brother couldn't handle her.

Before he could open his mouth, Keely said, "Back off, Tweetie. I scared Ren earlier. He's probably thinking I'm a loose cannon or something." She angled her head to look at him over her shoulder. "He'll learn I'm not. I don't do anything without weighing the consequences."

His jaw dropped open, then closed. Several times. Finally, he said, "You analyzed nothing. You just went after a fucking live grenade." He was the man, the trained soldier; it was his job to handle live grenades.

Tweeter laughed. "Oh, she analyzed it. Her brain is like a Cray super-computer. She can assess a situation and make a decision in a split second. Dad said Special Forces lost a good soldier when she was born female."

Keely stuck her tongue out at her brother. She'd stuck that same tongue out at him, and if she did it again, her ass was spanked.

"I still say I could've survived Hell Week if Loren hadn't caught me."

He shot a questioning glance at Tweeter who verified the incredible statement. "She made it through five days before they figured out she was there." At Ren's snort of disbelief, Tweeter clarified, "She shadowed them at Coronado, mirroring the first five days minus the team support. The instructors went apeshit. She lasted longer than half the class. Mom had fits and Dad was so proud he almost burst. Loren and Paul were freakin' instructors, and were livid she'd stayed under their radar so long. The only reason she got caught was because she saved one of the men from drowning with Loren's help."

"Fucking unbelievable."

Hell Week was called that for a reason. He'd made it, but never wanted to be that tired, hungry or cold again. His SEAL missions had been like vacations compared to the training.

"It's documented." Keely's glorious green eyes narrowed. "It was easy to infiltrate the training site. It's a beach, after all."

"Documented?"

"Yeah, I hired a videographer. I figured no one would believe me." Her lips quirked. "I'll get you a copy. My twin brothers' commentary is, uh, enlightening."

"More like profane," muttered Tweeter.

"Jesus H. Christ." Ren stood, hauling the tiny warrior to her feet. He then turned her to face him, his hands on her shoulders. He wanted her to acknowledge who was in charge from here on out.

Keely winced and attempted to shrug his grip off. He frowned at her sign of pain. He'd kept his grip purposely light.

"Are you hurt?" He released her shoulders. "You fucking did it when you dove for that damn grenade, didn't you? Or did it happen on the way here?" His gut clenched at the thought. He forgot all about the lecture he wanted to give her on not endangering herself and about following his orders. Instead he tilted her chin up so he could see her eyes. Yeah, she was hurting. Her green eyes were clouded with pain. "Answer me. Where are you hurt?"

She frowned then shook her head. "No, I'm…"

Tweeter cut her off. "Keely Ann Walsh! I specifically asked you earlier if you were hurt. Did you lie to me?" He grabbed her arm to pull her away from Ren.

Keely grimaced, her teeth audibly clenching.

"Leave off, Tweeter." Ren swore a blue streak under his breath as he shoved her brother's hand from her arm, then began to unbutton her shirt. "Vanko, any sign of activity?"

"None. I think we should do what little sis said and bug out. She makes a lot of sense."

Yeah, she did—but he was taking over—once he made sure she was okay. "In a sec. Keep your eyes peeled."

"Stop it." She slapped at his hands. "You are *not* taking off my shirt. I'm fine." Her teeth snapped together as she hissed, then winced.

"Yeah, sure you're fine," he grumbled under his breath. He ignored her pathetic attempts to avoid his fingers and continued to unbutton, then shove the blood-spattered shirt off her shoulders. What he uncovered had him swearing long and viciously. Tweeter did the same from his viewpoint behind her.

"Is it as bad back there as it looks from here?" His tones were clipped, deadly. He barely maintained control of the rage surging through his body. He wanted to find the bastard whose finger and teeth marks were all over her shoulders and the upper curves of her breasts and then kill the asshole in slow and painful ways. And what the fuck had she been thinking of coming to South America in this condition? She needed a fucking keeper.

Tweeter came round to look at the front. "Jesus-fucking-Christ, Keely. Who did this to you?" He looked at Ren. "This side is worse, but she has similar bruising and a bite mark on her left scapula."

Ren's eyes narrowed as he gently turned her to get a look. He swore some more.

"Bite marks?" Vanko stormed over from his post at the front door. He also examined Keely. His pale blue eyes darkened to the color of thunderheads. "*Dermo.* If the bastard's not dead yet, he will be."

Keely sighed. "I'm fine. I made it here, so it's not as bad as it looks." She swept them all with a glance that held strained patience. "We need to move out."

As she began to pull her shirt back up her arms, Ren halted her hands. "You *will* tell us who did this."

She paled, bit her lower lip. "Maybe."

"No maybe—you *will* tell us."

Her green eyes filled with tears and she let out a watery sigh that hurt him in places he hadn't known existed. She was giant-sized courage packaged in a dainty body. He wanted to carry her off to somewhere safe and keep all the bad things from ever daring to share the same air she breathed. From what he'd observed in their short acquaintance, she'd most likely fight and scratch him every inch of the way. Keely was a fighter and would resent his over protectiveness, but damn if he still didn't want to do it.

When she'd walked into the hovel of a bar and took control of the bartender, his brain had seized. He hadn't believed his eyes. All his higher-level thinking went AWOL and something primitive had taken over. Call it territorial imperative, alpha-male protectiveness, or whatever, but he wanted her out of the danger zone. No matter how smart or deadly she was—strawberry blonde sprites did not belong on missions in third-world hellholes.

Now, all he had to do was convince her to go home. He had a feeling Keely would prove to be very difficult.

He grasped her cold, trembling hands and placed them on his chest. He pulled the blood-spattered shirt up and over her battered shoulders and over her chest then buttoned it, careful not to touch her breasts or do anything to cause her any more pain—or embarrassment.

His gut seized at the thought that what they hadn't seen might be worse. "Vanko. Check outside. We're leaving."

Tweeter moved past him and Keely into the back room, then came out with her backpack and the weapons. "Here, boss." He held the equipment out. "I'm carrying my sister."

"No way, Tweetie." Keely grabbed her backpack and shrugged it on with barely a wince.

Ren swore under his breath. "Let us take care of you. You've done more than your share."

"Stop swearing. I can walk."

"Stubborn little minx." Ren resisted the urge to throw her over his shoulder. Vanko choked back a laugh and sobered when he glared at him.

Keely moved toward the door, her head held high, her tight, round ass moving so sweetly he couldn't help his little brain's reaction. *Shit.* Now wasn't the time to get a hard-on. He shifted his cock so it wouldn't rub against his zipper.

Tweeter noted the adjustment. A frown creased his friend's forehead. "Uh, Ren..."

"Not a word, Tweeter. Not one fucking word."

Tweeter shook his head and said something Ren couldn't quite catch. He expected he and his friend would have a come-to-Jesus meeting over Keely soon.

Vanko met Keely at the door and led her outside, gently cupping her elbow as if she were made of spun glass. He frowned. Vanko was a horn dog when it came to women. *Shit.* As op leader, he'd have to warn the handsome Ukrainian off. This was Tweeter's sister after all.

"Tweeter." He kept his voice low so the others couldn't hear. His sharp gaze never left Keely as Vanko turned on the charm. He fisted his hands at his side. "Tell me about your sister. She handles herself well for a civilian."

"You really meant 'for a girl,' didn't you?" Tweeter raised one brow. His eyes crinkled with suppressed laughter. "We all taught her—Dad, we boys, all Dad's grunts. She's a natural warrior—and scary smart."

"Where did she learn to handle a weapon so well?"

"She's good, isn't she?" Tweeter smiled like a proud father. "Dad taught her on small weapons. Loren and Paul taught her what they learned in SEAL training. She was so good, Dad bribed someone to let her go to Army Sniper School. She aced it."

Sniper School was almost as difficult as Hell Week.

"Well, hell." He shook his head. "She took out that bartender like a pro. What's her hand-to-hand training?"

"Paul taught her Krav Magra—and Dad had us wrestle her so she could learn how to defend herself in case some S.O.B. got a hold of her. Mom hated it all, but in the end had to admit it came in handy when Keely got breasts."

Ren choked, not wanting to think about her breasts. Of course his gaze went straight to them— and they were sweet and full on her petite frame, more than a handful. Then he thought about the unknown bastard who'd brutally marked her. She was so small, so fragile despite all her training. Some son of a fucking bitch had hurt her.

Tweeter added, "Ren, if all these questions are about if she can handle herself if we meet trouble in the jungle, the answer is affirmative."

"No, I saw that she could handle herself, but wondered how the bastard overcame her to hurt her that way? She took down the bartender easily and he had to outweigh her by a hundred pounds."

Tweeter shook his head. "Not many people could sneak up on her. She has a spider sense about things like that."

"Probably outnumbered her then." The image of men holding her down as they hurt her made him growl. He and Tweeter moved to join the others, picking up the rest of their gear from the table as they exited the bar.

"Yeah. I'll be calling my brothers in on this hunt. No one messes with our baby sister."

"I'll help. Anyone ever dares touch her like that in my presence and he'll lose a hand before he hits the fucking floor."

Tweeter shot him a narrowed glance. "Ren, we all protected her as she grew up. Then we trained her once she got big enough to understand she might not always have us around to cover her cute little tush. Even after all the training, we still try to protect her."

"Is there a point here?" He watched Vanko brush a golden curl from her forehead. He tensed and barely stopped himself from flying across the ground and slapping Vanko's hand away. *Shit.* He was not like this. He'd never been this possessive over a woman. He took in and let out one deep breath, then another, until the burning desire to rip Vanko's arm off left him.

"The point is—she hates us hovering and smothering her with protection. Very self-sufficient, my little sister." Tweeter looked at her and shook his head. "I'm not sure how she got out of the U.S. without Dad knowing. One of us always knows where she is and what she's doing. Drives her fucking nuts. Hell, when she went to MIT at the age of thirteen, I had to go and attend with her so I could keep the predators away..."

"Thirteen?" Ren pulled Tweeter to a halt. His gaze unconsciously traveled to Keely to check her status. She was fine. She and Vanko waited near the edge of the village clearing. Vanko wasn't touching her any longer. Good. He turned back to Tweeter, who studied him as if he'd never seen him before. He wasn't sure he wanted to know what his friend saw on his face. "Thirteen, you said?"

"Yeah, she's a genius. She has three doctorates—physics, math and computer science—and teaches at MIT. Applied computer sciences."

"That's why the NSA project." His gaze drifted

in her direction once more. She was eyeing him. She smiled and he found himself smiling back. Then she turned to Vanko to show him something in her hand. He frowned. Yeah, his friend Vanko would bear watching. Keely was under his protection now. His op—his rules.

"She just turned twenty-one, Ren." Tweeter's cool tone drew his attention from the other two.

He stared at Tweeter. "Twenty-one?" That made Vanko—and him—thirteen years older. "We need to get your baby sister home."

"Keely won't go anywhere she doesn't want to go. She has a temper to go with all that red in her hair—and she thinks she's six feet tall and an Amazon warrior and not the little pixie she really is. She'd fight an erupting volcano with a cup of water."

"Not on my op, she won't." He noticed Vanko running a hand up and down Keely's back. He'd really hate to kill the Ukrainian, but if the slick bastard didn't get his paw off her, he might have to. He growled as he moved forward. "I'll—we'll—protect her. She won't need to put out any fires."

Tweeter following him muttered something that sounded like "good luck with that."

"Vanko, take point." He pulled the Ukrainian's

hand away from Keely, then gently gripped her elbow and pulled her to him until she was plastered against his side.

"How's he supposed to do that, Ren?" She wiggled away from him, then looked up, her eyes narrowed. She was annoyed. He grinned. He must be a sick fuck, but he liked her pissed at him. Her eyes glowed like green fire—and all her concentration was on him, not Vanko.

"Yeah, Ren," Vanko said. "How?" The Ukrainian's posture was one anyone who'd fought alongside him would recognize—he wanted a fight. Ren was in the mood to give him one, but now was not the time, nor place. Keely's safety came first.

Keely stamped her foot. "Okay, let's stop all this testosterone bull-hooey. Listen up, boys. Stay off the path. Head due west, following parallel to the path, for approximately three and a half klicks. Vanko has my GPS and will definitely be taking point." She shot Ren a fierce look. It was a visual dare for him to disagree with her. "We'll be climbing at the end. The helo is in the village's marijuana field. It was the only clearing for miles."

"Who's the boss here?" He tapped the tip of her nose, accepting her unspoken dare.

"Me—since I rescued you and I know where the bird is. Problem with that, big guy?"

"Yeah." He grabbed her hat from Tweeter's hands and plopped it on her head. Her nose was red from the sun. "I'm in charge—you're a civilian consultant from here on out."

"Fine, if that's the way you want it." She tucked her hair up under the hat and moved to join Vanko.

Ren caught her arm and pulled her back to his side. "You're with me."

"Wonderful," she murmured, her lips thinning. "Men are Neanderthals."

He choked back a laugh. She could call him anything she wanted as long as she stayed put—next to him.

Vanko took the lead and Tweeter brought up the rear.

"Why stay off the path?" Tweeter asked from behind them.

Good question, and one he would have asked eventually.

"Mines."

Her tone was short and clipped. She was pissed. The woman didn't give an inch. In her place, neither would he. Then he groaned, remembering the explosion they'd heard earlier. The bartender had explained the absent villagers were blasting stumps to clear new fields. The explanation had made sense at the time. "How did you find that out?" He was afraid he knew the answer.

"Well ... something about the clear path from the field to the village bothered me. Tweetie calls it my spider sense. Anywho, I saw a trip wire." He stiffened and muttered "hell." She patted his arm, her annoyance with him disappearing as quickly as it appeared. "Chill, big guy. It was a red herring for the claymore planted a few feet ahead." His insides turned to ice at an image of Keely stepping on a mine. "So ... I got off the path, found some old rock pile that used to be a drying shed or something, got behind it and lobbed a rock on the mine."

"Then you waited like a good girl to see who or what the noise brought out," Tweeter put in.

Keely laughed. The sound skittered over his skin, burrowing inside him and chasing away the cold. His contrary cock grew hard. When in the hell had he ever gotten hard from a woman's laugh? Never—until now. *Shit. Shit. Shit.*

"My brother knows me well. We played this game enough with the other kids on the Marine bases where Dad was stationed."

"And who came out of the forest?" Vanko asked from point. The Ukrainian was paying too close attention to Keely.

"Two mercs." Keely looked around the jungle. "We should be coming up on their bodies soon."

"You killed them?" Ren gripped her elbow tightly. At a low moan from her, he loosened his hold and absently soothed the pain by gently massaging the spot with his thumb. He'd heard her tell them she'd taken out three total bad asses before coming to the bar, but it hadn't really registered. Well, how could it? He could barely accept what he'd seen her do. Then they'd gotten busy shooting people shortly after that little tidbit had been delivered. Now that the actual incident had been underlined, he was angry—and scared after the fact. She could've been killed before he ever found her. *Now where the fuck had that thought come from?*

"No." She glanced at his grip on her arm and narrowed her eyes. "Um, loosen up, big guy. I need that elbow." He gentled his hold, but did not let her go. She looked at his hand once more, then shrugged. "Anywho, you saw what I did to the bartender. That's what I did to them—and I used all of my flex-cuffs on them."

She didn't sound at all upset about having to subdue

two hired killers, just ticked off about using her whole supply of restraints. Every time she opened her mouth he had to revise his assessment of her abilities.

"How did they come at you?" he gritted out. Various scenarios flew across his mind's eye, and he didn't like any of them.

"One at a time, thank God. They were skinny. I could've taken them both at once, but I was glad they played it cautious—one man to investigate and one man to cover the rear." She grinned. "They were really shocked to see little old me."

All of a sudden she held up her free hand then stopped. He followed her lead, keeping a hold of her so she wouldn't go off to single-handedly challenge a unit of terrorists or something.

"Vanko. Hold it." His tone was low, urgent. He readied his weapon; Tweeter and Vanko followed suit. He didn't know what Keely heard, but her body language indicated she heard something. The jungle was oddly quiet. There was something or someone out there. She stood for several seconds, her head angled, listening, then tugged him to the left a few yards where she shoved some palm leaves aside.

The other two moved to join them. They laughed. He stood and viewed the scene with complete disbelief.

The two men lying on the ground, bound hand and foot, were typical mercs: tough, muscular and mean-looking. He wouldn't be surprised if the two wouldn't shoot their own mothers for money. "Skinny," his voice cracked with anger, "my ass."

Head tilted to the side, Keely scrutinized the two thugs. "Next to my brothers most guys are skinny."

"Your brothers aren't out to rape and kill you." He took several deep breaths until the sick feeling in his gut subsided. She could have been killed.

"Well, I should hope not." Her focus was totally on the prisoners. Her hands fisted on her hips. "Well, Jeez-Louise, the one guy moved around too much and dislodged the pressure bandage." She moved to go to the moaning man, but Ren tugged her back against him, his arm snaking around her waist like an iron clamp. His body instantly tensed everywhere her body touched his. *Oh hell, I'm in real trouble.* If his widely careening emotions hadn't convinced him, his body's instantaneous reaction to hers did.

Switching back to using his big brain, he said, "Let Vanko and Tweeter check them out." His nerves couldn't handle her approaching the men who would've raped then killed her.

"They can't hurt me. Dad taught me how to

immobilize prisoners really well."

His only responses were a grunt and his other arm coming around her from the other side until she was trapped within the circle of his arms. She wiggled, testing her boundaries. He tightened his hold until she settled against him. She'd soon learn not to fight the limits he set for her.

Vanko eyed his arms, an eyebrow raised. Ren glared at him. The Ukrainian smiled and shrugged, then moved to check out the two immobilized men.

As Vanko checked over the men, Keely fidgeted against him. "Let go."

"No." Her ass rubbed his hard-on and he clenched his jaw, cutting off his groan. Hell, he envisioned a lot of jerking off and cold showers in his future. Despite his big brain telling him to ignore her, he pulled her hard against his arousal and rubbed it against her tight, perky butt. Maybe that would teach her to stop wiggling.

She stilled as a small animal might when sensing a predator on its trail. Good. She got the picture. He eased his hold and allowed her to move away from the evidence of his desire. He choked back a laugh at her muttered "frick-fracking testosterone."

"Vanko? Status?" His words came out lower and

huskier than he would've liked. Tweeter's sister affected him too easily. On an op such a distraction wasn't good. He had to get his reaction to her under control, or better yet, get her back to the States as soon as possible. Out of sight. Out of mind. *Yeah right—that would work. He was toast no matter where she was.*

"Oh, she did a number on them, Ren." Vanko stood up. "Hands cuffed behind their backs and then cuffed to each other. Duct tape on their legs and gagged with pieces of their own clothing, then covered by duct tape. No way they could get loose. Good work, Keelulya"

"Thanks, Vanko." Keely beamed at the compliment.

Vanko's use of the diminutive version of her name placed her in the little sister or female relative category. Ren felt tension releasing he hadn't even known he had.

He attempted to look at the two mercs with the same level of professional objectivity Vanko displayed, but kept coming back to the purely emotional conclusion she could've been killed. He heaved a deep sigh and shook his head. Jesus, most women would have run in fear from the two ugly characters on the ground. Not her. She took them out and tied them up like a professional soldier. Fuck that, it made no difference that she was competent, she could still be hurt—and he would never allow that.

"What should we do with them?" Tweeter said. "Toss them on the path—maybe on one of those claymores they buried for us?"

The two bound men moaned and shook their heads, their eyes pleading.

"Tweetie, that's not nice." Keely wiggled out of Ren's arms and approached the prisoners. She nudged one of them with the toe of her boot. The man's eyes filled with what looked like fear. He whimpered behind his gag. "This is Pablo. Maybe I should interrogate him? Find out what he knows?"

Ren had to laugh as the man on the ground shook his head vigorously.

Tweeter lifted Pablo's head. "That's my baby sister you attempted to molest. I should just slit your fucking throat."

The man looked down at his gag, then up at Tweeter. Tweeter removed the gag.

"*Senor,* I did not molest your sister. Never would I do such a thing."

Vanko reached over and slapped the man on the back of the head. "Then talk, shithead. And we might leave you enough slack to get loose—eventually. The way I see it, you're both lucky some hungry jaguar hasn't followed the scent of the blood."

Keely backed away as Tweeter and Vanko asked questions. She bumped into Ren, then stopped, didn't move away. He frowned as she leaned almost wearily against him. This wasn't the Keely he'd come to know in the last hour or so. He slid supporting arms around her and braced his chin on the top of her hat-covered head. "You okay?"

"Tired. Hot. Achy. Wish I had snagged a couple more bottles of Coke." She angled her head and looked up. "I want my air-conditioned suite at the resort hotel. Waste of time asking these two anything. I'm betting they only knew they were hired to kill you guys and then they'd get paid. They probably have never even seen Reyo Trujo."

"I have. Ugly bastard. They aren't missing anything special."

"I know what he looks like." He stiffened against her. "Stop it with the protective posturing. Back in Boston, I read his CIA and DIA files, silly. Stop worrying. No matter what it looks like, I normally don't go haring off on dangerous missions. This was an exception. I'm an analyst. I program computers to search and recognize patterns, then analyze the data."

She started to add something, then hesitated. He nudged her. "What's wrong?"

"We need to talk about something I chanced upon when I was working for the NSA through MIT—it's the reason I sent my resignation to MIT. It has to do with all this—and more. It'll be easier to show you. I had my luggage delivered to the hotel and my laptop is there."

"If it isn't stolen," he muttered. The Triple Frontier, in particular, Ciudad del Este in Paraguay, was the largest black market and free-trade zone in South America. Light-fingered porters at the hotel probably made a living pilfering through hotel residents' luggage for marketable goods and ferrying them across the river border. The borders in this part of the world were looser than a pimp's morals.

"I have all the data on a flash drive in my pocket. All they'd get are the programs, which are also duplicated on my flash drive. Plus, they wouldn't understand them even if they could get past my security—which they couldn't. The computer would wipe itself if they tried."

He smiled. She'd sounded all stiff and huffy. "Shh, little warrior. I know you wouldn't leave anything around that was government sensitive."

"How would you know that?" she grumbled. "You don't know me at all." Adding under her breath, "And don't want to know me either."

"Ah, that's where you are wrong. I plan on knowing you … knowing everything about you." His tone was one he didn't recognize. The feelings that went with it were ones he'd never felt before, but they were real.

She wiggled and turned into his body, her hands braced on his chest, and looked up at him. "You really want to…?"

"Yeah." He couldn't help it. She looked so cute. He placed a chaste kiss on her sweaty, flushed cheek. He frowned. Taking her hat off, he lay his cheek against her forehead. "You're burning up. Are you sick?"

"No … uh, well, I don't think so." She scrunched her forehead then let out a weary sigh. "I really don't do heat well. And I'm thirsty." She pushed against his chest, shoving her lower abs against his cock. His unruly cock pulsed against her. She looked down and blushed. "Oh my…" She shoved harder, attempting to get away from his arousal.

His reaction was to gather her closer. She buried her face in his chest. "Stay there." He didn't like it when she tried to get away from him. His hand gently cupped the back of her head, his fingers combing through the wild red-gold curls. They were burning strands of silk. "Nothing's going to happen."

She muttered something under her breath.

He choked, then coughed. "Did you just use the f-word?"

Her head jerked up and she glared at him. "No. Now let me go. You don't like me. You're teasing me. You don't want me here. You are an … ungrateful … man!"

His little spitfire uttered "man" as if it were a nasty word. He couldn't help it, he laughed.

She hit his chest with one little fist. "The next punch will be the heel of my hand up your nose."

He released her because she asked and the other two stood grinning at them, not because he felt threatened. He tapped her nose with his finger. "You don't know anything about what I like, sprite. I wasn't teasing you. And you did use the f-word, little liar. I may have to tell your Mom." But she was correct, he didn't want her here. He wanted her in Idaho, on Sanctuary where it was safe. And he was very grateful she had come into his life.

"Fine. Do. She won't believe you." She turned her back on him and walked to her brother. "Well, did old Pablo share anything new and exciting?"

"No." Tweeter frowned and placed the back of his hand against her forehead. "Jesus, Imp, you're burning up and where's your damn hat?" He moved to pick her up.

Ren muttered under his breath and reached Keely in two steps and swung her into his arms before Tweeter could, then plopped the hat on her disheveled curls. "Let's get to that damn helo and get her out of this heat."

CHAPTER THREE

Keely was pretty darn sure she could walk, but Ren, the headstrong bastard, wouldn't put her down. And Tweeter, the traitor, didn't challenge his boss on the issue. She'd have something to say to her brother later about sibling loyalty.

Truth be told, she felt like dog poop. Her fever, and she did indeed have one, was partially a result of dehydration and the rest due to a possible infection from the human bite marks on the lower curves of her breasts, the deeper marks the others hadn't seen yet—and only Tweeter would see once they got back to the hotel. He could help her clean the wounds. She had a military field medical kit in her luggage; it included wide-spectrum antibiotics. Her Dad always said never go to any third-world country without a well-supplied medical kit. Once again he was proven correct. She'd have to remember to tell him when she talked to him.

But first they had to get back to the hotel. And if her spider sense was working one hundred percent, that wonderful occurrence wouldn't happen soon or easily.

"Ren. Tweeter. Vanko." She hissed in a low tone "Stop. Now."

Ren had somehow sensed her alarm before she'd spoken and had ducked under the frothy leaves of a giant fern. The others joined them.

"Put me down, dammit, and weapon up." She reached for the extra H&K Ren carried on his shoulder. He fought her for it for a few seconds until she pinched a nerve in his elbow. He swore at her but relinquished the gun. "I'm itching like crazy, Tweetie."

"She's correct. There are men waiting ahead," Vanko said. "I can smell cigar smoke on the breeze. How far to the helo, Keelulya?"

She grimaced. "It's maybe two hundred yards ahead. Over the small rise we're approaching."

They all crouched silently and listened. A cough carried on the wind. The low murmur of men's voices.

The clink of metal on metal.

She growled under her breath. "They'd better not be messing with my helicopter."

Ren looked at her askance. His lips quirked. Damn, he was good-looking when he lightened up a bit. He wasn't classically handsome, but then she'd never appreciated pretty boys. She'd always been attracted to men like her dad and brothers; tough, rough around the edges, protective, but gooey in the middle with their women. Ren met most of her essential requirements—time would tell on the gooey middle part.

Yeah, Ren Maddox could be a danger to her mental and emotional health. He definitely was a danger to her physically. He'd had an erection ever since they met. She was highly familiar with male penises of all lengths and girths and their tendency to pop up unannounced, having seen too many as she grew up with five older brothers and all their friends. Ren's penis was definitely larger than all her brothers' appendages. Damn the CIA for having such complete files. And his arousal hadn't subsided even during the firefight. That was just not normal. Why that particular fact made her womb clench and her mouth go dry, she wasn't sure—but damn, she wanted to find out. Timing sucked, though.

"Keely," Ren whispered against her ear. She

shivered—whether due to her fever or the feeling of his breath against her sensitive ear lobe, it was a toss up. "Stay here. We'll handle them. Don't come out until one of us comes for you."

"But, I can—"

Three "nos" came from the men. Outnumbered by testosterone as usual. Story of her life.

Ren brushed his hand over her back. She shivered again. She wanted to blame the reaction on her fever, but recognized it was his touch. "Please, just stay safe. You're feverish. Let us take care of you."

She nodded. Her lips thinned as the three left her. They'd better come back for her in less than ten minutes, because that was all the time she'd give them. There was cold water on the helicopter in a cooler and she wanted it. And nothing was keeping her from her nice, comfy, ice-cold, dehumidified hotel suite any longer than necessary. She'd take on fifty effing mercs to get her damn helo back.

Holding the H&K across her lap, she observed the three men meld into the forest. She sighed. They moved so well together, fluidly, a sign of lots of training. Her dad would approve. The way they signaled and choreographed their approach on the enemy reminded her of the war games she used to play with her brothers and Dad's recruits around Camp Lejeune. It had been hot and humid there, too. She'd never gotten used to the southern weather, which is why when she went away to college she'd gone north. Hell, even Boston was too hot in the summer, but she at least could go to the Cape to escape the city heat.

Short, rapid bursts of submachine gun fire startled her out of her feverish reverie. Damn, she needed to get with the program. Daydreaming was a good way to get her butt shot. She sprawled on her stomach, wincing at the evidence of even more bruising. Gutting it out, she snaked her way toward the rise. The guys might need back up, whether they'd admit it or not.

The gunfire came in sporadic bursts. In her mind, she visualized her three men moving constantly so the mercs or whoever had been waiting at the helo couldn't get a bead on them.

A furious spate of really foul Spanish sounded to her right. Too close. The sound of feet, maybe two sets, crashed through the undergrowth. They were less than ten feet away and heading for her position.

Furious shouts in Russian reached her. Vanko had seen her danger and alerted Ren and her brother. Quickly, she found cover behind the large trunk of a fallen tree. She placed the H&K to her side within reach. She extracted her knife and placed it next to the automatic weapon, then pulled her Bren Ten from its holster at her back. Close-in work demanded a handgun.

God, the fever was really making her dizzy. She blinked sweat from her eyes and kept her fuzzy gaze fixed on the place the enemy would break through. She took a two-handed grip on the powerful pistol, bracing her hands on the trunk. Then she waited.

The first man burst through the dense foliage. He spotted her immediately; her hat had fallen off during her crawl, her halo of red hair was a dead giveaway. Before the man could even raise his weapon, she popped off two shots. The first one hit him in the forehead, then the insurance shot, in the chest on his way down.

She let go of the gun with one hand and wiped away the sweat pouring down her forehead. She couldn't afford burning eyes at this juncture.

The second man, alerted by his companion's fall, dove behind a tree and began firing at her. His shots were wild and off the mark, but splinters from the trunk hit her cheek. Concerned about her bleary eyesight, she ducked down and played dead. She needed to draw him out. She wouldn't miss head-on. Plus, she knew from the sound of the other gunfire abating, that one of her guys would be coming soon.

Forcing herself to breathe slowly and calmly, she listened and waited.

"*Senorita*? Come out, I won't hurt you."

Yeah, like she was going to do anything that damn stupid. Her dad would tan her hide if she fell for such a trick. In her mind, she tried to anticipate what the macho idiot would do. Frontal attack or circle around? She'd have to play for both. Good thing she'd handled an H&K one-handed before. Shifting her Bren Ten to her left, her less dominant hand, she picked up the larger weapon with her right. All safeties off? She felt for them. Check. Everything was good to go.

Her ears ringing from all the high-caliber shots, she trusted in her spider sense. Her gut said bad guy was coming at her from the front and slightly to her right.

"*Senorita?*"

Dumbass. Now she knew where he was. She came up to her knees in one smooth mood, firing. There was no way to miss him with both guns blazing. A shot from her Bren Ten hit his shoulder, turning him away from her. She tracked his large body mass with the automatic weapon, firing a stream of torso shots. The man fell to the ground.

She ducked behind her fallen tree just in case none

of her shots had been kill shots. She stayed in place to see who would come next.

"Keely!" Ren's furious roar was a welcome sound. She slumped against the sturdy tree. She was too tired to answer him. He'd find her. Somehow she knew he'd always find her.

Two short bursts told her he'd made sure the mercs were dead.

"Yo, big guy? I think I killed them already." Her voice slurred. "Ren?" Was that weak, wimpy voice hers?

"Yeah, ya did." He stepped over the downed tree and knelt next to her. "Let go of the guns, baby." He tugged at the H&K. She let him have it, but tucked the Bren in her holster after flicking on the safety.

"I'm not a baby." She glared, but wasn't sure it was effective since she was weaker than a new Marine recruit after his first full day of training. "Hey, guys! All the bad guys dead?"

"You bet, sis," Tweeter said. "Dad would be proud."

"Yeah, stupid asshole thought I'd come out and surrender like some silly girl." She laughed and raised a hand to her whirling head. "Dad would've dropped the f-bomb all over the place if we ever did anything so damn dumb."

Tweeter hunkered down on her other side and cast

a concerned gaze over her. "Yeah, and Mom would've made out like a bandit when he had to buy her something in forfeit."

"Jewelry," she muttered as the world began to spin even though she was flat on her stomach. "Dad always buys her jewelry." She found Ren's frowning face. "The rain forest is spinning. Make it stop."

"Wish I could, sweetheart." He pulled her into his arms, turning her so she lay cuddled against his chest, then stood with her. An amazing feat of strength she would be sure to admire later—when she was safe and clean and rested—and not so dizzy.

Did he just kiss her hair? Oh yeah, he did. She sighed. She could get used to this kind of treatment. She snuggled her head into his chest. He smelled good, all clean, manly sweat.

"I'm going to get down on my knees and thank your father for teaching you how to survive." His voice sounded strained. "God, Keely, when Vanko said they were coming your way, I… I…"

Was that panic in his voice? Okay, she really was in trouble—he met the gooey center test.

"I'm fine. Stupid bad guys can't get the best of me. I'm a Walsh-trained Marine, sort of." Keely peered through her lashes at Ren. "You hurt, big guy?" She swiped at a tear that leaked from the corner of his eye.

"No, just … worried … about you." He pressed a light kiss near the corner of her mouth.

She licked her lips. "You taste good. Feel good, too." Her words were more and more slurred—and what was she saying? He'd think she was easy or something. Damn, she was really sick. She wiggled closer to his warmth. "Cold now. So tired. I want my hotel room and … and…"

"And what?"

"The biggest frick-fracking Pepsi you can find."

Ren pressed her head snugly against his chest. "I'll find Pepsi if I have to go to Buenos Aires to get it."

She patted his chest. "That would be nice. Still have the GPS, Vanko?"

"Yes, Keely. I'll get us to Puerto Iguazu."

"Good man." She nuzzled Ren's bared throat. Yeah, he really smelled good. All musky male heat and something citrusy. She tasted his throat with her tongue. The big strong man shuddered; she liked that. Yep, Ren was a warrior with a gooey center and tasted like a man margarita. Yummy. She yawned. She had to tell them something before she succumbed to the fuzzy darkness. Oh, yeah, hotel.

"Sheraton in the National Park. Rooms are in

Tweeter's … and my names—"

"Go to sleep." Tweeter's voice came from somewhere in the dark, hot fog that swept through her brain. "When did you last sleep?"

She frowned. "Over thirty-six hours ago?" She yawned again, her jaw cracking. "'Scuse me. Adrenaline crash … Tweetie?"

"Yeah?" Her brother stroked her arm as it lay over Ren's shoulder.

"Med kit in luggage. You—just you—take care of me."

As everything faded to solid black, she heard a "like hell, baby" from the man who carried her.

Chapter Four

Ren waited in the hallway outside the top floor set of suites Keely had the foresight to reserve for them at the Iguazu National Park Sheraton. He glanced at the small woman lying so still in his arms. She hadn't regained consciousness since the attack in the rain forest. Not even the loud rotor and engine noise of the Kamov had roused her. He'd alternately prayed and sworn under his breath during the entire trip to the hotel. This was a perfect example of why women didn't belong on battlefields or black ops missions.

Red flags of fever were the only color on her face. The rest of her skin was pasty white and damp from the sweats that had alternated with chills. If he had to guess, she was running a temp of at least a hundred and two. She had an infection somewhere. He only hoped it was one treatable with the antibiotics they had on hand and not some tropical bug she picked up on her valiant, but mad dash to warn them.

Vanko stuck his head out the door. "It's clear. Her brother is running a cool bath to get her temperature down. I will find her luggage and seek out the medical kit."

Ren nodded and hurried toward the sound of running water. As he entered the bathroom located off a large, luxurious bedroom, Tweeter stood up from the side of a spa tub big enough for all four of them and held his arms out for his sister. "Give her to me."

"No." For some goddamn reason, he couldn't bear to let her loose, not even to her brother. He didn't want to examine his feelings on the issue now, he just knew he had some and they were strong. "I'm staying. It'll take two of us to bathe her and then check out the wounds."

"Ren… Keely won't like this … and I'm not sure…"

"Fuck off, Tweeter. I'm staying," he all but snarled at his friend.

Tweeter's lips thinned, but he said nothing as Vanko

entered the room with a standard-issue Marine field medical kit in his hand. The Ukrainian looked from one to the other of them. "Is there something going on here I should know about?"

"No." Both he and Tweeter spoke at once.

Vanko shrugged. "O-o-kay. Here is the kit. It seems to have everything we'll need. I can always go back to Keelulya's very connected supplier and buy additional antibiotics from him, if needed."

Keely's supplier, Bazon, was a smuggler and very likely a former merc himself, but the tough old guy had seemed genuinely upset at the "little golden miss's" illness. He'd even had his son drive them to the hotel— no charge.

"Put the kit on the counter, Vanko." Ren stroked some stray curls off Keely's forehead, his fingers lingered, stroking her pale skin. "Then could you call room service and order us some food? See if you can find Pepsi—and maybe some soup an invalid might be able to drink." He looked away from her pale face to glance at her brother. "Anything else you think she'll need?"

Tweeter stared at him as if he were examining a newly discovered species. His face went from angry to a blank mask Ren couldn't read. "Get lots of straws,

Vanko." Tweeter turned to shut off the water. "She hates needles and I don't want to start an IV for hydration if I don't have to. She'll drink from a straw even half-asleep."

"She'll get a fucking IV if she fucking needs it," Ren gritted out. "If I have to, I'll fly her to fucking Buenos Aires to a fucking private hospital."

"Take it easy, Ren." Tweeter's demeanor was composed as he moved to unbutton Keely's shirt. "I've seen her like this before. She doesn't do heat well. It's mid-summer here for chrissakes and humid as the lower rungs of hell. She came from freeze-your-ass-off Boston and had little time to acclimate. Plus, she's hurt and needs fluids; even more she needs rest, some antibiotics—and later food."

Ren threw Keely's way-too-nonchalant brother a fierce glare. He shoved the man's hands away and took over the undressing. "Get out of here, Vanko. It'll be bad enough when she knows I've seen her naked."

He heard the Ukrainian move away, then stop. "Let's clear the air, Ren. Are you claiming Keelulya for your own? Because if you aren't, then I would like to remain and you can leave." The challenge in Vanko's voice was unmistakable. Even Tweeter stiffened.

"Just exactly what are you saying, Vanko?" Ren

wanted to tear his colleague's heart out through his throat.

"That I would like the chance to care for Keelulya and explore a relationship with her."

Shit, his friend was serious. So? Was he claiming Keely? His head told him it was too soon, but his gut said "hell, yeah."

"Yes." He stared first at Vanko, who frowned, but nodded, then at Tweeter, who still had the damn blank expression on his face.

"I won't have her forced or pressured, Ren," Tweeter finally said.

"I don't force women, and you damn well know it."

Keely whimpered and Ren soothed her with nonsense words and soft strokes of her head while he glared at her brother.

"Yeah, I know that." Tweeter unsnarled some of Keely's curls as they fell over Ren's arm. "But I have never seen you so possessive of a woman and Keely, while smarter than almost anyone I've ever known, is young for her age. We tended to overprotect her as she grew up."

Ren snorted. "I bet." He sighed. "I won't rush her, okay? That's all I can promise. But I plan on being around—a lot—so she can get used to me."

Tweeter's lips quirked. "Well, she already likes you."

"Really?" Ren paused in the act of removing her bloody shirt. He nestled her fragile body against his. "How can you tell? I mean she's opposed me at all junctures so far."

"She hasn't shoved your balls up your throat."

"Why would she? I haven't made a move—yet."

"Oh, yeah, you have. You've had the hard-on from hell since you met her."

Vanko choked, then coughed. Ren shot him a glare. The Ukrainian had the balls to smile.

Tweeter continued, "She allowed you to hold her against you—and your boner. She also let you carry her. Trust me, she's never allowed anyone to do that."

"She'd have let you carry her." Ren figured she was merely treating him as she would one of her brothers.

"No, she wouldn't have. Keely has a lot of guts and a gigantic sense of pride—she would've walked until she dropped before letting me pick her up." Tweeter stared at him, shaking his head. "You are an anomaly, my friend. I've seen her reactions to all sorts of men— me and the brothers trying to protect her, Dad's training recruits keeping their distance under the threat of pain and mutilation, geeks treating her like a buddy, assholes trying to get in her panties, and bullies trying

to hurt her. You don't fit into any of those categories."
Tweeter laughed.

"What's so funny?" Ren glared.

"You'll have to deal with the whole damn family.
Prove yourself worthy, no matter what she says or feels."

"No problem. But first we need to get her well, then
home to Sanctuary, and we aren't doing that standing
around here shooting the shit." He turned and glared
at a grinning Vanko. "You still here?"

"Leaving." The Ukrainian exited the bathroom,
shutting the door behind him.

Ren held Keely as Tweeter ripped the bloody-
beyond-salvation tank top over her head. With no bra
to impede his view he got his first good look at the
bruising—and bite marks. "Fuck, just fuck."

"Oh holy shit." Tweeter took in the infected bites
and assorted bruises on Keely's lower breasts. Tweeter's
concerned gaze caught his. "Let me give her a loading
dose of antibiotics in a shot while she's out of it. Once
we cool her off and clean those wounds, I'll help you
get some fluids down her. We'll mash any future meds
in some applesauce or ice cream until she can swallow
them on her own. That's how Mom always got our
meds down us when we were little. Keely will eat it like
a little bird, I promise. She'll be fine. Just fine."

His friend sounded as if he were trying to convince himself as much as Ren.

Ren nodded. "Strip her pants off, then take her. I'll strip off and climb in the tub to hold her."

"Ren…"

He sighed. "Don't argue, please. I can't explain it, but I *need* to hold her, to care for her."

"Fine, but you'll have to deal with her outrage and embarrassment, because I won't lie to her."

"I didn't ask you to." After tossing his clothes to the side, he climbed into the tub. His body shuddered at the cold water, but he'd been colder during Hell Week. He'd sit in a tub of fucking ice if that would make Keely well. He held his arms up for her limp body, flushed with fever.

"Here you go. Easy." Tweeter gently lowered Keely into his arms.

He held her against his chest for a second, before maneuvering her around so that her back was to him and her bottom between his thighs as he lowered her into the cool water. Her body convulsed in shivers as the water hit her overheated skin. She whimpered but remained unconscious.

"Shh, it's okay. I've got you. You're safe." She quieted and relaxed into his embrace. He buried his face on her shoulder for a second, inhaling her unique scent. He could find her in a dark room by sense of smell alone. With an arm firmly anchoring her against him, he said, "Hand me a cloth and some soap. I'll start cleaning the wounds."

Tweeter handed over the items, then pulled out a pre-packaged syringe and an ampule containing what Ren knew was a wide-spectrum antibiotic.

"What dose are you starting with?"

Before Tweeter could answer, Ren's attention was caught by a particularly deep bite mark on the lower curve of her right breast. "God-damn-mother-fucking-son-of-a-bitch!" His fist clenched around the washcloth. "What kind of inhuman bastard would hurt her like this?

Keely's brother knelt by the tub and efficiently gave her a shot in the upper arm. "A dead one. But first, my brothers and I will want a little 'talk' with the fucker." He took another cloth and began to bathe his sister's legs. His hand halted almost immediately. "Aww, fuck, just fuck."

At the look on Tweeter's face, at the tone in his voice, Ren stiffened. Icy fear traveled his spine. "What?"

"You can't see from there—" Tweeter choked back what sounded suspiciously like a sob. "Between her legs

… on her inner thigh."

"No!" He howled the word. Had she been raped?

The bathroom door banged open and Vanko rushed in. "What's wrong with the little one?"

Ren was so upset he didn't even think to order Vanko to leave the room. He just pulled Keely into his arms, laying her across his lap, then gently spread her legs. Bruising on her inner thighs looked like finger marks. He traced the ugly evidence of her legs being forcibly held apart. He scanned every millimeter of her skin up to the red-curl-covered mound. There was a multitude of bruises.

His heart sank as his anger built. He growled continuously now, like a jaguar on the prowl. But it was the teeth marks just above her mound which had him swearing in every language he knew.

"I wish to be on the hunt for the *sukin syn*." Vanko, his eyes a mirror of an inner inferno, turned away, leaving the room and closing the door gently.

Keely began to shiver in his arms. "She's not so flushed now. Take her, Tweeter." He couldn't look Keely's brother in the eye. Couldn't say out loud what he knew they all had concluded—whoever had hurt her, had also probably raped her. The external evidence was there; the internal evidence, possibly long gone since the infection from the bites had time to set in. Only Keely could tell them for sure what really happened, and when, and he wasn't sure he could hold it together to ask her the hard questions.

Now all he and her brother could do was deal with the resulting damage. No wonder she hadn't wanted to talk about her attack earlier. She had to hold it together until they were out of danger. And she had. So much courage in such a small package.

Tweeter pulled Keely from Ren's arms and cradled her as he knelt by the tub. Bracing her on his thigh, her brother gently began to rub her dry with a fluffy towel, wrapping her in a thick terry cloth bathrobe once he was done.

By then Ren had sluiced off and shrugged on the other bathrobe. "Give her to me. We'll lay her on the bed. Dress the wounds." He spat the words out like bullets. He was so enraged he wasn't sure how much longer he could contain the anger building inside him. He needed to hit something. No, he needed to kill someone, preferably the man, or God forbid, men, who'd done this to her. Right now, he had to maintain calm for Keely.

"Ren?" Tweeter held his sister close to his heart. "Don't ever hurt her—I'd hate to have to kill you."

Ren nodded curtly, taking her from Tweeter's arms into his. He strode into the bedroom and gently lowered her on the turned-down bed. Vanko had set an ice bucket filled with chilled cans of Pepsi, a handful of straws, and a covered bowl of what smelled like a chicken soup of some sort on the bedside table. He turned as Tweeter brought some antibiotic ointment and bandaging supplies to the bed. "She will tell us who did this, won't she?"

"Oh, yeah. In fact, she might not have to. I'll get on her laptop and plug this flash drive in." He held up a purple and pink thumb drive. "She'll have used the plane trip to write reports. My sister is nothing if not A-type—no matter what happened to her, she will have documented it. I figure she probably sent me a coded e-mail about it, but I don't trust the Internet security here to access my account."

"If it's not on there?"

"She'll tell. I have a feeling it's way more complicated than just her being … attacked."

"You think her assault has something to do with the trap set for us?" Ren frowned. He didn't like the sound of that at all. His fingers absentmindedly stroked her hair as it lay like a fiery golden-red wave against the cream-colored pillow.

"Maybe not directly. But knowing my little sister, she opened up a can of worms, reported said wormy situation to someone, and then everything went tango uniform." Tweeter sat on the opposite side of the bed and gently opened Keely's robe to get at the weeping bite marks. "Keep her still, boss. This stuff stings. I also want to check and make sure the bruising isn't broken ribs."

Ren cursed softly. His gaze never left Keely's face. He held one of her limp hands in his as her brother doctored her wounds. Small mewling whimpers were the only reaction to Tweeter's probing fingers and the stinging ointment.

"Ren?" Vanko's voice came from the doorway.

He didn't turn around. "Yeah, Vanko?"

"I spoke to the room service girl. There is an in-house doctor if we need him. Also, the young lady knows the local *curanderia*. Maybe I could get some ointment for the bruises and wounds? I have often found that some of the rain forest products are very healing."

"Good idea." He looked at Tweeter. "Do we need the doctor?"

"Yeah, just to be sure that … um, well, you know the … ahh, shit. Yeah." Tweeter looked at his trembling hands. "God, I'm a fucking mess. My baby sister… God, she's Walsh-tough, but she never should have come here without going to a doctor. Shit, just shit. How am I going to tell Dad and Mom? Fuck, Ren, she came to save my hide."

He understood Tweeter's feelings of guilt for what his sister had suffered. Somehow it was all tied together— the trap, her attack in Boston and, goddamnit, SSI. His own guilt lay on his heart like a lead blanket. He hoped the flash drive had some insight for them. He had a driving need to seek retribution.

He closed Keely's robe then pulled the top sheet and fluffy comforter over her. He turned to Vanko, whose face was etched with concern. "Get the doctor. Get the ointments, too. And see if there are any shops open." He glanced out the floor-to-ceiling windows with their glorious views of the mist-covered falls. Dusk had fallen. "Keely will need clothes. We will also—we'll be here until Keely is well enough to travel to Idaho."

Vanko's eyebrow arched. "We are staying here while the little one goes to Sanctuary?"

"Trujo has to be taken care of—once and for all." Ren hated to think of what might have happened if Keely had arrived after the firefight had already begun. "Call Price and Trey and get them down here." He glanced at Tweeter. "Keely will go home to Idaho with her brother. You okay with that?"

"Oh, I'm fine with it." Tweeter shot an affectionate look at his sister, who'd curled up on her side like a kitten. "But she won't be. She'll think she has to stay here and cover the intel end, which she is exceptionally good at, by the way."

"I have no doubt, but she can do intel at home. I want her out of it, far away from Trujo and his fucking band of murdering thugs."

"Whatever you say, boss." Tweeter tugged the duvet even further up around Keely's shoulders. "But be prepared to be argued into the ground."

⸺

REN SAT AT THE SUITE's dining room table and ate the room service food Vanko had ordered. It could be five-star gourmet fare, but to him it was just tasteless fuel.

Vanko had gone shopping with the assistance of the very attractive room service girl he had befriended earlier. The *curanderia* was the girl's grandmother and lived on the outskirts of the park area. She also knew a shop owner who would open up for the kind of business they promised. Money talked.

The doctor, a gray-haired, old school local, hadn't

batted an eye when he and Tweeter stood by the door for Keely's exam. Nor had he cared that she was still unconscious while he checked her out. While battered and abused, there had been no internal signs of bruising or tearing which would have been present if she'd been raped. All the damage was external. Ren had all but gone to his knees with relief. Tweeter had cried.

He glanced toward the open door to the bedroom where she lay asleep. He'd managed, with Tweeter's help, to get some water and soup broth down her, then the antibiotic tablets crushed into mango sorbet. It had definitely taken both their efforts since a febrile Keely tossed and turned and whimpered in a semi-state of consciousness. He'd had to go in several times in the last couple of hours to hold her through similar bouts of restlessness. Her sleep, while no longer fevered, continued to be fretful. Only his touch seemed to soothe her. He smiled—unconsciously she accepted him. It was a start.

He glanced at his watch. In another thirty minutes he'd get some more meds down her, then maybe he'd lie next to her and take a nap—that way he'd be there in case she needed him to soothe her through whatever disturbed her sleep. At least that was the way he rationalized it to Tweeter who'd smiled knowingly and said "sure, Ren."

"Boss." Tweeter gestured for him to come to the end of the table where he had Keely's laptop open. "You need to read this. It all started years ago, but baby sis's project for NSA allowed her to find the patterns just recently—said patterns jumped out at her since SSI seems to have been involved in several of the incidents, all National Clandestine Service contract jobs."

He pulled up a chair and read the screen. He glanced at Tweeter, a frown creasing his forehead. "Shit. We had several close calls on those cases. Lost a good man on one of them."

"Yeah." Tweeter ran a hand through his dark blond hair. "So, to summarize, it looks like my sister discovered a pattern of someone high up in the Department of Defense, most likely in the DIA, selling out special forces teams and private contractors like us to the enemy they were sent to eradicate and/or collect on-the-ground intel about. Keely reports said patterns of bad acts to NSA as required by her contract with them. They say they'll handle it, but Keely continues to monitor and the bad acts continue. Then two days ago or so, she stumbles across the trap set for us—and decides enough is enough."

"Trujo wants us out of the way because we've

interrupted his major lines of drug distribution while working in conjunction with several S.A. countries," added Ren. "So, he contacts the government baddie and has him send false intel to NCS, our government employer, who asks us to meet and evaluate a new informant on al Qaeda activity in the hot Triple Frontier area."

"Baby sis—who loves me a lot—hot tails it down here when she can't reach me."

"But she said she called Sanctuary and spoke to Quinn. Why didn't she have him call us off?"

Tweeter frowned, then something crossed his face that had Ren's gut clenching. "She suspects a mole at Sanctuary and she doesn't know anyone there she could trust."

He nodded. "I don't like it, but that makes sense. She could've made our situation even worse. The trap could've been sprung earlier. She wouldn't take that chance." He slammed the table, making the laptop bounce. "We've got a fucking traitor in SSI. But who?"

Tweeter shook his head. "I don't know. I've trusted all those guys at my back." He scrolled down some more files, then clicked on another one. "Yeah, she documented her suspicions after she spoke to Quinn. She has a plan for catching whoever it is, though. She always has a plan."

Ren read the screen. "Yeah, that'll work and it should lead us to the DoD turncoat to boot." He snorted. "She even has it set up that NSA will pay us for the work. Hmm, I see she had planned to come back with us to Idaho anyway. So I don't have to worry about forcing her there." He glanced at the bedroom. "She's restless. I'll go give her the next set of meds and see if I can get her to drink." He hesitated. "Um, what did your mom do about bathroom breaks when you were out of it?"

Tweeter's lips twisting with amusement, he stood up. "I'll take care of it, boss. If she roused enough to see you putting her on the john, she might break your nose. I'll call you in when it's all clear." He pushed away from the table and strode toward the bedroom and closed the door.

Ren pulled the screen around and scanned files. He wanted to know what had happened about the time she decided to leave for South America to warn them. Who the fuck had brutalized her? Her bruises dated to about that time.

Finding a file dated two days ago at the bottom of the list, Ren opened it and began to read. His jaw clenched as he read the detailed and succinct description of the attack in a dockside warehouse Keely had managed to live through. She confirmed the doctor's conclusion— external bruising but no penetration. It was all there in black and white—and he saw red.

Pushing away from the table, he left the file open for Tweeter. He walked to the window and stared at one of the most beautiful waterfalls in the world and attempted to let nature calm his anger. It didn't work.

The door to the suite opening and closing had him reaching for Keely's Bren Ten, which he had put in the pocket of his robe.

Vanko, loaded down with packages, walked toward him.

"Drop the packages and read the screen on the laptop. Also read the other two opened files. Then go with me to the hotel gym. I need to do something to get rid of this rage or I'll start tearing the suite apart with my bare hands."

Vanko nodded and sat at the table and began to read.

Ren strode toward the packages and found some sweat pants and a t-shirt that would fit him and do for a good bout of kick-boxing—and hallelujah, a bottle of single malt Scotch. He put the clothes aside and opened the alcohol. Grabbing a glass from the bar, he threw a couple of cubes in it and poured two fingers of Scotch. Tossing it back, he poured two more fingers, then fixed a drink for Vanko. He took both drinks and sat next to Vanko as he read.

His friend glanced at him, his eyes darkened with rage. "How could she even think to leave the country after … that…" He pointed to the screen and the report of her abduction and abuse at the hands of four men whom, she'd surmised, had been hired by the DoD traitor to silence her, thus confirming her findings had been spot on. "The fact she managed to escape and kill two of them, then travel here to warn us—I cannot wrap my mind around it."

"Never again," vowed Ren. "She'll never have to fight like that again."

"We will definitely hunt the remaining animals down." Vanko clicked the other files and read swiftly. "Ahh, the little one stumbled into a very nasty nest of vipers. But I see she has a plan—a good one." Vanko looked at him. "If directed by her from the safety of Sanctuary, she should be fine."

"Read the next file." Ren tossed back the rest of his Scotch, the warmth not managing to take away the chill of knowing he harbored a traitor in his midst.

"*Dermo.*" Vanko grabbed the drink Ren had made

him and drank deeply. "She has a plan to catch this piece of excrement also, yes?"

"Yes."

The door to the bedroom opened and Tweeter walked out. "All personal needs are taken care of—and she took her meds and drank like the little angel she is. And, thank the Lord, her fever finally broke." He smiled at Vanko, then frowned as he sensed the tension in the room. "What is it?"

"Read this file." Ren opened the one about Keely's attack. "Vanko and I are going downstairs to the workout room to toss each other around for a while. Guard your sister. I'll be back to take over so you can go hit something, too."

"Will I need to hit something?" Tweeter approached the laptop as if it might bite him.

"Oh yeah. Killing some fuckers would be better, but hitting will be on the agenda."

Ren threw off the robe and walked naked to pull on the clothing he'd chosen to wear.

"Jesus-fucking-Christ!" Tweeter pulled out his cell and viciously punched in numbers.

"Who are you calling?" Ren walked to join Vanko who held the door to the hall open.

"My Dad. He needs to get some damage control

going. There are two fucking dead guys in a Boston dockside warehouse. They're probably smelling by now. Dad needs to make sure there's nothing there to incriminate Keely."

"Shit, I didn't think of that." He rubbed a hand over his face. "Should we detour Trey and Price to Boston and have them handle it?"

"No, you need them here. I want to get Keely to Sanctuary as soon as possible. Dad and some of my brothers can handle it. Trust me. If Loren or Paul are stateside—and by the notes Keely made, she had issued the family distress call—they are, then the twins and Dad will take care of it."

Ren nodded. "Good. I don't want Keely touched by any of this any longer."

"That might be hard to stop, Ren. She placed herself in the eye of the storm," Tweeter said.

"And I'm taking her out of it." Ren followed Vanko out and shut the door firmly.

His warrior sprite would not be used as bait. No way. No how.

CHAPTER FIVE

Keely woke up slowly. Turning to lie on her back, her gaze skimmed the surroundings. She was in a bedroom, a large, airy room with ceiling fans providing a light breeze. Floor-to-ceiling windows covered by shades filtering the sun took up one whole wall. Under her were soft-to-the-touch sheets on a comfortable mattress. A feathery light duvet covered her body.

She peeked under the bed covers and found herself in a cotton tank top and sleep shorts. Thank God, someone had bought her some clothing. She'd left Boston too fast to pack a proper bag; she hadn't wanted to take the chance the person or persons who'd had her kidnapped might not manage to do so again. She'd grabbed her computer and her med kit and fled.

Vague memories surfaced. They weren't the nightmare ones of Boston, or even those of her hurried trip to Argentina and the events in the village, but more recent, pleasant—unbelievable—memories. Ren holding her in a tub, bathing her, touching her intimately, touching her gently.

Her cheeks burned as other hazy scenes flitted across her mind's eye. Ren feeding her. Sponging her feverish, naked body. Rubbing cooling ointment on her bruises and wounds. Holding her against a lot of hot, firm masculine skin. All the while he cared for her, he alternately crooned soothing nonsense and swore vilely at the men who'd harmed her.

He'd slept with her! Cared for as if she were precious to him. Why? She could've sworn the man thought her a nuisance—and wanted her gone. Maybe her subconscious made up all the images. She was attracted so she dreamed about him.

She sat up and looked to her left. She rubbed her hand over a man-sized depression in the mattress pad. She swore she could still feel his warmth on the sheets. Leaning over she inhaled. Citrus and a male musk uniquely Ren's. Sweet Jesus! He'd slept next to her; it hadn't been a figment of her imagination, so the other memories must be real as well. He'd taken care of her day and night. Her cheeks burned even hotter at the thought of him nursing her through the fever.

For how long? She glanced at a bedside clock radio—for three days! How could she lie next to an *uber*-alpha-male for close to seventy-two hours and not awaken? Man, she must have been really sick. And where had her brother-protector been? Had he lost his mind? He never let men close to her.

Swinging her legs out of bed, she stood. Whoa, big mistake. The room tilted. Her arm shot back to catch her if she fell. Taking a couple of deep breaths, she waited to orient herself to the use of her legs once more. When she thought she could take a step without falling on her face, she headed for the bathroom. She wanted a shower, clothing and food. Lots of food—and the Pepsi she vaguely recalled the men promising her if she'd only wake up.

The thought of the sugary caffeine nectar from the gods had her diverting to the main room of the suite. A quick glance showed no one present. She spied the familiar red, white and blue cans sitting on the bar. Like an addict needing her next fix, she made a beeline for them. Filling a glass with ice, she popped open a can and added the soda to the glass, stopping to sip the foam from time to time. She moaned and swore she felt the caffeine and sugar hitting her blood stream. After several sips of the drink, she almost felt like herself again.

With the glass in her hand and an extra can in the other, she listened for signs of life in the other rooms. The suite was very quiet. The guys were probably sleeping, after all, they'd taken care of her for three days.

But then Ren had obviously slept next to her, so where was he? Had he gone out?

She frowned. If he was going after Trujo, he'd need her help. The *narcotrafficante* was slipperier than the eels found in the drainage canals alongside the roads in Puerto Iguazu. She knew where the bastard holed up in the Triple Frontier. She'd researched the notorious and powerful drug lord for the NSA. She'd show the guys her findings. They needed to see what they'd be up against. Three men versus a small army did not slant in favor of the good guys.

Now to see who was here, because neither her brother nor Ren—who'd obviously displayed more than brotherly concern for her person over the last three days—would have left her alone and helpless.

Ren. Just thoughts of his scent and warmth

surrounding her in bed made her heart race and her womb spasm. His devotion to her care could be just gratitude on his part, but it felt like more. His actions seemed lover-like as in male-to-female love and not the paternal or sibling kind. Of course, there had been his ever-present hard-on in the village and the rain forest—that physiological response was definitely not the reaction of a brother. Her only conclusion? He was sexually attracted to her. But was there more there than just lust? And how did she feel about it if there were?

Ren as a lover? Her mouth went dry and her vision blurred—probably just low blood sugar. She took a sip of Pepsi. She'd never really thought about taking a lover before. For one, she was young and had overprotective men surrounding her most of her life. Secondly, there had been no time. Her college classes and later her teaching and research had taken up the majority of her time. Third, she was not a believer in casual sex; she wanted a long-term, loving relationship like her parents had. And, finally, most of the men she'd met either treated her like a freak because of her genius or like a sex toy.

Keely shuddered at the memory of the four men who'd kidnapped, abused, promised her rape, and, ultimately, death. She'd killed two of them. After their buddies had gone off for food and to report to their boss, the two left had attempted to rape her. When they made their move, they'd underestimated her. They freed her hands and feet, then one held her for the other. Freeing her had been a major mistake, and she took advantage using all the dirty tricks her brothers had taught her. Weakened by their abuse, it had been a perilous fight. Killing them was the only way she could free herself and escape. It had been a close call, one she would only admit to herself. She regretted having to kill, but there had been no way she'd allow them to rape her. Plus, she had to escape to warn her brother.

Idly, she wondered if the police had found the bodies in the dockside warehouse. An anonymous phone call before she boarded the plane in Boston had given the police the general location.

Thrusting the thoughts of the kidnapping and its aftermath back under old news, she set her drink aside and carefully opened the door to one of the suite's three other bedrooms. Empty. At the second try, she found her brother sprawled on his stomach, clothed in just his boxers, on top of the bedspread. The sun beat on his naked back through the large windows. She could see the sweat beading on his skin even in the air-conditioned room. Damn humidity. She flicked on the ceiling fan and then tiptoed to the window and lowered the shade in an attempt to cool off the room even more.

Before leaving to take care of her other needs, she leaned over and kissed him on the top of his messy, dirty blond hair. "Love you, Tweetie."

He mumbled something unintelligible and settled back into sleep. She smiled. Only an earthquake would wake this brother. The others, like their dad, were trained warriors and slept lightly. Tweeter would have been a SEAL like Loren and Paul, the two oldest boys, except for the fact he was the youngest, had a genius IQ, and had been deputized to attend MIT with her as her protector. There were predators everywhere, even at the prestigious university. And he had protected her, devotedly. When she turned eighteen, she lovingly told him to get his own life—and he joined the Maddox brothers at SSI.

Shutting the door to his bedroom behind her, she checked the last room and found it empty, but with signs it had been occupied—Vanko's room.

Ren was nowhere to be found in the large suite of rooms. God only knew where he was. So she guessed she was on her own for seeking sustenance. She glanced at the clock over the bar. Almost lunchtime. She bet there was an eating area by the pool. Her stomach growled loudly at the thought. She patted her flat tummy. She needed fuel, especially if she had to handle three alpha males determined to be overprotective where she was concerned.

Her short-term goal set, she retrieved her drink and re-entered her bedroom.

The shower felt wonderful and the toiletries provided by the hotel were more luxurious than any she used at home. She emerged, smelling like a tropical rain forest, all earthy and flowery at the same time. Running her fingers through her wet curls, she was glad she hadn't quite rinsed out all the coconut-smelling conditioner. It would keep the frizz-quotient down.

She found a unique pottery jar on the counter and lifted the lid. It was an ointment. She sniffed it. The smell brought almost erotic memories of Ren's large hands gently massaging it into her wounds and bruises. The cream must be some sort of a miracle drug because the five-day-old evidence of her attack had faded so much she had to squint to see anything. The bite marks were also no longer infected, but she chalked that result up to the meds her brother and Ren had gotten into her. She wasn't sure when she had her last dose of antibiotics, but she'd find the med kit and get a tablet to take at her meal to be safe.

Her body clean, lotioned and treated with the miracle cream, she walked into a large closet and found several outfits for her. The guys had been busy. She couldn't find a bathing suit so added that item to her mental to-buy list. The pool called to her. She was a water baby and wanted a swim so badly she could taste it. Searching in all the built-in drawers, she could find no underwear, either. Typical male oversight. She'd have to remedy the deficit as soon as possible. She could go without a bra, but hated to since her breasts were full and needed the support. And going panty-less was not an option, but she could make do until she could get to the shops.

She took an aqua-colored sundress off a hanger and pulled it over her head. The dress had a built-in bra and it fit just fine. Although it showed more cleavage than she normally would. Shoes? She looked around and found a pair of turquoise-jeweled thong sandals. Very chic—and perfect.

Whoever had bought the clothes had excellent taste. For some reason she sensed it hadn't been Ren. He just didn't seem the type of man who knew what clothes would suit a woman. And she knew it hadn't been her brother. He'd never buy her anything that showed her breasts so much—and he'd have bought her underwear. So that left Vanko.

She grinned. Bet the flirty Ukrainian had had fun. That was one man who enjoyed women. He'd dallied with her outside the village cantina, but she'd sensed it had all been in play. She'd take him along when she went to buy more clothing. They'd have a good time. Plus, this was a rough area of the world and she wasn't stupid enough to go shopping in the street markets alone. One kidnapping had been more than enough.

Walking back into the bedroom, she located her backpack. She pulled out a travel wallet on a strap and checked to be sure she had traveler's checks. She would cash some at the front desk; she could charge most things to the room, but she needed cash for tips and such. The antibiotics were on the bedside table and she put the bottle in the small purse. Then she went into the main living area of the suite. Spying her laptop on the table by the window, she went over to see what the guys had accessed. Hitting a key, she woke it up and saw with satisfaction they had read it all. Good, she wouldn't have to talk about what happened and why she'd done what she had. The explanations had all been in her reports. Closing the laptop, she looked around and located a key card for the room on a chest by the door. She picked it up and put it in her travel purse.

As she went to leave the room, she thought about a weapon. She couldn't see her Bren and it wouldn't fit into her small purse any way. Her knife was also too big. She shrugged. She should be safe in public space in a resort hotel, but she'd leave the guys a note so they wouldn't go apeshit when they found her gone.

Hurrying over to the desk, she wrote a note telling them where she'd be, the time she left, and the time she expected to be back. Taking the note pad, she propped it against the laptop, then left. She was hungrier than she could ever remember being. She hoped the restaurant had burgers, 'cause she needed red meat.

———

KEELY APPROACHED THE HOSTESS STAND at the poolside restaurant. She could've eaten in the main dining room, but the blue water of the Olympic size pool and the breeze blowing in from the falls beckoned her.

"*Hola, senorita.* One for lunch?"

"Yes." Keely scanned the area, ignoring the lascivious stares of men as they stripped her naked with their eyes. Uncomfortable with the avid scrutiny, she asked, "Could I have a private cabana, please?"

"It is not a problem," the pretty brunette said with

a smile. "Please follow me."

Keely walked behind the hostess, aware that a majority of the male eyes followed their progression through the poolside restaurant.

Damn, maybe this hadn't been a good idea. Her hair was like a beacon. She should have called room service, but wanted, no needed, to get out, to act like a tourist—to be normal. She hoped her indulgence wouldn't come back to bite her very naked butt.

The hostess gestured to the table. Keely smiled and slipped her ten dollars. "Please close the draperies."

"I understand, *senorita*. Your hair—it is very beautiful. The men, they cannot resist looking, wanting to touch the fire."

"Thank you. My fiancé—*mi novio*—likes it well enough." And where in the heck had the idea of a fiancé come from?

The hostess's gaze moved to her left hand. Her ring-less left hand. Busted already.

Damn, she'd have to get a ring to underline her lie. It would be better for her to be engaged and considered off-limits while she was in South America. Not that a ring or the threat of a fiancé waiting in the wings would stop all men, but it would most of them.

"Your server is Teresa. She will be with you soon.

Enjoy your meal." The hostess laid the menu in front of her then left, releasing the sheer draperies to close Keely inside.

Even though the draperies were tissue-thin, their closure gave her some peace of mind. Yet the men would still be there later, watching for her departure. Maybe there was a back way out?

A few seconds later, a young girl entered, smiling shyly. "The dress it is very beautiful on you. Senor Vanko and I thought it would be." She poured water into one of the crystal goblets on the table.

"You helped Vanko buy my clothes?" She looked at the girl and guessed them to be of an age. Teresa was petite with small breasts and hips, dark-haired, dark-eyed, with a beautiful full-lipped smile. She could see Vanko flirting with her.

"Yes. The men, your *novio*, especially, were so concerned. They had the doctor in to see you."

Her *novio*, huh? Wonder whose idea that had been? The men must have realized how awkward it would look to have three men in the same suite with her. They'd come up with the same fiction she had to protect her. Had it been Ren's idea? Her gut said it had. The thought warmed her.

Teresa pointed toward Keely's bared shoulder. "I

see my grandmother's salve helped the bruises and other marks."

"It is a wonder drug. Does your grandmother sell it in the market?"

"No, no. She is the local *curanderia*. The people, they come to her house. I take Senor Vanko there and he explain what happened and she make for you." The girl smiled. "Each person needs their own special magic, *si*?"

"Yes." Keely held out a hand and the girl placed hers in it. "Thank you. I would love to meet your grandmother and take more of this ointment home with me. I bruise easily."

"Men can be brutal pigs." Teresa bit out the words as if she knew of what she spoke. Looked as if they shared something else in common.

"Not my men." She didn't want the girl to think Ren, Vanko or Tweetie had hurt her.

"I understand. Your men are honorable."

"Yes, they are." She gently squeezed the girl's hand, then let it go. Her stomach's angry growl reminded her of why she was there. She laughed. "Do you have hamburgers? I'm starved."

"Yes, the finest Argentine beef." Teresa wrote on her pad. "What would you like with that?"

"A salad. Your house dressing. Fresh fruit. A Pepsi or Coke—oh, and make the burger well done, with mayonnaise on the side."

"It will be done. I will bring the salad and your drink right away."

"*Gracias*, Teresa. And later, could I ask you to take me to the shop where you and Vanko bought the clothing? I need some more items."

Teresa nodded and grinned. "Like lingerie? Senor Vanko turned very red when I mentioned such."

"That surprises me. He is very much a flirt."

"*Si*, he is, but he said your *novio* would not like him purchasing such intimate items for you. So he bought none."

Keely flushed at the thought of Ren purchasing underwear for her. Would he pick practical or sexy? She shivered, remembering his long-fingered touch as he rubbed ointment into her breasts. She'd bet on sexy—black or red. "Yes, my *novio* wouldn't like it at all. Let me know when you have some free time. I'd be happy to pay you to accompany me."

"No need to pay. Maybe Senor Vanko could go along? To guard your hair?" Teresa grinned and winked.

"Maybe." She laughed at the mischievous twinkle in the Argentinean girl's eyes. Teresa left the cabana in a swirl of gauze draperies.

Almost immediately after Teresa's exit, a youthful waiter with a glass of something fruity and most likely alcoholic entered the cabana. "From the senor for the senorita." He bowed and began to place the drink before her.

One of the leering men had sent her something to drink? All the lectures from her dad and brothers about men drugging unsuspecting women's drinks came to mind. Did she look stupid? She shook her head and waved the drink away. "No, thank you. I don't accept drinks from men I don't know. My *novio* would be very upset." More like livid.

"Senorita, please." The young man pleaded, his tanned complexion almost pasty with fear. "The senor will be very angry. He will think I upset you."

Teresa entered with a salad and the soft drink and began to argue with the waiter in rapid Spanish, the dialect so heavy that Keely couldn't follow most of it. She got enough of the gist and had to stifle laughter. The very sweet Teresa was reaming the poor guy a new asshole. The girl described in detail the physical attributes of Ren, Vanko and Tweetie then told the young man he had more to worry about from the senorita's men than the senor.

The waiter, his face now beet red, bowed and left the cabana, taking the drink with him.

"Teresa, *gracias*. Maybe I should go back to my suite. I'm obviously attracting unwanted attention. Could you have my lunch boxed to go?"

In fact, Keely's neck had begun to itch like crazy. Something bad was about to happen. She didn't want innocents caught in the crossfire, plus her weapons were in the room.

"Yes, that might be good." Teresa frowned. "The senor Tonio mentioned is a very bad man. He takes what he wants. *?Entienda?*"

"Yes, I understand." She massaged her temples. All of a sudden she was tired. "I just wanted to have a normal lunch like a normal tourist."

"You are not normal." Teresa waved a hand toward Keely's head. "Your hair, it is an attraction. Your body, also—it spoke to the men as you walked into the restaurant." She shook her head. "You must not walk around the resort without one of your men, senorita."

"I agree."

Teresa turned to leave. "I will hurry the meal and pack it for you to take."

"*Gracias*. I still want to shop with you—later when Vanko can take us."

"Good. I will enjoy that." The drapes parted and Teresa left.

Closing her eyes, Keely laid her head against the high-backed chair. Unwanted tears filled her eyes. Damn, why couldn't she have a boring, simple life? She'd always had to watch out for predatory males. She'd been fairly safe in Cambridge at MIT, or had been until the crap with the DoD turncoat and the NSA had begun. But everywhere else, she'd had to make sure she dressed down, covering her feminine assets.

Men were pigs, as Teresa said. Well, all men except for her brothers and maybe Ren and Vanko. She snorted—no, they were pigs, too, just not to her.

"Senorita?" A low, raspy male voice spoke. Every nerve in her body went on alert. Her brain screamed danger. The dangerous male was close—too close. How had a man sneaked into her space without her knowing? She must be more tired than she realized.

Keely opened her eyes. Damn, there were two of them! Large thugs with guns holstered—looked like Beretta submachine pistols—but showing under their lightweight jackets. They stood in front of her table and between her and the exit. Their heavily muscled bodies touched the table's edge. She'd bet the taller one had enough reach to grab her across the table. She slowly nudged her chair back.

While the expressions on their faces would suit a statue, their eyes glittered with menace—and lust. They were highly aroused as the tents in the front of both their light wool dress pants showed. *Well, this was just frick-fracking great.*

As their libidinous glances took in her face, hair and cleavage, she slid the steak knife from the table with her left hand and then transferred it to her right under the cover of the tablecloth. She held the weapon against her right thigh in the folds of her full skirt. The knife was not a perfect throwing knife, but it would do. She might be able to take one man out and get past the other into the open where someone might come to her defense.

"Senor Trujo would like the pleasure of your company for lunch. He was not happy you rejected his drink." The taller of the two men spoke. Both thugs frowned as if she had insulted them personally.

"Senor Trujo?" A sudden chill swept over her body and it took all of her control not to shudder. Did the *narcotraficante* boss know she was associated with Ren and the others? How could he? She'd never met the Argentinean drug lord and had only been "associated" with Ren and SSI for a few days. Even if the DoD traitor had mentioned her to the pissant drug lord, Trujo still should not have connected her to SSI.

Fate had a horrible sense of humor—and even worse timing.

"I do not know Senor Trujo. I do not accept drinks or lunch from men I don't know. My *novio* would frown on it. Beyond that, it is just a stupid thing to do."

The shorter thug looked to her left hand which lay on the table. "I see no ring."

Damn, she really needed to buy a ring—and would just as soon as she got away from these two Neanderthals.

"We just got engaged. Last night. He's buying a ring now. He is meeting me for lunch to celebrate." *Way to think on your feet, Keely.*

The two men looked behind them as if they expected to see her fiancé approaching.

"He can come find you. Senor Trujo's table is the best in the house. We will see your *novio* when he arrives. Come," the smaller man held out his hand, "Senor Trujo does not like to be kept waiting."

"I'm leaving. Going back to my room. Please get out of my way." She placed her left hand at the edge of the table and pushed her chair further away using her feet. Then she stood, keeping the knife in her right hand hidden in her skirt.

"We cannot allow you to do that, senorita." The taller of the two men reached for his gun.

Keely brought her right hand up and threw the steak knife. It hit the man reaching for his weapon in the upper arm. As he bellowed his rage and grabbed at the knife to pull it out, she shoved the table at the other man. The edge hit him in his groin, a direct hit on the obscene bulge in his pants. She muttered, "Pervert."

The man she'd knifed came around the table, reaching for her. He grabbed her arm in a bruising grip. She used his forward momentum to throw him over her hip. He landed on his head at the back of the tented cabana. He hit so hard the supports shook wildly.

Keely ran for the opening. The shorter man attempted to grab her with one hand while he held onto his aching manhood with the other. He was livid with rage and swearing in Spanish; he'd gladly hurt her if he could catch her. She twisted and avoided his grasp then kicked out at his knee, sending him to the ground.

Keeping her gaze on the downed men, she blindly pushed through the draperies and ran into a large male body. Instinctively, she thrust her hand up toward the face, hoping to break this new attacker's nose.

"No, none of that, you little spitfire. I'm the good

guy here." Ren's growling voice soothed her instantly as his arms surrounded her in a tight embrace.

"Ren?" She trembled in his arms, her face turned into his chest.

"Yes, baby. It's Ren." He held her with one arm around her waist as he soothed her back with his other hand. "Who are these fucking assholes?" He sounded mean—no, he sounded deadly. Her trembling lessened. She was safe. He wouldn't let anyone hurt her.

She looked up at him. His eyes burned with the need for retribution, but she knew he'd want her out of the danger zone and out of the public eye before he did anything. She stroked a shaky hand along his tight jaw. He was containing his rage as the wild pulsating muscle in his jaw attested, but she sensed it wouldn't take much for him to let loose his wrath.

"Come closer," she spoke softly. He leaned down until his ear was against her lips. His narrowed gaze never left the two men, who, she sensed, now stood, breathing heavily behind her.

"What?" His breath whispered over her ear.

She clued him in on the situation in a low tone. "They are Trujo's men. The creep sent over a drink. I refused it. They came over. Tall guy announced Trujo wanted me to have lunch with him. He can't know who

I am, can he?"

His gaze switched to her, gentling as he scanned her face. "No." He paused, thought some more, then swore viciously under his breath. "No—how could he?" His head jerked up and turned toward the main pool dining area. She knew he looked for his enemy.

"That's what I thought." She rested her head on his chest. His heart pounded loudly. Inhaling, she luxuriated in his scent; it calmed her just as it had for the last three days. She nuzzled the opening of his shirt at his throat, then touched the tip of her tongue to his sweaty skin. Spicy and lemony all at once. She liked it. His taste, like his smell, steadied her.

His hand moved from her waist to press her face into his chest, his fingers threaded through her curls. It was a blatant act of possession. He spoke to the two thugs over her head. "Who dared approach my woman?"

The way he said "my woman" should have struck every stubborn, independent nerve in her as wrong, but instead it thrilled her. He'd claimed her, even if it was just for show and her protection.

And, God knew, she felt safe, even with two dangerous, armed thugs behind her.

"What's going on, Ren?" Vanko's voice was a

welcome addition to the tableaux. Now there were two against two.

"Keely? Did those bastards touch you?" Her beloved brother's voice added to the mix.

Teresa must have called the suite when she saw the danger. Bless her heart.

Keely turned within the circle of Ren's embrace, her back against his chest, her butt against his groin. They fit perfectly. She shook off the incongruous thought, time enough for that later, now she had to concentrate on the current tense situation.

The man at whom she'd thrown the knife glared at her, but his anger was icy and under control. This was a man who could wait for revenge. Cold vengeance was the worst kind; you never knew when the avenger would turn up. She shivered.

Ren rubbed her arm, his chin resting on the top of her head. "Keely, you okay?" He placed a small kiss just below her ear. Goose bumps raised on her arms.

"Now I am. Just a little chilled."

"Vanko, give me your jacket." Ren took the proffered jacket and placed it around her shoulders, then pulled her back against him.

The bleeding thug's frigid gaze was fixed only on her. His complete disregard for the three men ranged around her confirmed he was the more dangerous of the two and that she had made a bitter enemy. "This is the *novio* you told us about?"

Despite the added warmth of Vanko's jacket and the security of Ren's arms, she shuddered at the evil look the taller man shot her. "Yes." Her voice was soft, hesitant, then she coughed and said more firmly, "Yes. This is my *novio*." She refused to show fear to this man. He'd jump on it, use it against her.

Ren's arm tightened and he brushed a kiss on the top of her curls. "Easy. I've got your back."

"I will tell Senor Trujo. We are sorry for frightening you, *poco gata*. We will leave now." He gestured to his companion, who rubbed his sore groin and shot a dagger-like glance at her.

The asshole had called her "little cat" which in colloquial Spanish equated to "little bitch"—as in prostitute. Ren stiffened, then cursed at the insult to her, showing he knew his gutter Spanish as well as she did. His anger was obvious in the viciousness of his swear words.

"I don't think so." Ren's voice halted the two men's departure. "I want to meet your boss, personally. Take me to him now. His invitation and your threatening actions and verbal insult to my fiancée are inexcusable."

"No!" She wiggled and turned within his arms, her hands flat on his chest. His heart thudded under her touch. She could almost smell the adrenaline changing his scent. His body was gearing up for a fight. "I'm ... fine. I ... am ... fine. Let it go, please? For me?" She added in a low tone. "For now."

He bristled. A muscle in his jaw twitched. A low rumble sounded in his chest, akin to a large predatory cat's angry growl. She stroked his pecs, attempting to soothe him, pressing small kisses over his shirt. He obviously wanted to meet with Trujo, taking only Vanko and Tweeter along. She had to convince him of what a bad idea that would be—she had intel they needed to see before any meeting took place. They'd be outnumbered, outgunned. Trujo's estate was an armed camp. She couldn't let them go without proper planning—and more backup.

"Keely. Baby." Ren's voice pleaded. He took one of her hands and brought it to his lips to kiss. He stopped then frowned as he fingered a new red mark on her arm where the tall goon had grabbed her. He swore again, casting a fulminating glance at the man closely observing them. Then he looked back to her, his eyes narrowed, smoky grey-blue in their anger. "You fucking had to defend yourself. So hell yeah, I want a meet with the fucker. The other stuff is just side bennies."

The fact he wanted to meet Trujo more on her behalf than on his own terrified her even worse. Still, all her reasons to delay the meet were valid. "I was scared. I over-reacted. Please?" She buried her face in his chest, tears wetting his silk shirt. "Please." She stroked him with her free hand.

"Keely … sweetheart … it's okay. God, stop crying." Ren swung her into his arms, then addressed Trujo's men over her head. "Don't ever let me see either of you even look at my woman again. I won't be so forgiving next time."

Keely peered through water-logged lashes. The taller man nodded, then pulled the other man with him. Vanko closed the draperies, shutting out interested onlookers. Tweeter stood next to them, a concerned glance on her.

"Keely, stop crying. You're killing me here." Ren rubbed his cheek against her hair.

She sniffed. "Sorry. I'm hungry—and still tired— and I wanted to pretend just for a while I was a tourist— and they ruined my lunch." She all but wailed the last part of her sentence.

"Senorita? I have your lunch all packed for you."

Keely raised her head. Teresa had entered the

cabana and wiggled her way past Vanko. She held a large bag. A luscious cooked-meat smell filled the tent-like structure. "Thank you for calling the guys. Those men would've tried to take me away."

Teresa smiled. "Senor Trujo, he run like the scared little boy when he sees your *novio* come running. Trujo is an evil man. It is bad you attracted his notice."

Ren squeezed her more tightly against him. "Thank you, Teresa. You've been a big help. My fiancée will be flying home to the States tomorrow with her brother, so Trujo will not have a chance to approach her again."

"I'm not leaving—" she stopped when Ren sealed her lips with a kiss. A hungry, tongue-thrusting kiss unlike any she'd ever had. This was *so* not brotherly. Just as she was getting used to his tongue, touching it tentatively with her own, he stopped.

He leaned his forehead against hers and breathed heavily. "That was out of line, sprite. I apologize."

"Ren!" She tried to pull his mouth back against hers.

"No, now isn't the time." He turned with her still in his arms and strode to the cabana opening. His gaze took in the pool area and all the interested looks turned their way. "At least you had the sense to get a private table. The men in this place would love nothing better than to eat you with a spoon."

She pinched his tanned, hairy arm. "Watch it, big guy! I had every reason to think I should be safe in public in a goddamn Sheraton!"

"Shh, you're right." He kissed her cheek. A brotherly peck this time—damn him. "I'm sorry. When we got Teresa's call, we'd just read your note and were coming to join you for lunch. We'd reached the same conclusion. You should've been safe."

An apology? From the look on her brother's face this wasn't usual behavior for Ren. And from her vast experience in dealing with the alpha males in her family, a lecture and the laying down of the rules were the normal responses when she'd frightened them. Lectures and rules *without* apologies only came when the ones delivering them knew you'd still love them even when they were being dominant know-it-alls. She'd gotten both from Ren, which could only mean he must not want her ticked off at him. She smiled.

"Which was obviously wrong on all our parts." Tweeter paced them on the right with Vanko on the left.

"Are you all armed?" she asked in a hushed tone. "Those guys had Beretta semi-automatics under their jackets."

"We're armed. We can handle anything those two might dish out." Ren glanced down at her as they entered the elevator. Vanko and Tweeter followed with her brother carding them for the top floor. "What did you throw at the big goon? Your knife is still upstairs."

"A steak knife. It was very sharp and had decent balance."

Ren and Vanko laughed as Tweeter said, "Way to go, Imp."

"And the smaller one? What did you do to him?" Ren idly stroked her cheek.

"I shoved the table into his ugly dick." She threw an irate glance at the three of them. "The bastard had a hard-on the size of Baja. Pervert."

"I'm so proud. Dad will be too." Tweeter felt her forehead with the back of his hand. "You got another fever?"

She let go of Ren's shoulder and felt her forehead, then sighed. "Probably. Too much excitement for my first day out of bed. Probably also why I cried all over Ren. I never cry unless I'm tired ... or hungry ... or low on caffeine." She stopped talking when Ren chuckled. She'd never heard that exact sound from him before. It sounded like amused affection. "Um, yeah, fever ... I have an antibiotic capsule in my purse. I was going to take it with lunch." She looked around suspiciously. "Who has my lunch?"

Vanko grinned and held up the bag Teresa had made. "It's here, Keelulya. I promise not to eat it."

"You'd better not. I'm starving."

They exited the elevator and approached their suite. Tweeter opened the door and went in to clear the place. Vanko had drawn his gun and watched the hallway while Ren held her closely as if he wanted to absorb her into his body. It seemed like hours before her brother stuck his head out and said, "All clear."

Ren sat her in a chair at the dining room table. Vanko placed the bag with her lunch in front of her.

"Pepsi, sis?" Tweeter called out from the bar.

"Yes, please." She opened the bag and found the container with the burger. Opening it, she took a bite and started to chew. "Yuummm."

Ren laughed at her. He sat next to her, his thigh touching hers. "I'm hungry, too. Can I have a bite?"

Was he teasing her? If he was, it was irresistible. She held her burger up for him. He leaned in closely and his mouth descended, first taking a nip of the tip of a one of her fingers then a bite of the burger from the spot she'd torn into.

"Good—to both bites," he murmured, licking

his lips. His smiling gaze captured hers and held her prisoner.

Tweeter put the Pepsi on the table, breaking the intense connection. "Who wants to order from room service?"

Vanko said, "No need. Teresa is bringing up several of the burgers and some other dishes she thought we big strong men would like."

"She's nice—don't take advantage of her." Keely eyed Vanko and Tweeter—and then Ren. She wanted to make it clear the Argentinean girl was off-limits. Teresa was too innocent for the likes of these warriors. Vanko was a lady killer. Her brother, all her brothers, had a similar reputation. As for Ren, his files at the FBI and CIA and all his military records classified him as practically a monk. He was acting against type in his recent assiduous care of her, and she found it hard to believe that she was woman enough to change his lifelong relationship patterns.

But as with any statistical pattern, there were always outliers. Outliers were unpredictable and never followed the rules.

"She is a nice girl," Vanko said. "But she is just that—a girl. I am like a big brother."

"Uh-huh, pull the other one," she said around a bit

of beef, "she thinks you're a hunk."

Vanko laughed. "I am flattered. What do you think, Keelulya?"

"She doesn't think of you at all." Ren grabbed her hand and brought her burger back to his mouth, taking another bite.

"Stop eating my food." She snatched her hand back. "Or … or … I'll eat some of yours."

"You can eat anything of mine you'd like." He winked at her.

She choked, coughed, then blushed, quickly taking a sip of Pepsi. She'd have to reread his files, maybe she'd missed something about him being a rogue—either that or he was the statistic that disproved the numbers.

Tweeter slapped Ren on the back of the head, hard enough for Ren's head to jerk forward. "Stop talking dirty to my sister."

"She knows what I meant." Ren looked at her and smiled. "Isn't that right, Keely?"

Oh yeah, he was definitely flirting. Her gaze inadvertently drifted to the front of his lightweight trousers. His package made Trujo's goon's Baja-sized bulge look dinky. She licked suddenly dry lips and reached again for her soft drink.

"Imp, I'm telling Dad and all the brothers. Stop

looking at Ren as if he were Christmas, Easter and your frigging birthday all rolled into one."

She looked at her brother and stuck her tongue out.

All he did was laugh and say, "Now that's mature."

Chapter Six

Ren kept an eye on Keely as the four of them finished their lunches. She put up a good front, but her recent experiences had taken a toll on her, physically and emotionally. She could protest all she wanted—he wanted her out of South America and safely ensconced at the Sanctuary compound. He expected his brother Trey and another SSI operative—Price Teague—to fly the SSI jet into Puerto Iguazu later in the afternoon. After the plane was refueled, Tweeter could fly his sister back to the States.

"You're staring," Keely said.

"You're tired," he countered.

She shrugged. "Maybe, but that's not getting you off the hook for thinking you can just pack me up and send me away like a helpless little girl. I'm a woman—an adult—and I can make decisions for myself."

"Not this time." He stroked a particularly persistent curl out of her eye.

"You … are not … my boss." She pointed her finger at him. "I don't even let my brothers dictate to me anymore."

"Anh." Tweeter drew everyone's attention. "That's not so. You let us dictate in times of danger—and this qualifies. Trujo's men tried to abduct you in broad daylight, sis."

"Did it look like I was being abducted?" She narrowed her eyes and swept them all with a withering glance. "Well?"

"No, Keelulya," Vanko said, "but I read the report you made of your other abduction. Ren, he is worried, and wants you safely at Sanctuary where our people can watch over you while we go after Trujo."

"There's a spy in Sanctuary who works for the blasted traitor at DoD. I blew the whistle on all the DoD bastard's lucrative and murderous sidelines, he can't continue his bad-ass actions without exposing himself. Now, he's gunning for me. He had me once already," Keely shuddered visibly. "I'm safer with all of you. I trust you … I don't know the people at Sanctuary."

Her logic had Ren and the other two stumped for a second. Muttering several pithy comments on sprites-too-smart-for-their-britches, he tipped her stubborn little chin up so he could see her eyes. "Tweeter is going with you. You'll be staying in my house—with him—until I get there to take over—"

"Your house?" she interrupted. "Why not Tweetie's place?"

"Because."

"Oh, well, that makes sense … not." Keely stabbed at a piece of fruit on her plate. He winced. He hoped the fruit hadn't been a stand-in for one of his body parts. "Okay, let's say I go back to Idaho with my brother and stay in *your* place," she waved the fork bearing a piece of mango around. "Who'll help you and Vanko go after Trujo? I showed you the layout over lunch. My estimates of his army are on the light side, but even low-balling the numbers, you'll be at a distinct disadvantage. Trujo has to be on high alert since you escaped his trap and are most likely out to get him."

A loud knock on the door interrupted the answer he was going to give. Vanko went to open the door. The voices were familiar and expected.

Ren smiled. "My answer to your question just walked in the door. Meet my brother Trey and one of my other operatives, Price Teague."

Keely stared at the two men, her eyes narrowed, examining them as if trying to assess their loyalties. He could have assured her that Trey and Price were above reproach, but she'd have to learn to accept his decisions on faith. He could explain every little detail of his plan to take out Trujo, but he didn't work that way.

"Okay, I grant you—you now have four men, but you're still vastly outnumbered. My ability to strategize would be invaluable."

"Probably, but it ain't happening." He refused to budge on the point. She was out of there later tonight—after she rested for a few hours.

"Is the little gal afraid for us?" Price walked to the table and all but leered at Keely.

Ren bristled. "Yeah, the little gal—Tweeter's baby sister—is worried. And she is off limits, Price. So back off." He noted he'd beaten Tweeter to the explanations and warning by a split second.

Keely with a big smile on her face held out her hand and said, "Yeah, he's my *novio*, just ask him. Very bossy, too. So back off." She winked at Price, who laughed and took her hand gently in his and kissed the tips of her fingers.

Ren reclaimed Keely's hand, hauling her and her chair even closer to him. "Watch out, Keely. Price is a ladies' man. There isn't an eligible female in the whole of Idaho County that hasn't been approached by him." He added under his breath, "And bedded."

"Well, since there are less than point three people per square mile in the whole of Idaho County, and most of them male, that isn't saying much, brother." Trey came over and took Keely's hand. "Pleased to meet you, Keely. Quinn told me about your call. I tried to get back in touch with you, but couldn't. I called your dad then."

"Holy crap," muttered Keely.

"Why crap?" Ren looked from her to her brother. "Tweeter called him when we got to the hotel room while you were sick, baby."

"Baby?" Trey mouthed to him. Ren frowned and shook his head and mouthed "Later."

"Double holy crap." Shooting an accusatory glance at her brother, Keely said, "Tweetie! You know what will happen."

Keely looked really upset, even more than she had in the middle of the cantina firefight or dealing with the two vicious bozos by the pool.

Tweeter nodded, a satisfied smirk on his face. Ren had a gut feeling they were about to be descended upon by the rest of the Walsh clan.

"When will they get here, big brother?" His little warrior glared, a really mean look he hoped to never see turned on him.

"In an hour or so. They flew in right behind Trey and Price." Tweeter looked at Ren. "I figured you could use the extra firepower. Keely put out the alert to Loren and Paul, so they'd already arranged leave from their SEAL team and were on their way to Boston to see what she needed. When I called Dad, he was already in Boston with Devin and Andy, having been called by my brothers. Then…" Tweeter grimaced.

"What?" Keely moaned.

"Sorry, Imp. Whoever abducted you had your townhouse trashed."

Keely moaned and turned paler if that were possible. Ren pulled her onto his lap and stroked her back.

"Go on, finish it, Tweetie," she said, her voice tight with unspent emotion. Her head nestled on his chest. He liked that she trusted him enough to seek comfort in his body. "Did Daddy and the boys go to the warehouse?"

Ren sensed her heightened tension and kissed her sweet-smelling curls while continuing to rub her back. His brother eyed the gesture and smiled, nudging Price whose face displayed shock at the sight of him cuddling a female. He glared at them, hoping they'd keep their damn traps shut in front of Keely.

"The fuckers cleaned up after themselves at the warehouse. Dad spoke to the Boston PD and while they found some trace evidence—mostly blood—mostly yours…" Tweeter eyed Ren warily as he snarled several swear words, "…and some unidentified blood, there were no bodies."

"Some bastards had Keely and bloodied her?" Trey looked almost as angry as Ren felt. "She had to kill to escape?"

"Yes." Vanko's accent was thick, an indication of his extreme anger. "Keelulya was tortured—they were going to kill her because she uncovered an asshole for hire in the DoD."

Trey and Price looked Keely over, this time, no leers, no knowing smirks, but with a newfound respect in their eyes.

"She came down here at great risk to herself to warn us about the trap," Ren said. "We surmise Trujo paid the traitor to arrange sending us here." He rubbed his cheek against her forehead. Fuck, she still had a fever. His plan to get her home looked even more warranted in light of her continued illness. "She was bruised—developed an infection in her wounds—and still made it to us in time." He praised her not only for his men's benefit, but also for hers. He wanted her to understand he did appreciate her sacrifices. "Then she helped us fight off the mercs sent to kill us. She's managed to escape death too many times over the last few days. But no more—I'm sending her home with Tweeter. Out of the danger zone."

"Yes … all right, I'll go." She sighed, her warm breath touching the sensitive skin at the base of his throat. "I'm still running a fever. I'd be a burden."

"You would've gone anyway, even if I had to sedate you." He brushed a feather-light kiss across her temple.

"Maybe." He stiffened against her. "Down, big guy, it's a moot point now—I'm going. My biggest concern was the outnumbering thing, but with Daddy and the other brothers coming plus Trey and Price, you should be fine. You can use my contact, Senor Bazon, to get anything you'll need to fight Trujo. By the way, the Kamov? I paid for that ordnance for the belly guns. Use it."

Trey pulled up a chair and sat so close to him and

Keely that he was ready to shove his brother on the floor.

"It's fine. He's fine. Don't," Keely whispered, unconsciously moving closer to him and away from his brother.

Trey noticed her movement, swore softly, then moved back. "Sorry, I was crowding you. So—did I understand correctly? You flew a fully-loaded Russian military chopper to go to my brother and the guys?"

She nodded.

Trey looked at him. "Where did she get an attack helicopter?"

Vanko answered. "From one of the meanest looking arms merchants I've ever had the pleasure of doing business with."

"Senor Bazon is not mean." Keely sat up and glared at Vanko. "Did you upset him? Do I have to go down and mediate, then arrange weapons for you all?"

"No, little girl, you do not." A low masculine voice came from behind them. "I can get us any weapons we'll need."

"Daddy! Mama!" Keely wiggled off his lap, shoving Trey out of the way in her rush to get to a huge mountain of a man who stood in the entry of the suite with four equally large men ranged alongside him, all of them towering over a red-haired woman even smaller than Keely.

The five Walsh men glared at him, before turning to surround the littlest Walsh warrior in a hugging and kissing huddle. Keely's mom eyed him with piercing green eyes identical to Keely's. Her fiery emerald stare rivaled those of her husband and sons for fierceness. Of the six Walsh arrivals she scared him the most—so much so he had to remind himself to take a breath. She blinked, releasing him from her spell, then elbowed her men out of the way so she could take her daughter into her arms.

"God, I'm a dead man," Ren muttered.

"Nah." Tweeter leaned in close so his words would not carry. "I told them you were a good guy. But I expect Dad and Mom will talk to you about Keely. They had a lot of questions about you and your business. Mostly I think they want to assure themselves that you won't hurt her in any way, shape or form, and that includes most especially her feelings."

"I'm not going to hurt your sister. I'm merely protecting her."

"Keep telling yourself that, my friend. You were a goner two days ago when we both realized Keely would only respond to you in the middle of her nightmares."

Tweeter had a point—damn him. Ren was just beginning to examine his feelings toward Keely. It would be a lot easier to examine those emotions without five large and overprotective Walsh males and one very scary Walsh female breathing down his neck.

"Thanks for vouching for me."

"No problem. Baby sis and I will be collecting."

"What?" Ren said.

"Keely has this idea for an electronic security dome. It would be perfect for Sanctuary. We could work off the perimeter security and add a third dimension, giving us a holographic image of the entire property. No one could approach by land or air without setting off a warning." Tweeter looked like a kid anticipating Christmas morning and lots of presents. "Plus, it will give us two-way radio capability from the furthest point of Sanctuary to the Bat Cave without worrying about terrain and weather interference. Give me the go-ahead and I can keep her busy and happy—and out of trouble—until y'all get home."

"Go for it, but try to be as cost effective as possible. We aren't made of money." SSI did well, but overhead was high.

"Hey, you're getting one of the foremost applied computer scientists in the world working on a project that has never been done before—for free. She's willing to give us the patent. The military applications are unlimited. We'll be rolling in cash once we prove it works."

"She can keep her patent. I've been thinking about offering her a job at SSI since she quit MIT because of us." Well, he lied. The idea had just popped into his head. But the more he examined the idea, the more it felt—right.

Tweeter nodded. "Sounds good. She can live with me. I don't figure we want her driving back and forth from Elk City or Grangeville like the other employees."

"No, she won't be living off Sanctuary." She'd live in his house with him, but those details could be worked out later—once he examined all the ramifications of asking her to cohabit. He wasn't sure what he'd do if she said no.

A smile on his face, Ren watched as Keely hugged each of her very large brothers. She and her mother were midgets among giants. Each brother treated her as if she were made of spun sugar. They had to know she was a mini-Amazon, after all they'd trained her. But there was something about her that made a man want to protect her—or possess her. He was one of those men. He frowned. He didn't like the idea of allowing anyone else protect her, not even her family.

Tweeter rambled on. "Don't worry about cost. What we're going to do to Sanctuary we can do with stuff we already have. Keely and I have been corresponding about this for a while and so I just added stuff to previous electronics order. We should have most of what we need to do the wiring and laying of cable."

Ren shifted his attention back to Tweeter. "Um, and how is that going to happen?" He thought of the rugged and dangerous terrain surrounding their compound. Remembered the bitch of a time it had taken full grown men to string the perimeter security conduits and build in the solar power and battery arrays to power the perimeter alarms.

"Keely and I have rock-climbed all over the world. She's an expert. Man, you should see her. She's like a frigging spider. And since it is cold in Idaho right now, she'll be in her element. Haven't you guessed? She's a winter sprite."

Just thinking of some of the climbs on Sanctuary, treacherous enough in dry, warm weather, but deadly in the snow and icy conditions that covered their part of the country the majority of the year, he shuddered.

"There had better not be a new bruise or bump on her when I get home." He uttered the words in the form of a warning. Tweeter had better heed it or pay the consequences. He didn't care if the man was Keely's brother. He walked away from Tweeter to meet the rest of Keely's family.

"Ren!" Keely ran to him and tugged his arm, dragging him to meet her family.

"Daddy. Mama. Loren, Paul, Devin, and Andy. This is Tweetie's boss, Ren. He's sending me to Idaho with Tweetie so y'all can kick Trujo butt."

Ren had to laugh at Keely's fierce frown. She really wanted to kick butt, too. The fact she was leaving without too much of a fight had him thanking God. He hadn't wanted to have to force her, but he would have.

He stroked a hand down Keely's back and settling it at her waist before holding his other one out to her father. "Colonel Walsh, sir. I'd like to thank you for teaching your daughter how to take care of herself. Mrs. Walsh, I promise that as long as she is under my protection at Sanctuary, Keely will not have to use any of those skills her father taught her."

Keely's father took his hand in a bruising grip and shook it. "Don't count on it, son. Keely is a magnet for trouble." Her mother and four brothers nodded, grim looks on their faces. "This traitor who's decided my little girl is a person to be eliminated—"

"Is a dead man." Ren's words came out as a rumbling snarl.

The Walsh family nodded their satisfaction at his statement.

"Knowing my daughter, she already has a plan on how to track the bastard and lure him out." Colonel Walsh stared at him. "You'll inform me when this is to happen—and I will be there with my boys and several carefully selected former Marines. Understand?"

"Yes, sir. I have no problem with that."

Keely sighed, a happy smile on her face. "I knew my family would like you." She hugged his arm against her breast, her obviously braless breast. His damn cock hardened and throbbed. He only hoped none of her family noticed.

Her mother gasped, her green gaze tracing a path from Ren's bulge to his face. "You might want to let go of him, Keely. The man, um, needs his space."

"Mama, he's been like *that* since I met him." She fluttered her lashes at Ren, an impish grin on her face. "I think it's a permanent condition."

"What the fuck—" One of the twins, Loren or Paul, snarled and fisted his hands. Ren prepared to move Keely behind him in case a fist was thrown.

"Paul! Language!" Molly Walsh held out her hand. "Pay up."

Payment in the form of a quarter was handed over by the red-faced giant with a muttered, "Sorry, Mama."

Colonel Walsh laughed. He gently stroked his wife's flame-colored hair, his gaze on his daughter. "Behave, Keely-girl."

"Sure, Daddy." She smiled sweetly. "Ren's like you guys." She paused, letting everyone wonder if she was still talking about infinite hard-ons or something else, then added, "A hero. Plus, he let me fight alongside him. We kicked butt."

"We sure did, sprite. But to save me—and your parents—from prematurely going gray, you'll be on the SSI jet out of here later this evening with Tweeter."

Keely's mother's face lit up like the morning sun and she winked at him. Fuck him, she approved of him. He pulled out a quarter and handed it to her.

She laughed. "You don't have to pay for thinking the f-word, you know."

"Wasn't sure about the rules, ma'am."

"Call me Molly—keep your money." She smiled at him. "I'm sure I'll collect from you enough in the future. Ex-military men just can't help themselves."

"I look forward to it, Molly." He sensed Keely

sagging against him. He gently turned her and tipped her chin up so she looked him in the eye. "You're ready to drop. Why don't you lie down while Vanko, Tweeter and I bring the rest up to speed?"

She nodded, then yawned as if his mentioning her tiredness made it so. "Okay, but if you need me to sweet talk Senor Bazon into getting you the good stuff and not the third-world leftovers, let me know. He likes me—says I remind him of a rain forest pixie."

He chastely kissed her forehead, aware every single Walsh eye was on them, then turned her toward the bedroom. "Want me to bring you a Pepsi?"

"Later." She started toward the bedroom. She moved like a man's wet dream, all female curves in a pint-sized package. All the male eyes in the room were on her. She stopped and turned. "Someone needs to buy me some panties. I'm not flying all the way to Idaho without panties. It isn't decent. Oh, and some blue jeans and a long-sleeved shirt. It's winter in Idaho, for chrissakes." Then she smiled, turned her sweet ass, which everyone now knew was naked under the dress, and entered the bedroom and shut the door.

Ren turned to meet the narrowed, but he sensed, amused gazes of the Walsh clan. "What?"

"You sure you're ready to keep my little girl out of

trouble, Ren?" Colonel Walsh smiled, a big shit-eating grin. "She's a pistol, just like her mama."

"Kennard Walsh!" Molly punched her husband in the stomach with a tiny fist. "I am not."

All five brothers muttered various renditions of "Are, too, Mama," earning them a lethal feminine glare promising retribution at a future date.

Devin Walsh pinned Ren with a knowing look. "You be careful around my baby sister. She's been known to kick a guy's balls into his throat when provoked." The nonverbal message in that warning was "don't hurt my sister."

Trey and Price, silent observers to the Walsh family reunion, snorted in disbelief, but sobered when they saw Vanko nodding agreement with Devin's words.

"That little bit of a gal can take down a full-grown man?" Price asked.

"Yes." Vanko's head jerked emphatically. "Just today she threw a steak knife at one of Trujo's men and emasculated the other and made good her escape just as we arrived to rescue her."

"When the fuck did this happen?" Colonel Walsh asked.

"Kennard, language. How do you expect the boys to clean up their language if…" Colonel Walsh cut off

Molly's lecture by picking her up and kissing her. Ren saw lots of tongue and sensed major amounts of love and passion in their embrace. The Walsh boys groaned. As the kiss continued, Tweeter muttered, "Get a room, Dad."

Keely's parents broke off the kiss. The Colonel plopped his wife into a chair and pulled out a quarter handed it to her. "Sorry, pumpkin."

Molly, flushed from the heated kiss, took the money. "As you should be, lover."

Laughing, Ren replied, "The incident occurred a couple of hours ago, sir. Keely went down to grab some lunch at the pool restaurant and we were joining her when it happened. She had the situation under control. We were just backup."

"That was when you decided to send her home with Stuart?" Molly smiled at him with approval.

He had to think a second about who Stuart was— no one ever called Tweeter that and lived. "No, the decision to send Keely back was made before that. The lunch situation and Trujo's interest in her just underlined the need. The bastard has his eye on her now—and her connection to SSI makes the situation even worse." His lips thinned and his nostrils flared. "He will never touch her while I live. He should have never been able to breathe the same air she did."

Every Walsh head nodded in agreement.

"Show us the set up and bring us up to speed, Ren," Colonel Walsh ordered as he picked his wife up, sat in the chair and settled her on his lap.

As Ren pulled out the diagrams Keely had made and copies of her intel reports, a furious scream came from the bedroom, followed by the sound of something big hitting the closed door.

Icy fear shot through Ren's body as he moved toward the sounds of fighting coming from the room. "Keely!"

Assorted weapons appeared as every man moved en masse. Molly, a big semi-automatic in her hand, passed the other men, pulling alongside of Ren. She looked the perfect picture of a mother rushing to protect her child. He now realized Keely got her fighting spirit from both sides of the family.

"I've got this, Molly." Ren waved the advancing mini-Titan back.

Whatever Molly might have said was cut off when the bedroom door flew open and a man came flying out, landing on the carpet, just missing Ren and Molly. He pushed Keely's mother toward one of the twins, who grabbed her and shoved her toward his father.

The downed thug sprang up and turned to run but stopped, his jaw dropping open as he saw all of them. "Hell." He sat on the floor and buried his head on his upraised knees. "Senor Trujo is going to kill me." The man was the shorter goon from the restaurant; the one Keely had emasculated.

"Not if I do it first, fucker." Ren looked toward the bedroom and the sounds of the continued fight. "Keely!"

"I'm busy." She sounded more irritated than anything. But she was sick and tired—and, hell, he was here. She didn't need to be fighting.

Ren saw red. "Fuck it. Keely!" He started toward the bedroom and had to dodge another airborne body—the tall man she'd previously knifed.

Keely followed this one out. Her fiery golden hair flew all over the place and her pale face had flags of red on her cheekbones from exertion—or from her fever. He didn't know and didn't care; she needed to rest, not fight hired killers.

The tall man lay on the carpet in a bloody heap. She kicked him in the ribs. "Call me a little bitch, will you?"

Ren hadn't thought she really understood what *poco gata* meant in Spanish, but she obviously had. The man she'd stuck with a steak knife was probably wishing he'd forgotten all about her. Ren scanned her body, looking for obvious injuries. "Fuck it, Keely. You're practically naked!" She was in one of his t-shirts—and nothing else. Every man knew she had no underwear. The thugs had probably gotten an up-close-and-personal look as she tossed them around. That image pushed him from mad to furious.

"I'm wearing your shirt. And don't think I didn't hear all those f-bombs flying. Mama, he owes you—make sure you collect."

Keely sure as hell didn't shrink away from his wrath. Ren managed to avoid smiling at the feisty warrior sprite and pulled a throw off the couch to wrap around her like a sarong. As he enfolded her body in the fluffy material, he spotted new marks on her arms and face that promised to bruise later.

He snarled. "Goddamnmotherfuckingsonofabitch!" His breaths came fast and hard while his hands clenched and unclenched at his side. Every primordial instinct pushed him to avenge the harm to his woman.

"Ren, no. I'm fine." Her voice was low, soothing, a tone aimed at taming a raging beast. She held his arm as if she could prevent him from moving.

He stroked a finger lightly over the red mark on her

face. "No, baby. He terrorized you. He fucking touched you, hurt you. I can't let that go." He gently shoved her toward her mother. "Go to your Mama, baby, and hide your eyes. Molly, you might want to hide your eyes also." Turning, he found his brother backing him up. "Get Keely an ice pack, Trey. I have to kill someone."

"No." Keely stepped into his body, blocking him from the downed thug, and buried her face in the middle of his chest, her small hands grabbing fistfuls of his shirt. "No. He has broken ribs. I heard his jaw snap. I twisted his testicles and penis when he was on top of me."

"He. Was. On. Top. Of. You." Ren was proud of himself. He didn't roar. He glanced at the piece-of-shit-excuse for a man who lay on the floor, bleeding and moaning as if he were going to die. He turned his narrowed eyes back to his little Amazon. "Explain." He rubbed her back to still her shaking.

Keely sighed and took one of her hands off him and shoved it through her thick, messy curls. "Just stop it with the snarl in your voice. While impressive, it's pissing me off. I handled the situation. It's done."

"Keely." His voice was calm, but he knew she had to feel his trembling as he struggled not to move away and kill the bastards where they lay. "Tell me how you handled it." Then he'd decide just how much more hurt he needed to impart to the assholes.

"They wanted to take me out the balcony and then to Trujo. I said no. They said yes. So, I took out the little one first and then he—" she pointed to the other one, "knocked me on the floor and tried to put a carotid hold on me, so I twisted his dick and balls. He hit me in the face…"

Ren swiped a gentle finger over the mark on her cheek and took the ice pack Trey handed him and put it on the rapidly swelling bruise.

She gasped and winced, then continued her matter-of-fact narrative. "…but he, like all men, had to check to see if he still had all his working parts. That was his mistake." Her mother choked back a laugh behind them. "I had him after that. Daddy and the boys taught me how to fight from every position known to man. The a-hole—sorry, Mama—didn't have a chance once I got leverage. I am *very* good at physics."

She leaned her forehead on his chest. He held her close with one arm, the other hand still holding the ice pack to her face. She continued with a sigh. "I handled it. And while I truly appreciate that you want to handle them some more, it is unnecessary. Now, I'm really tired. I need an ibuprofen or something—and my Pepsi—lots of ice. And I need to be held, first by my Mama, then by you, especially you. Daddy can take care of cleanup."

He sensed every Walsh going on alert at her words. Fuck 'em. She wanted to be held by him, she got him. The fact he'd have held her anyway without her asking was beside the point.

She sniffed into his shirt. He felt wetness. "Okay, baby. God, please don't cry. You're killing me."

"I don't cry—hardly ever. Ask my family. It's just that I don't feel good." She sniffed. "Crying is a wussy-assed girly thing to do. And I am not a wuss. I'm a frick-fracking Walsh warrior."

Handing Trey the ice pack, he swung Keely into his arms, then reached for the cold pack again. "Hold this on your face, baby. Your Mama and I will put you to bed, get you some meds and the Pepsi, and then after I talk some more with your Dad, I'll come in and lie next to you until you go to sleep. Okay?"

She sniffed and took over holding the ice pack against her face. "I knew you'd see my point of view."

"You won't always get your way, Keely." He whispered against her hair.

She muttered something under her breath. He had to smile—it sounded like "Wanna bet?"

CHAPTER SEVEN

One week later, Sanctuary, Idaho

"Tweetie, hand me that last transmitter stake."

Ignoring the increasingly blustery wind and the feathery flakes of snow whipping around her with more intensity, Keely reached back a Thinsulate-gloved hand. Her other hand, encased in an extra layer of down-filled glove, gripped the rope holding her in mid-air, two thousand feet above the canyon floor. Her brother hung alongside her, carrying the once-heavy pack and spotting her.

"Here ya go, Imp." The stake was slapped into her hand. "Bracing you."

As he had for the last fifty stakes, his body snugged

against her back as she practically sat on his strong thighs. She hammered the stake into the hole she'd created seconds earlier. She sprang the hooks that dug the stake further into the rock wall. Satisfied it was anchored well, she plugged in the electrical conduit they had strung from stake to stake. The green light went on, showing it had power. The power source was a solar-powered battery array secreted on a six-thousand foot crag and cleverly built into the rocks.

"Signal?" She grabbed the rope with both hands, after putting on the other down-filled glove over the thinner one. Air temperature was a balmy twenty-two degrees with a wind chill of minus twenty. Frostbite was a given in these conditions, and both she and Tweeter had multiple layers to protect against it. She swiveled to face her brother.

Tweeter scanned the computer tablet protected in its own down-filled sleeve. "Yeah, it's working. They all are." He beamed at her. "Damn, I can't wait to see the holographic image on the table we built in the Bat Cave."

The Bat Cave was the underground operations center located in the sub-basement of the Lodge, SSI's main building and a gathering place for Sanctuary residents. Sanctuary itself was a hundred square miles of some of the roughest terrain in Idaho. Two years ago, Sanctuary had received town status from Idaho County.

Tweeter already had a fairly impressive security set up, but had jumped at the chance to make it even better. When she'd first mentioned a year or so ago the potential of a holographic imaging table to display a complete picture of the whole of Sanctuary, ground-to-sky, he'd almost swooned and begun to collect equipment for the day they could work on it together.

The day had arrived. After their arrival from Argentina—and after her mama, who'd ridden along, had gone back to Georgia—she and Tweetie planted sensors and strung cable and electrical conduit during the blustery days and built the array in the Bat Cave at night. Finally, they were done.

She lifted her face to the gray wintry sky. She loved the snow and cold, but a blizzard was coming and they'd needed to get the system operative before it hit. Thus, the concerted push today. There was already seven feet of snow on the ground and four more predicted with high winds to complicate matters over the next twenty-four hours. And it was only late October. She smiled at her brother. "We'll work on fine-tuning the table's reception and testing the signals. The bad weather should be a trial of how well the system works. Bad guys don't wait for nice weather to attack."

Tweetie patted her cheeks. She barely felt his hands. He pulled her wool balaclava over her face, covering the exposed skin. The hood was one of the men's and far too big for her, so it kept slipping. She really needed to get her own winter clothing if she were going to stay at Sanctuary—and it looked like she would be. Her brother told her Ren intended to offer her a job. She intended to take it. She was highly attracted to the head of SSI—and knew he felt the same about her.

"Looks like we should head back. Wouldn't want Quinn to send out a search party." Tweetie spoke over the Motorola headset so they could keep their faces covered and wouldn't freeze their lips to their teeth trying to talk in the sub-zero temps.

"He'd do it, too," she replied. Quinn had already sent search parties out twice since she'd been here. The older man was in charge of employee safety when neither Ren nor Trey was here to keep an eye on things.

She had to admit that she and her brother tended to get caught up in what they were doing and forgot about time—and checking in regularly. Ren had called once while they were out and had reamed Quinn a new asshole, or at least, that's what the salty old Marine had told them.

She shivered at the thought of Ren's increasingly possessive and protective attitude. He'd spoken to her every evening. He wouldn't tell her what was happening in South America, but cross-examined her on her return trip, her mama's thoughts on his home, and her living in it, her sleep patterns, what she'd eaten, and how she was adjusting to Idaho life. Most women would find him too controlling, but she was used to that kind of behavior, having lived with it all her life. Using her mama's fine example of how to handle dominant, know-it-all males, she'd never found it a problem to do what she wanted, when she wanted, even under the eyes of six Walsh males and all their friends. It was all a matter of knowing when to give in and when to assert one's self.

"Earth to Imp. Need help climbing?" Her brother reached for her pulley system. They might be two thousand feet above the canyon floor, but they still had one thousand feet to climb to the top where their two-seater snowmobile was parked.

"Yeah," she held out a shaky hand, "all of a sudden, I'm beat." The remnants of her injuries and the subsequent illness from her abduction still managed to bother her when she was fatigued. Of course, she hadn't breathed a word of her continuing weakness to Ren on the nightly calls. She wasn't stupid; he'd have had Quinn tying her to the bed and had Quinn's wife Lacey, a nurse, caring for her.

She couldn't afford to rest and had purposely pushed her physical limits to get this wiring done. The weather and the terrain hadn't helped. She and Tweeter had been banged about yesterday and today in gusty winds as they climbed and installed cable all over Sanctuary's borders. Added to the physical demands of the job, she was still acclimating to the altitude. It was amazing she wasn't flat on her back with exhaustion and acute mountain sickness. But whatever she suffered, it would all be worth it. Her gut and itchy neck told her the system would get a trial by fire—and soon.

"Shit, Keely," her brother's voice held concern, "why didn't you say something? Ren will have my ass if he comes home and you're down sick again."

"Just tell him I forced you."

Tweetie snorted. "Yeah, like that makes a difference. He'll still blame me." He reached for her lines and turned her so he could see her eyes through her yellow-tinged snow goggles. He frowned. "When we get back, skip the bar and grill tonight. Get Scotty to pack you some food to carry back to Ren's place so you can turn in early. Scotty can mix his own damn Mojitos and crap."

"Nope, the bar is fun—and a way for me to unwind." She grinned behind the hood protecting her from the biting wind. "Quinn challenged me to a game of darts. He can't believe I keep beating him. Lacey loves that I can put his Marine ass in place. Plus, if I win tonight's match, he's promised to teach me how to play poker."

"Quinn cheats, sis. I can teach you how to play poker," Tweetie said in his big-brother-knows-best tone as he pulled them both up the face of the rock wall with ease.

"Once I have the fundamentals down, you know he won't have a chance. It's mostly probabilities." Thinking of the bar, a frisson of unease skittered down her spine. Something had happened at breakfast. Something she'd pushed to the back of her mind in her need to get the wiring done and the security system operational. "What would Ren do if one of his men was, um, bothering me?"

"Who's bothering you? And when, for chrissakes? I'm with you all the fucking time."

"Stop it with the f-word, Stuart Allen Walsh. I'll collect for Mama in absentia." She braced a hand to assist over a jagged area so the ropes would not fray. "Besides, it happened at breakfast when you're still sacked out, slug-a-bed."

"You get up too damn early. Now fess up—who is the fucker?" His snarl was almost the equal of Ren's and dared her to chastise him for his use of the f-word.

She wasn't really afraid of the man bothering her, more like wary and suspicious at his all-of-a-sudden lechery. Oh, heck, who was she kidding? She was more than wary and suspicious. The man's actions reminded her of the four who'd kidnapped her in Boston. Two of those were dead and she'd created computer sketches for the two still at large and had a program running to check them against law enforcement data bases. This guy wasn't one of them. He'd been at Sanctuary while she was held prisoner in Boston, but he was of the same breed of low-life predators—a jackal. She could handle most assholes, and had proven so time after time. But she wasn't at her best now and this particular guy was huge—and had more training than she. She wasn't stupid enough to think she could take him *mano a mano* and win; the bastard had the habit of sneaking up on her. Only Scotty's presence had stopped the man from touching her, taking what he said he wanted.

Why were some men such animals?

Tweetie climbed up over the edge of the cliff and hauled her up the last several feet. When she was on terra firma, he took her shoulders and shook gently. "Stop avoiding my question? Who was the asshole?"

Anger and worry were in his eyes. God, he was so sweet. He was the best big brother and had sacrificed so much of his life for her. She hated being a burden once more. Maybe she was overreacting to the man. God knew, she was tired and still recuperating. Plus, she had another reason to keep an eye on the guy and didn't want Tweetie or Quinn kicking him off Sanctuary just yet. She should have kept her mouth shut.

She shrugged. "It's not important. I'll just make sure other people are around. He hasn't done anything, just talked about it."

"He who?" Tweetie tipped her chin up with a heavily gloved hand. "We're not leaving here until you tell me. They'll find us next spring, frozen to this very spot if you don't cough it up soon."

The wind was swirling the snow around them, causing periods of mini-whiteouts. Visibility was maybe ten feet and getting worse. The trip back to the Lodge would be extremely tricky, but doable. Even without a final testing, she knew they could follow the new system's transmitter signals all the way back. The system was fully functional, but she wasn't ready to reveal it to the other SSI personnel until Ren gave her the okay. Only she, her brother and Ren knew what they'd been doing for the last week.

She lowered her lashes; the snow was stinging what part of her face was exposed by the loose balaclava. Her goggles were fogging; she flipped on the battery-powered heater built into the high-tech eyewear to keep the lenses clear.

Tweetie all but growled. "I'm waiting, sis."

Okay, so they really needed to leave. They couldn't get lost, but they could get caught out here. There was always the chance of hitting a hidden rock or driving off the edge of a cliff in the limited visibility. Some of the trails were very narrow and hugged the edge of cliff walls.

She sighed. Stalling could get them killed. She'd have to tell him her suspicions. Her brother didn't make threats idly. "It's one of the new SSI recruits here for training." She peeked at his eyes; they were filled with fiery, blue sparks. "He's hitting on me. I've told him no."

He hissed a nasty word. "The bastard should know to stay away from you. You're living in Ren's house— that means you're off limits." He shoved her toward the snowmobile; its protective tarp was covered with a foot of snow at least.

"Am I off limits?" Keely was intrigued. She knew Ren was overprotective and had decided she was under his care—the last week's worth of nightly phone calls had proven that point—but other than that, he hadn't said word one about his future intentions toward her. Heck, her brother had been the one to tell her she had a job at SSI if she wanted it.

Now, she wasn't stupid, just young. Ren's constant hard-on when he was around her and other body language indicated he wanted her—a lot. Her mama had noticed the attraction and lectured her in very explicit terms about safe sex and intimate relations with large men. Keely still blushed whenever she thought about her mama's detailed talk and the personal experience that necessarily preceded all that knowledge.

Personally, she had no issues with Ren's lust. She'd been in lust with him since she'd first met him. She admired and respected his alpha qualities and had been half-way in love with him from reading his files. She knew she could handle him as easily as her mama had handled her equally macho dad. And that relationship had been loving and hot for over thirty-five years and six children.

"Keely, are you listening to me? Ren will go apeshit over any man who even sneezes in your direction." He turned her into his body, sheltering her from the brunt of the vicious wind gusts.

"This particular jerk mentioned a lack of a ring. He doesn't think I'm off limits."

"Ren needs to get his fucking ass home." Her brother snagged her arm and helped her fight the headwind that seemed to want to blow them back over the edge of the cliff they'd just scaled. Together they made their way slowly to their transportation.

"Well, the jerk bothering me has been rather explicit as to why he thinks Ren isn't the man for me—and that he is. I think he's full of bull hooey and just feeling me out to see what I'd say or do. I think he's the spy inside SSI."

Tweetie's hand on her arm tightened at her words. He pulled her to a halt next to the snowmobile. She continued with her conclusions. "He seems too foolish to be the brains. I mean why hit on me? If he's supposed to kidnap or kill me or even just observe and send back intel to his boss, then it's stupid to call that kind of attention to himself. He'd have to assume I'd tell you or Ren about him."

Tweeter growled. "Which one is it?"

"Un-unh." She shook her head. "I'm handling it for now. I don't have enough evidence to prove he's leaking info to the big bad guy in D.C. The deep background checks are in the works. I don't want to scare him off—or get him tossed off Sanctuary—until we know for sure whether he's working alone or with a group."

"So, it's one of the terrible trio?" Tweeter's eyes narrowed.

She didn't bother denying it. The terrible trio—as they'd named the three recruits—had triggered her internal alarm from her first day on Sanctuary. They made her neck itch like crazy. Heck, even her mama had commented on them, said they were smarmy. The fact they were recent hires just solidified her suspicions. They'd all hired on about the time she'd reported her initial findings to the NSA on the patterns in the failed NCS missions. NSA had told her not to worry her little golden-red curls about it. Cretins.

Upon meeting the three men, she'd told her brother about her spider sense. SSI's initial-hire background checks hadn't gone much past the trio's military records. In her opinion the background checks hadn't gone deep enough and she'd shared her conclusions with her brother and Quinn. She offered to create a better program for SSI and did so, then immediately set about piercing the lies built upon lies in the threesome's backgrounds. Proving her itchy neck was once again one hundred percent spot on. Once Quinn knew the three had been less than honest, he made sure their trainers kept them away from sensitive security information vital to SSI's operations.

Every evening for the last week, she dug even deeper to find out who the three really were by happily hacking into secure computer systems all over the world. Last evening, she'd finally hit pay dirt. She found proof that the guy hitting on her, Rod Bannon, was a soldier of fortune who hired himself out to the wrong side more often than not as did his constant sidekick, Tripp Jordan, one of the suspect trio. The jury was still out on the third guy, Jose Vences; he'd lied about his experience and credentials, but so far she hadn't found any evidence of bad acts in his background.

She now had a double-check running on all the information she'd found to verify its veracity. She didn't want to accuse anyone wrongly and wanted an iron-clad case to present to Homeland Security and the FBI. She was also interested in seeing if she could backtrack from Bannon and Jordan to anyone in the DoD. She wanted the S.O.B. who'd tried to kill her, her brother, Vanko and Ren. No one messed with a Walsh.

"We need to get the intel on those three to Ren sooner, rather than later. Plus, if one of them has set his sights on you, Ren will kick his ass off for that alone."

"And we can't let him do that—yet. If Bannon and Jordan are spies, we have to prove it and try to turn them to get to who hired them." She climbed onto the passenger seat after Tweeter ripped off the tarp and put it away. "The program should've finished the verification process by the time we get back."

Tweeter patted her arm. "Arms tight around my waist, sis. We'll be running full out. The storm is getting worse."

She circled his waist with her arms and leaned her forehead on his back. "Maybe Ren will have returned." God, she sounded like some lovelorn teenager. She'd missed Ren and his warmth and scent surrounding her in bed. She hadn't slept well since she'd left South America. Recurring nightmares about the Boston incident kept her tossing and turning. In them, this time, she did not escape. Ren's nearness kept the night terrors away and replaced them with erotic dreams. She wanted to belong to Ren Maddox, and only him, in every carnal way she'd ever read about. Unfortunately, she got the impression he planned to move slowly. She'd have to speed him up some. She knew what she wanted—Ren in her bed, making love to her every night.

Tweetie switched on the snowmobile. "Quinn said Ren called earlier. I forgot to tell you. They're going to try to beat the blizzard. Although if they haven't landed by now, they might not be able to."

"Let's go. I need some of Scotty's five-alarm chili to warm me up." And she needed to see if Ren was home. Maybe tonight she could sleep soundly—in his arms.

"Sounds like a plan to me." Tweeter gave the powerful snowmobile gas, accelerating quickly through the white wall of snow and ice crystals.

———

"WHERE IN THE HELL ARE they?" Ren paced the main room of the Lodge. He'd been back in Sanctuary for two hours and the weather had deteriorated measurably. He hadn't flown through one of the worst storms in Idaho history to arrive and find Keely out in it, risking her sweet neck.

"They're fine." Quinn Jones, the third in command at SSI behind him and Trey, sat in a leather club chair in front of the huge stone fireplace, nursing a pre-dinner scotch. "Each and every time I sounded the alarm on them in the past week, we found them safe and sound.

They just forget the time while they're working. By the way, what are they working on? Is it a secret?" The older man took a sip of his scotch, his narrowed gaze fixed accusingly on Ren.

Ren winced. He'd kept Quinn out of the loop. Keely's talk of spies had him being extra-cautious. Not that he suspected Quinn, but the less the older man or anyone knew about what Keely and Tweeter were doing to upgrade the early warning security for Sanctuary, the better. Ren didn't want the spy coming across the information and then trailing after Keely and Tweeter and ambushing them. A sniper's bullet could travel a long way and could not be defended against.

He moved to sit in the chair next to his long-time friend. "It's a secret for now. Not even Trey knows." Quinn relaxed his affronted posture at that admission. "I'm concerned about the other problem I told you about." He'd spoken at length to Quinn from South America about the potential of a mole on Sanctuary— and the need to know where Keely was at all times in order to protect her.

"The little gal has been burning the candle at both ends." Quinn eyed him over his glass. "She's doing deep background checks on the new recruits—three of them in particular. I have to say, she has good instincts.

The same three she's suspicious of smelled hinky when I first met them. They look good on paper, but if they are ex-US Special Forces, I'll eat my saddle." Quinn was an old cowboy from Texas, even the Marines couldn't train the country boy out of him.

Ren leaned in closer. His voice low, he asked, "Which three? And what do you think they are?"

Quinn glanced around the room. His gaze zeroed in on a spot in a side room open to the great room where the billiard and game tables were located. Most of the Lodge's activity was centered there at this time of the day since Scotty didn't serve food until six o'clock on the dot.

Ren turned casually following the line of Quinn's stare. He found six men hanging around the pool table. A boisterous game of eight-ball was in progress. Trey and Vanko were there along with four new men. "Which of them is Keely looking at?"

"Rod Bannon, he's next to Trey. Jose Vences, the guy taking a shot. Tripp Jordan, standing behind Vences. The other guy, Risto Smith, is a good man and came highly recommended by people we both know and trust. Bannon and Jordan are definitely trouble. Smell like washouts who went merc. Vences just doesn't have the chops of ex-military and not sure where he's coming from, but he ain't what he advertised on his application." Quinn turned, a smile lurking in his eyes. "Keely said their backgrounds are as fake as a stripper's tits."

"She didn't put it that way, did she?" Ren's lips quirked at the thought of the little innocent saying such a thing.

"Nah, she called them asswipes." Ren choked back a laugh. Quinn grinned and continued. "She seems to have picked up some colorful terms from her Marine daddy. Shocked the shit out of me hearing such a crude term coming from such sweet lips. Just goes to show you how upset she was, I guess."

Ren shook his head, turning once more to observe the three. He murmured, "Are they spies? What do you think, Quinn?"

The older man said nothing for a while, studying the men just as Ren had. "Bannon would get my vote. Maybe Jordan. Vences, my gut says no. Yeah, he lied, but he's too eager, too helpful. The other two think they're hot shit. Uh ... noticed Bannon hanging around Keely at breakfast a couple of times—didn't like the smell of that, either."

Ren turned to look at his friend. If Quinn said it didn't smell right, then it really stank. Every muscle tightened at the thought of Bannon near Keely. "What did the fucker do? Did he touch her?" He gripped the arms of his chair, forcing himself not to leap up and tear the bastard's face off.

Quinn's calm, dark gaze fixed on Ren's hands. "Might want to let up on the chair. You'll leave dents."

"Fuck the chair. What did Bannon do to Keely?"

"Nothing yet as far as I could glean. Mostly talk and coming on to her. Scotty was there and kept an eye on the situation. Said Keely handled it well." Quinn chuckled. "Scotty said the little gal is one cool customer. I suspect she wants to get the goods on the three so you can toss their asses off the property—so she kept it cool."

"Where the fuck was her fucking brother when all this fucking happened?" He let go of the chair and stretched his all-of-sudden cramped fingers, wishing they were around Bannon's thick, ugly neck.

"Tweeter and Keely have been out every damn day in the worst weather I've seen in these parts in years, working on whatever they've been working on—so to answer your question, at five o'clock in the morning when said approaches occurred, Tweeter was sleeping."

"Fuck that. Keely was there, he should have been. I'll kick his ass," muttered Ren.

"Back off, boss man." Quinn laid his hand on Ren's shoulder, forcing him to sit all the way down. Ren hadn't even realized he was half out of his chair. "She handled it. Scotty was there. She knew it and made sure Bannon knew it."

Ren rotated his head and shoulders in an attempt to alleviate the tension. He'd let it go—for now. He'd keep an eye on the situation, and if Bannon so much as breathed on Keely, all bets were off. He'd tear the asshole's head off and stuff it down his bloody stump of a neck. The image made him smile. "What have they told everyone about their daily trips into the wild?"

"At first, they told everyone they were snowboarding." Quinn snorted. "They took out boards the first few days, but the weather got treacherous. So then they changed their story to snowmobiling."

Ren nodded. "Sounds plausible."

"Yeah, except it has been colder than a witch's tit here for a week and the wind could blow your ass down. Everyone *knows* the two geniuses are doing something, but no one can imagine what. There's been quite a bit of speculation. I suspect that's why Bannon put the moves on Keely two days ago, prior to that time he kept his distance. He wants to shake something loose for his boss in DoD, maybe?"

"Maybe." Ren growled. Instead of chasing Trujo's ass all over South America, unsuccessfully, he should have been here protecting his sprite. Keely had needed him and he hadn't been here. Well, he was here now, and her little ass was never going to be out of his sight, if he could help it. "Where the fuck are they? There are fucking blizzard warnings out."

Shouts from the game room indicated the pool game was over. Trey ambled toward them, Vanko trailing him. The two men joined them.

Ren angled his head toward the pool table where the three suspects cued up another game with the other new guy, Smith. "What's your take on Bannon, Vences, and Jordan?"

Trey frowned. "Bannon and Jordan are blowhards, more show than go. Vences is young and naive. Can't believe the kid was an Army Ranger. Noticed you didn't ask about Smith, but Risto is solid gold, served in Afghanistan with a friend of mine. A fucking hero many times over."

"Keely's okay with Risto, the other three, not so much." Ren turned from his brother. "Vanko, what's your gut telling you?"

"Same as Trey's. So, Keelulya's neck is itching again?" Vanko grunted. "Her itchy neck is better than most intel."

Ren smiled. "Yeah, it is. She's doing deep backgrounds on them according to Quinn."

"Where are Keely and Tweeter?" Trey looked around as if he expected to see them in the Lodge with the other Sanctuary inhabitants getting ready for the evening meal. Many chose to eat in the main dining room rather than fix something in their lodgings.

"Outside." Ren's smile left his face as his experienced gaze took in the white-out conditions through the large floor-to-ceiling windows overlooking the mountainous terrain in which Sanctuary was nestled. He'd landed the SSI jet at the small airport outside of Elk City in conditions he normally wouldn't attempt. He'd been driven by the need to see Keely, so he'd chanced it.

"Well, shit." Trey looked toward the window. "Should we go out and look for them?"

"How? Where?" Ren pounded his fist on the arm of his chair. "Sanctuary is over a hundred square miles. Where are we supposed to look?"

Price joined them. "I couldn't help but overhear. I just came from the Bat Cave and I think I know where they are. They're heading in."

"How do you know that?" Quinn sat up in his chair.

Price grinned and sat on the arm of Vanko's chair. "Whatever in the hell those two have been doing while we chased Trujo's ass all over the Triple Frontier has produced a holographic image map of all of Sanctuary. I saw a blip moving from the north and heading on a straight line for us—well, as straight as you can get in this area. They look to be about twenty miles out."

"This the secret?" Quinn looked at Ren.

"Yeah." Ren stood up. "Show us, Price."

The others stood and joined Price as he led the way to the Bat Cave entrance, which only the inner core of SSI could access. Some of the other SSI employees might work in the Bat Cave under Tweeter's supervision, but none of those employees had clearance to be there without one of the directors.

Price used his hand imprint and retinal scan to open the elevator and the five of them entered the elevator and rode to the sub-basement. When the doors opened on the lower level, the men all gasped at once. Ren could understand why. There, on a large table in the center of the room was a holographic representation of the whole of Sanctuary, from border to border and ground to sky.

They moved to the table as one.

Ren followed the path of the small blipping signal

coded with a set of letters and numbers that had to be Tweeter and Keely as they made their way back to the main compound.

"Fucking amazing," breathed Trey. "My God, Ren, this is brilliant. I've only seen the likes in sci-fi movies."

Ren frowned. "What are these blips coming in from the east? They don't have a code." Twenty or more blips edged into the hologram and moved steadily on a heading that would bring them to the Lodge.

"Shit. Someone is coming into our territory from the National Forest lands," Price said. "Unplanned guests?"

Ren quickly plotted speed and trajectories, then swore. "Fuck, just fuck. Keely and Tweeter will intersect the bogies before they make it back to safety." He looked to Quinn. "Try to raise them on the two-way." To the others, he said, "Gear up. We're going to intercept the uninvited visitors."

Chapter Eight

"Tweetie." With the howling wind and the loud thrum of the powerful snowmobile engine, Keely shouted to make herself heard over the headset. "We've got company according to the readings on the laptop. Bogies coming in from the east just to the south of us. They'll cut across our path before we make it home."

"Shit." Tweeter swore some more and she didn't even think to chide him for all the f-bombs he dropped. "Switch to the alternating emergency frequencies, sis. We need to warn the others."

Keely, keeping one arm securely around her

brother's lean waist, balanced the small laptop between their bodies as she keyed in the new set of alternating frequencies on her headset. Thank God for digital technology. She heard Quinn's welcome voice hailing them, issuing a warning about the unknown visitors to Sanctuary.

"Hey, Quinn. We see them on our portable comp," she told the older man.

"Keely, are you okay?" Ren's welcome voice warmed her more than Scotty's five-alarm chili would've.

"We're fine, big guy." She leaned harder into her brother's body as he took a corner on one skid. She shoved the laptop into the front pouch of her parka so it wouldn't fly off on another such turn. "How did you see the intruders? Is the table working?"

"Yeah, baby, your table's working. Now you and Tweeter find a hole and hide in it. The guys and I are coming out to see who's visiting in this kind of weather."

"Can't be anyone friendly, that's for sure," Tweeter said. "We're going to Cave A5. I'll weapon up and meet you."

"Keely?"

"Yes, Ren?"

"Stay where Tweeter puts you—please?"

She sighed. "No one ever wants me to have any

fun."

"I want you safe. And Quinn told me you haven't been resting. We'll discuss making false reports to me on your welfare later. For now I want you to rest and stay put until I come for you. Hear me?"

"I hear you." She rubbed her forehead on her brother's back. "I'm glad you're home, Ren. I missed you."

Silence on the connection seemed to last forever when Ren said, "Missed you, too, baby. Stay safe for me."

Tweeter chuckled and a beep told her he'd switched off the outside chatter so it was just the two of them on the headsets. "You lied to Ren about your health? You are in so much trouble."

"We'll see." She squeezed her brother's waist. "This Cave A5? Does it have a sniper rifle or two?"

"Yeah, why?" Tweeter hesitated, then said, "Ahh, sis. No. You promised to stay put. Ren will pull my guts out through my nose if you do anything to endanger yourself."

"I didn't promise and I won't let him blame you. Besides, there's no danger in sniping from a distance. I counted the blips—there are too many of them. Ren and the guys will need the advantage of a sniper. Tell me about the rifles."

"Shit, shit, shit." He heaved a sigh as he took a turn leading upward into what looked like a dead end. "You'll want the AWM .338 Lapua Magnum in these conditions."

"Oh, sweet. Good in temps to forty-six below. Accurate as hell, less susceptible to wind conditions—and we sure as heck have those. Now where will we put me? Is there a place I can dig in—elevated—about what would you say? Fifteen hundred meters or so from where Ren and the guys will be intercepting the bogies?"

Tweeter's only response was a grunt which she took for agreement with her site plan. He pulled into a sheltered area. The fierce gusts died down, blocked by the high rock walls on each side of the trail. The snow was deep, but at least it wasn't blowing around causing visibility issues. Her brother switched off the engine, then got off the snowmobile. "Sis, help me cover this up."

Keely got off the snowmobile and helped him cover the vehicle with the Arctic camouflage tarp. She followed him to a rock wall where he entered a code on a hidden key pad; the wall, really a steel door, slid open. They entered a small cave. Pathway lights illuminated as they moved through the space to another set of doors. This entrance was keyed to a retinal scan.

Tweeter shoved his goggles onto the top of his head then leaned into the scanner. "Remind me to put you in the system."

"I already did." She took her goggles off and slid them up her arm, then removed her heavy outer gloves.

"Like when?" He aimed a skeptical glance at her before opening the door.

"Hey, you sleep a lot, and remember I designed a lot of the equipment you're using, big bro." She followed him into another room. This one was lined with steel walls and was ultra-high-tech. It was warm, about sixty degrees, and illuminated by recessed LED lighting which had been activated by the opening of the door.

Tweeter strode to a cabinet and pulled out the sniper rifle first designed for the Swedish army and later used in Afghanistan due to its ability to withstand extremes in conditions from intense heat in the desert to freezing cold in the snow. "Is this too heavy for you, Keely?" He handed her the Lapua. It was fully assembled. He pulled out several loaded magazines and some extra rounds, stuffing them in a carry bag designed for the weapon when disassembled.

"No. I can handle it."

"Good." Tweeter pulled out a submachine gun and ammunition, a serrated battle knife and sheath, and a handgun.

"Got another knife in there for me?" She peeked around his shoulder. "Just in case, give me a handgun."

Her brother pulled the two items out and handed them to her. "And let's not have a 'just in case.' Stay the maximum distance away and cherry pick. Ren will kill us even for that much involvement. I know you can hit the pip out of an ace of spades at a thousand meters, but Ren doesn't."

"You'd think after my demonstration in South America, he'd know better." She checked over the weapons and muttered. "Stupid man."

"Ya'd think, but that's Ren." Tweeter pulled out some protein bars and a couple of bottles of water from a cabinet built into the sleek walls. "Need any energy bars?"

She took two and a bottle of water, which she guzzled. Cold weather dehydrated a person easily. The water would only freeze outside. She'd save the bars for later while she waited for her shot.

"Tweetie, you'll call it. When you want me to start taking out targets, let me know. I'll wait until you give the go-ahead. That way, Ren won't know the difference if I don't have to shoot."

Her brother tweaked her on the nose. "Don't worry about the boss. You'll talk him around. Me? He'll kick my ass. And I wouldn't blame him. I'd do the same if I were in his shoes. But since I'm your brother, and I know you're a better shot than any of us boys, I want you at my back. Ren will learn how capable you are the longer he knows you—plus the dead bodies will prove your case." He took her face between his hands and stared her in the eye. "No wounding. Go for kill shots. This is war."

She swallowed hard, but nodded. God, she'd be killing again. But it was in defense of Sanctuary—and of Ren. And Ren would be here to keep the nightmares away.

"I'll do what needs to be done. Just don't get dead. Dad and Mama would be really pissed." She hugged him. "Now let's get me in place." She pulled out her laptop and glanced at the monitor. "Our guys have dug in about two thousand meters from here. Find me a nest and then go help them."

———

Keely nestled down in the snow, the white Arctic snowsuit Tweeter had pushed on her protecting her from the worst of the cold. She had hand warmers layered between her Thinsulate glove liners and her outer Arctic-grade mittens. She'd only take the outer mitten off when she was ready to pull the trigger.

The sniper rifle felt good. The Zeis scope was perfectly engineered for cold-weather, dusk and nighttime sniping. She had a grand view and could see the intruders edging into her peripheral vision from the east.

Tweetie had left ten minutes ago and should just be coming in behind the SSI team. She monitored their chatter, waiting for her brother's go-ahead. She had the exact range thanks to the GPS app on her computer, the new program she'd created for the hologram table and the hand-held computer for the high-tech rifle. The wind would be the only variable in her shot and it was minimized by the weapon and the caliber of the ammunition. This particular gun had been created for these conditions.

The sound of submachine gun fire echoed up from the valley. She looked through the night-vision scope. The bogies had fired first, confirming they were up to no good and fair game for killing. The SSI operatives held their fire for now, luring the bad asses in.

"Come on, Tweetie. Give the sign." Her mitten off,

her gloved hand was steady, her finger on the trigger and her eye glued to the scope. She breathed slowly, waiting patiently for the go-ahead. She had her sight glued on the lead snowmobiler. Absently, she wondered why killing from a long distance didn't seem to bother her as much as close up. It should—killing was killing—but it didn't, at least not in the heat of the moment. Later she knew it would haunt her dreams.

"Go, sis." Tweetie's whispered signal had her taking a bead on the lead guy's temple.

She took a breath and as she released it, she pulled the trigger. He was down. She lined up her next shot and took it as easily as she breathed. She didn't have to look to see that she'd placed the first bullet right where she'd aimed—in the front lobe of the bad ass's brain. If he wasn't dead now, he soon would be. Her dad had taught her well. He'd always said: "No use shooting, Keely-girl, if you don't hit what you're aiming for."

"Stay under cover, guys," she muttered into the head set. "I've got them, and I'm well out of range of their weapons."

"Keely—" Ren's voice held anger—and something else—fear.

"Leave her be, Ren," Vanko said. "She has excellent position, and she just took the two in the lead out."

Keely squeezed off her third shot. "And now the third. She's right. They cannot reach her with the weapons they have."

"Ren, I'm fine." She took a breath, waiting for her next shot. The intruders seemed to be circling around, regrouping; she couldn't single out any one and didn't want to waste ammo. "I'm over twelve hundred meters away. Let me put them on the run, and you guys can follow and do clean up." Finally, some fool broke away. She took the shot as he attempted to approach the entrenched position of the SSI team. She was four for four.

"Damn, she's good," another of the team said. "If you don't snag her, I will." It was Trey, Ren's brother. She smiled.

"Keep your mind off my woman and on the fight, brother."

Whoa! Her womb clenched, her heart pounded, forcing her to back away from the next shot. Ren had claimed her in the middle of a frick-fracking battle. He sounded pissed about it, too. She breathed slowly for a space of several seconds, then put her eye back to the scope. No shot yet. She waited until the next target entered her range and pulled the trigger. Automatically, she ejected the empty five-shot magazine and slapped in a full one.

As she set up her next shot, she wasn't sure what alerted her, but something had. A slide of shadow over shadow in the reflected early evening light off the snow. A soft swooshing sound of loose snow displaced by boots. Whatever had caught her attention, it indicated someone approaching her position. Someone, no, more than one someone, was coming at her from behind.

Where the heck had they come from? And how had they known where she'd be? She hadn't known her position before ten minutes ago. No one from the fight in the valley could have made it up to her position so fast. Was it one of the traitors from within Sanctuary? Or did the invaders have two teams and had had the same idea about placing a sniper up high?

Slowly, she reached in her jacket pocket, where she'd secreted the handgun next to another hand-warmer to keep the weapon from freezing. She flicked off the safety and as she rolled over she brought out the gun and shot the man bearing down on her.

"Shit." She missed. The man was injured, but still moved. She fired another round into his head to be sure.

"I'm made." Her calm tone belied the loud thudding of her heart. The primitive part of her brain told her to run, but her training had her planning her moves so she could take the other man out. "Don't know how or who, but I'm moving to higher ground."

"Keely!" Ren's voice was loud in her ears, but she forced herself to ignore the myriad emotions in his tone as she did what she needed to do to survive. Her neck just didn't itch, it felt as if fire ants swarmed over it. The other bad guy hadn't taken the hint of his buddy's death and was stalking her rather than fleeing, indicating that whoever he was, he really wanted her. This guy, however, was more cautious than the one she'd shot.

She collapsed the bipod on her rifle, snagged the bag of ammo and mags, then moved laterally and up the slippery ledge upon which she'd been perched. She exited faster than she'd like under the worsening conditions. One wrong foot placement and she could go over the edge and fall a thousand or so feet to the valley below.

A wild shot hit a tree branch near her head when she zigged instead of zagging. She turned, switching the Bren Ten to semi-automatic and let off a fusillade of shots in the direction of the shot. She dove behind a rock just as her pursuer returned fire. He had what sounded like a submachine pistol, which trumped her Bren for firing capacity. *Shit.*

"Keely!" Ren's voice was now an angry roar.

She winced. "Don't yell, for chrissakes," she muttered into her mike. "I can hear. Can't talk, he's getting close."

Since her handgun was out of ammunition and reloading would make her dead, she swung the sniper rifle around and pointed it in the direction the shooter would have to come to finish her off. While the weapon wasn't made for close-in work, it had deathly stopping power at this short range. It was like using a cannon instead of a pea shooter. She wanted the sucker dead.

Her pursuer came around a bend at full speed. Stupid—maybe he was less cautious than the other guy. Men always underestimated her. He probably thought she'd keep running. Sometimes you just had to dig in and wait. She was good at waiting. She'd learned from the best strategist in the Marine Corps—her Dad.

The muzzle of the sniper rifle braced on a boulder, she shot him in the torso before he even caught a glimpse of her. The force of the shot knocked him back, off his feet, and carried him over the ledge she'd almost flown up to get away from him. If the shot hadn't killed him—and since it had decimated his torso, it should have—the fall would. She looked over the edge and saw that he had fallen to a ledge just below her former sniping position. He wasn't moving.

Listening, she heard nothing but the whistle of the wind, her heart pounding in her ears, and the sound of gunfire from the valley echoing off the mountainside. Even better, her neck had stopped itching. She let out a deep sigh. "I'm clear. Hear me, Ren. I'm clear. Watch your ass."

His answering growl was unintelligible.

Keely took several more deep breaths. She had to slow down her heart. A wave of dizziness assailed her. She leaned against the icy boulder for support. Adrenaline overload. Hypoglycemia, too. She was burning calories like a bunny on speed. She fumbled in her pocket and pulled one of the protein bars out. She tore it open with her teeth, then ate it in three bites, shoving the wrapper in her pocket. A small bite of snow kept her from choking on the dry granola and fruit. Taking calming breaths, she sat and waited for the sweet fruit to take effect. It took a minute or so but the high-carb bar did the trick. She ate the second bar more slowly, knowing she was still burning calories like a son of a bitch.

Finally, her brain registered the continued gunfire from the valley, and the danger to her team centered her. She needed to stop being a wuss and help the guys. She searched for another perch from which to take out baddies. Spotting a ledge that looked to be approximately in the same spot but fifty feet higher than her last one, she crawled to it and dug in, then assessed the scene. She put in a full magazine, then calmly spoke into the mike. "Setting up for more long-range."

The male chatter in her ears was mere white noise as she released the bipod. The intruders were attempting to swarm and overpower the SSI position, thinking the sniper was history since she had not taken a shot for a while. "Sorry, fellas, but you lose. I'm still here."

She found her targets and began taking them out like bonus-point characters in a personal shooter game. First one. Then two. Three. Four. Five. She ejected the empty magazine and shoved in a full one and emptied the next five rounds into five more of the enemy. She ejected the magazine and shoved in another full one, then paused to observe the action below. With the concentrated semi-automatic fire from the SSI team, the few remaining bad guys, whoever in the hell they were, ran.

Just to be safe, she reloaded the empty magazines with cold but sure hands. She didn't want to take a chance on being empty in case she needed the rifle again. She then reloaded the handgun before breaking down the sniper rifle and sticking it in the bag Tweeter had thought to bring along, making it much easier for her to hike out. She could reassemble the rifle in the dark and cold in less than a minute if she had to.

She shoved the handgun into her right parka pocket to keep it warm. She then tugged on her outer mittens with their hand-warmers, not realizing how cold her hands had become. And finally she checked to make sure her knife was sheathed on her left thigh.

"Guys?" She headed for Cave A5, which was just up and over the ridge, about a quarter mile away. The snowmobile had had to take a longer way around to get her to the position from which she'd first shot.

"What, sis?" Her brother answered—not Ren.

"I'm heading for the cave."

"I'm almost at your position, baby." Ren's low growling tone warmed her. "Stay put. I want to make sure the asshole you filled full of … Jesus Christ, baby, what the fuck did you shoot him with?"

Ren was below her. He'd found the guy she'd taken out with the sniper rifle at close range. She grimaced; she could just imagine how torn up his torso was from the bullet, let alone what the fall had done to the rest of his body. She choked back the granola threatening to come up her throat. Aftermath was a bitch.

"The Lapua … I couldn't…"

"That would do it. Just stay put. I'll swing by to pick you up."

"No, Ren. I can come down. I'm getting kind of tired, but I can make it." And that was the understatement of the century. It felt as if her legs weighed a ton. Her head hurt and she was running on fumes. If she had to fight off anyone else, they might just win the next round.

"I'm coming up. Meet you at your first position. Keely…?"

She knew he'd heard her exhaustion and needed her reassurance she really was all right. "I'll really am fine. I wasn't shot."

Keely gingerly picked her way down a rocky path only a near-sighted mountain goat could love. She couldn't believe she'd practically flown up this same route only minutes earlier. Adrenaline and a shooter on her butt probably had a lot to do with it.

The conditions were shitty—and getting absolutely crappier. Several times she had to practically crawl over icy spots. Finally she reached her original sniping position. Ren was already there. His back was to her. He was checking out the first guy she'd shot.

"Ren."

He turned and strode toward her, gathering her into his arms, rifle bag and all. His voice cracked as it came over the headset. "God, baby. I aged a hundred years when you said they'd made you. I thought I lost you."

Was that love making his voice waver or bad headset reception? She couldn't tell. His face was buried in her parka as his arms held her as if he'd never let her go. His words spoke of more than protectiveness, though. She smiled as she snuggled into his body, her arms around his waist. He was like a furnace. She sighed at the warmth he provided.

"Baby? Keely?" He leaned back and looked at her. His eyes narrowed. "Aww, shit, sweetheart. You're out of it, aren't you?" He rubbed her arms, warming and comforting her at the same time.

Speechless at the fervent look in his eyes, she nodded. She wouldn't identify it as love—yet.

He swung her into his arms, snagged the rifle bag she'd dropped, and headed down the path to his snowmobile parked at the navigable trail's end.

Trey was there, riding shotgun. "Should we try to make it back to the Lodge?"

Ren rubbed his cheek against her wool-covered head. "Baby, you okay with camping out in A5? There's food, heat and bedding."

"I'm fine, Ren, really. Just tired, hungry and cold—and that was before we had to stop and fight. Some food and sleep, and I'll be ready to fight again tomorrow."

"Not if I can help it," he muttered. "Tell the others what we're doing, Trey."

"They're holed up in A8," Trey reported after giving her brother their sit rep. "They chased the few remaining bogies back into the National Forest. They're monitoring the perimeter, using the computer set up in A8."

"My holographic table worked good, huh?" Keely yawned and swayed as Ren put her down to mount the snowmobile.

His arms immediately came around her to hold her up. "It worked great, baby. Trey, help her get on behind me."

Ren's brother picked her up and placed her on the snowmobile, guiding her arms around Ren's waist. He took the rifle bag and slung it over his shoulder. "Hold onto Ren, sweetie."

She nodded and curled her fingers around the front placket of Ren's survival suit. She buried her face in his back, the down fill as soft as a pillow.

"Are you secure?" Ren's low voice vibrated through

her body even as his voice came over the headset.

"Yes. Let's go." She rubbed her cheek against his back. "Will you hold me when we sleep tonight?"

"Nothing could stop me."

"Good." She drowsed in a state between half-asleep and half-awake or she might not have made the next admission. "I haven't slept well since Argentina. I don't ever want to sleep alone again."

"And you won't have to." His words followed her into a deep, cold darkness.

"Trey," Ren entered the inner room of A5 and placed Keely on a low divan, "set up two of the air mattresses, would you? And sock up the heat."

Trey moved to adjust the thermostat. "Why not three air mattresses?"

Ren heaved a sigh. "Because I'm sleeping next to her. You have a problem with that?"

"What's the deal, Ren? You playing with that little gal—or are you serious?"

He turned from loosening Keely's survival suit and glared at his brother. "Why do you want to know?"

"Fuck, Ren, why would you think? She's Tweeter's sister. You don't mess with a friend's little sister. You'd emasculate any fucker who did that with our baby sister."

Ren let out a harsh breath. Trey didn't want Keely for himself. God, he'd never been jealous before—it was a bitch of an ugly feeling. "I'm serious. Okay?"

"How serious? In case Tweeter asks me."

"Tweeter already knows, as does his family."

"But I don't and neither do the other men on Sanctuary."

A valid point, and one he would clear up as soon as they got back to the Lodge. No one would touch Keely and remain on Sanctuary. "Ring-on-finger-a-passel-of-kids-forever serious, is that good enough for you?" He glared at his brother. "Now, shut the fuck up. Our voices are disturbing her."

Trey lips twisted into a smug smile. "Ass. I knew you had a come-to-Jesus meeting with the Walsh men in Boston after the warehouse…" his brother's mouth thinned and something deadly swept over his face at the mention of Boston "…but I wanted to hear it from your lips."

Ren pushed back the images of the seedy dockside warehouse, the implements of torture, the metal table with restraints, the blood, Keely's blood, on the table and the concrete floor … no, he wouldn't go there. Only knowing Keely was safe in Idaho with her brother,

Quinn and Scotty watching over her had gotten him through the two days they spent in Boston with her father and brothers following up on her abduction after the failed search for Trujo. The resurrected images made him want to kill someone—and Keely needed only tenderness from him now.

"Trey … just fuck it."

"God, I'm sorry, Ren … it's just what we saw… I can't forget and Keely needs…"

"Yeah, I know. Keely needs love and gentleness. And, damn, Trey, I'll do my best to make sure she never has to … aw, shit, you know."

"Yeah. And I'll protect her with my life, brother. You can count on me."

Ren nodded. He gently finished undressing her, making sure none of the dark emotions brought forth by the heinous images came through his touch. He left Keely's leggings and sweater on. No way was he stripping her, even down to her ski underwear, with his brother in the same room. Not only would she be embarrassed, but he didn't think he could handle his brother looking at her body in the form-fitting Thinsulate layer. He used her snowsuit as a blanket until the bed was ready.

Trey had one air mattress blown up and winter-weight bedding laid on top of it. "Get your and Keely's bed made. I'll make some broth and hot chocolate. She needs fluids and sugar."

"Thanks." Ren leaned over and shook out the flannel sheet for the air mattress, then layered another flannel cover and added a comforter. All the amenities of home. "I'll wake her to eat when the food is ready. She got like this in South America. I can feed her if she doesn't wake up all the way."

Trey stopped preparing the food and turned, an incredulous look on his face. "You fed her in South America?"

"I cared for her completely, with Tweeter's help, for almost two full days and nights. She was really out of it." Ren shot an affectionate look at her motionless form. Her color was better now that the cave was heating up and her breathing was even. "She takes on too much, and then just peters out. Tweeter told me she tends toward hypoglycemia. Plus, she's just so damn tiny and delicate. She's not built for the kind of fighting she's been doing." He forcibly shut a mental door on the memory of the warehouse as it threatened to come to the forefront of his mind once more. She was safe, here, with him. He repeated the phrases like a mantra until he could contain the rage.

Trey turned from preparing the food. "She may be delicate, but she took out those bogies like a professional sniper."

"She is a professional sniper." Ren smiled at his brother's look of shock. "She attended Sniper School. I'm still waiting on my DVD copy of her Hell Week experiences." He chuckled as his brother choked on his hot chocolate. "Yeah, I had the same reaction, but the Walsh twins took me aside before we left Boston and told me all about that—and some other things."

"What other things?"

Ren grimaced. "They threatened to cut my balls off with a dull knife if I hurt their sister."

"That's when you told them you were serious, I bet."

"Damn straight." A murmur and a little groan had Ren hurrying to Keely's side. "Hey, sweetheart, you okay?"

She blinked at him and smiled. "Fine. Hungry. Not so cold. Nice … cozy." She yawned, closed her eyes, and snuggled into the snowsuit he'd covered her with. "Sorry. Tired. Sore."

Trey walked to his side and stared at Keely. "She's out of it, isn't she?"

"Uh-huh." Ren scooped her into his arms and

carried her to the bed he'd made for them and tucked her in, pulling the down-filled comforter over her. He stroked a finger over her still-chilled cheek. "Baby, can you eat for me?"

"Sure." Her eyes remained closed. "Hold me."

"On my agenda. But first you have to eat for me, okay?" He brushed a kiss over her lips. Her tongue came out to touch his mouth. He shuddered. Such a small touch and he was hard as a rock. "God, Trey, I've never felt like this before. She slays me."

She smiled and murmured at his words, but didn't open her eyes.

His brother clapped him on the back. "About time you found someone. You've always been too much of a loner. Now, feed your woman. We all need to rest. Tomorrow will be a long day dealing with the Sheriff."

"Not worried about that." Ren stood and stripped to his ski underwear, then walked to retrieve a tray loaded with cups of broth and hot chocolate, sorted through the utensil drawer and found a straw and added it to the tray, then took it back to where Keely lay. "Dan will accept our story, plus those assholes were loaded for more than hunting wildlife. Never saw so many illegal automatic weapons in my life."

He slipped into the bed with Keely and pulled her

onto his lap, making sure to keep the comforter tucked around her small form so she wouldn't get chilled. "Shove the tray closer to me, would you, Trey?"

His brother did, then knelt next to them. "Need any help feeding her?"

"Nope." He took the cup of hot chocolate and took a sip. Perfect. He grabbed the straw and stuck it into the cup, then prodded her mouth with it. "Sip, Keely."

Her lips took the straw like a baby taking a bottle and she sucked as he held the cup for her. "Want some soup, baby?" She shook her head and kept sipping the chocolate.

"You weren't kidding." Trey lay on his side on his air mattress next to theirs. "Just like feeding a baby."

"She's used to it." Ren tugged on the straw as Keely hit bottom on the chocolate and sucked air. The straw released from her mouth with a little pop and a hiccup. "Tweeter told me when she was little and sick their mom would feed them this way. Hand me the broth." Trey shoved a cup of broth closer to Ren's hand. "Another straw and she'll drink this also." He tasted the soup to make sure it wasn't too hot. "Drink it, sprite." She frowned and shook her head. He nuzzled her forehead, placing tiny kisses above her delicately shaped red-gold brows. "Come on, baby—for Ren."

She sighed and parted her lips and let him place the straw inside. She sucked a few sips, then let the straw fall from her lips and turned her face into his neck. A full-body shudder preceded her going boneless in his arms.

"She's done." Ren kissed the top of her head, rubbing his cheek against her curls.

"God, you really are in love with her, aren't you?" Trey took the cup from him.

"Yeah."

"Does Keely realize that you're a Neanderthal and you'll smother her just like you did our sister?"

"I'm not going to smother her, just protect her."

Trey laughed. "She doesn't need you to protect her. She does a pretty good job on her own."

"Who cares what you think, turd?" Ren resorted to the nickname he'd given Trey as a kid.

"Butthead," Trey replied. "Night."

"Night." Ren smiled. He put his cup on the tray and ordered the lights to low. He shifted Keely until she lay on her side next to him and he could curl around her, her butt snuggled against his hard cock. He anchored her with one arm over her waist and his other under her pillow. She sighed and melted into his body. "Sleep tight, sweetheart." He brushed her cheek with a kiss and closed his eyes.

———

Whimpering and moaning woke him from a dream of him and Keely on an island, naked and making love in a hammock. Her thrashing of arms and legs had him ordering lights on. "Keely. Baby. It's okay. You're safe." The sounds she uttered as she begged the men in her nightmare to stop hurting her made him want to kill. "Sweetheart, shhh. It's Ren. I've got you."

"What can I do?" Trey's low, concern-filled voice came over his shoulder.

"Nothing. She works through it in her subconscious and I hold her. Eventually my voice and touch gets through."

"She's dreaming of Boston, isn't she?"

"Yeah."

"Ren?" Keely opened her eyes, tears streaking down her cheeks. "I'm sorry."

"Nothing to be sorry about, baby." He kissed the tears from her face. "You want more hot chocolate?"

"Uh-huh, if it's no trouble." She snuggled her head under his chin, her fingers clutching his shirt.

"No trouble at all, Keely." Trey got up. "I'll make you a cup."

"Thanks, Trey." Her lips moved on Ren's throat, causing him to swallow and wish his pesky cock would behave. Keely needed gentleness, not a horny man poking her with his dick.

"Want to talk about the nightmares?" He stroked her back with the same soothing circular motion that had worked in South America.

"No." She shook her head, her hair tickling his chin and catching in his beard growth.

"It might help."

"I'll deal." She patted his chest. "Thanks for caring—and holding me."

"My pleasure. Here's your chocolate." He pulled her to a sitting position and took the cup from Trey. "Thanks, bro. Here Keely." He handed it to her. "Got it?"

She nodded and held the cup with both hands and took dainty sips, pausing to lick the marshmallow foam from her mouth. He silently groaned, wanting her tongue licking him anywhere she wanted. He'd promised her family not to pressure her—and after seeing the hellhole she survived, he'd promised himself as well. She needed a slow courtship and time to heal.

When she finished the cup, she handed it to Trey, who'd hovered on her other side. His brother would help him protect Keely, as would Vanko and Price, who had also seen what Keely had survived. Nothing bad could ever be allowed to hurt or touch her again. His heart couldn't handle it.

CHAPTER NINE

Next morning

"Keely." Ren pulled the snowmobile up to the front porch of his home. "Go in and take a bath—rest. I need to deal with the aftermath of the battle."

Trey had left before the two of them awakened, returning to the main compound to arrange for the collection of the dead from the previous evening's fight and to deal with the Sheriff until Ren got there. Ren, as a Special Deputy Sheriff for Idaho County, specializing in terrorism, would have to deal with the authorities.

"Will I have to speak with the Sheriff?" Keely's green eyes were dull from too little sleep and too much stress.

The look of resigned acceptance on her face pierced his soul. She'd done what she had to do, but it drained her physically and emotionally. He'd like to keep her away from such situations in the future. All he wanted was to wrap her in comfort and security and protect the hell out of her. Realistically, he knew, as Trey had intimated last night, they'd call upon her again. She was one of the best snipers he'd ever seen. His brother had contacted him before Keely had awakened and reported that every single one of the men she'd taken out at over twelve hundred meters was a kill shot to the head.

"Ren?" She touched his arm. "Will I have to talk to the authorities about all the men I shot?"

"No, baby." He pulled her into his arms and stroked her back. "I'm a Special Deputy. The Sheriff is ex-Special Forces. He knows what SSI does. This isn't the first time we've had dead bodies at Sanctuary from a firefight." He pulled back and saw her worried gaze. "I'm betting each and every one of those dead men were mercs." And he'd also bet that they would have either criminal military charges or civilian criminal records. Honorable men did not trespass armed to the gills.

"I'll work on that if you can get me fingerprints or photos. Plus, those two who came up on my nest… ?"

He nodded his encouragement. He wanted to hear her theories. "I don't think they were part of the group in the valley."

"We'll find out." It was unlikely there were two separate groups attempting to invade Sanctuary at the same time, but it was always a possibility. It was one he wasn't going to overlook; Keely's instincts had been batting a thousand since he met her.

She stroked one hand down his stubbled cheek. "Thank you."

"For what?" He turned his head slightly and kissed the palm of her hand.

"For holding me last night." She lowered her lashes. Her cheeks pinkening. "I really do like sleeping with you. It makes me feel … happy—and safe."

Holding her made him feel more than happy—it made him content. There was a sense of rightness in the act of holding her while she slept. He just wished he could take away her nightmares. "Aww, baby. You were so restless and moaning—and crying." He kissed one hot cheek. "I … I … wanted to soothe you but wasn't sure what to do."

"You did just fine, big guy." She wiggled away from his arms. "Now, I'm going to soak in your big-ass tub and then go over and eat one of Scotty's huge omelets.

After which, I will go to the Bat Cave and look at the data searches I had running on the terrible trio—as Tweetie and I have named our suspected spies."

"Keely," he held onto her arm so she couldn't turn to leave. "Take a nap. You didn't get much rest, and I'm worried you still have a fever."

"I'm fine, Ren. Really. I'll rest when you do." She forestalled any further lectures by turning her back on him and climbing the steps to his contemporary version of a log home.

"Keely?"

She stopped at his door and angled her head to look at him. "Yes?"

"We detoured by Boston and, along with your dad and brothers, packed up what was left of your stuff. Well, it's not much ... uh, the boxes are in the great room. I think there's some girly bath stuff and the like in there."

Keely's face lit up. She ran down the steps and leapt into his arms. He held her to him and reveled in the joy crossing her face.

"Thank you. Thank you." She peppered his face with kisses. "That was so considerate."

Too quickly, she dropped to her feet, ran up the steps and into his house. He wiped a silly-assed grin off his face. God, she made him happy—and whole. Once he took care of business, he'd grab Keely and they'd take a "nap," where he'd begin the sensual wooing of his little warrior. A more sexual smile crossed his face at the thought of a naked, sweet-smelling Keely in his big bed. He'd taken the liberty of smelling all her girly bath stuff as he packed it—the scents were warm and musky and had made him hot.

He groaned aloud at the thought of how she'd taste as he kissed her from her tiny toes to the tip of her curly head. He knew what she looked like naked from taking care of her night and day in Argentina. At the time, he'd filed away the images of her creamy white skin, her full rosy-tipped breasts, and the golden-red curls on her mound. He'd have been a foul monster to lust after her while she'd been so sick. But now, every treasured image resurfaced in living color—and he could hardly wait to revisit her body, this time healthy and alive for his touch.

But first, he had business to take care of. He had to protect Keely from any consequences of her skilled defense of Sanctuary and its people. He mounted the snow mobile and headed for the Lodge where he knew Sheriff Dan Morgan would be waiting to sort through the mess the intruders had brought with them.

Dan wouldn't give him any trouble, but the county commissioners were another matter. He and Dan would need to put together a report that demonstrated that Keely had saved the lives of innocent—and tax-paying—citizens. He'd have Tweeter start on the background searches on the dead intruders. The sooner they could show the invaders were not law-abiding citizens, the better.

———

AFTER HER VANILLA-SCENTED BATH, KEELY examined the contents of the packing boxes—all five of them. The cretins who'd trashed her townhouse hadn't left her much: some bath items, some cosmetics, some books, and miscellaneous things she'd packed in a storage unit the intruders either hadn't known about or didn't have the time to invade. All her clothes were gone, every blessed stitch. She'd need to go back to Boise or Coeur d'Alene and hit a mall and supplement the few items she and her mama had picked up on the trip to Sanctuary with Tweetie over a week ago.

The good news part of the debacle was that she'd be able to buy sexier underwear to please Ren instead of the teenage holdovers she'd worn previously. She also needed to buy more winter clothing than she'd had in

Boston. Winter lasted a lot longer and was a lot rougher in Idaho. She planned to tell Ren that she'd work for SSI as long as she could live on Sanctuary—with him.

Ballsy, yes, but she had a gut feeling he wouldn't mind.

She refused to cry over the loss of the majority of her possessions. She'd done more than her quota of crying over the deaths she'd caused; the loss of material things ranked pretty damn low on the grand scale of life's potholes.

Closing the lid on one box of books, she stood and stretched. Now to hit the Lodge and eat. She'd grabbed an apple and a Pepsi to get her blood sugar up enough to make it through her bath, and she still had almost fallen asleep in the warm, scented water. She could sleep later. After she refueled, she wanted to see just who Bannon, Vences and Jordan really were. Although Vences didn't make her neck itch as much as the other two, she suspected he was lying about something. The other two had ratcheted her spider senses up to high alert. They were at the very least felons, and at the worst plants.

Pulling on her parka and gloves, she left Ren's house, locking the door, and took the path leading to the back of the Lodge and the kitchen entrance. She liked to eat in the kitchen when she was by herself. Bannon, Jordan and Vences paid her way too much attention when she sat in the dining area. Vences probably did it to be one of the guys, but the other two, she sensed, wanted to hurt her. Whether they were ordered to do so or depravity was just in their nature, she wasn't sure yet. She'd bet their deep backgrounds would show some sort of sexually deviant crimes. They gave off that kind of vibe.

Entering the back door, the smell of spicy-so-hot-it-melted-tonsils chili hit her nostrils. The omelet she'd thought about asking Scotty to make flew out of her mind. Her mouth watered and stomach growled at the thought of Scotty's meaty, hot chili.

"Hey, doll," Scotty called out. His broad, ruddy face broke into a smile he seemed to only show her. The ex-Navy cook, whose much-younger fiancée she had yet to meet, had practically adopted her when Tweeter had first introduced them. No one would bother her with Scotty around.

"There's the love of my life," she teased. "When are we gonna skip this Popsicle stand and run away to the South Seas and open a restaurant on the beach?"

"You name the date, princess, and we're gone." He came over and hugged her, scanning her face as if to assess her condition. He placed the back of his hand against her forehead. "Low-grade temp. What in the hell have you been doing to yourself? Before she left to go back home, your mama made me promise to take care of you." He tugged her over to the island counter and lifted her onto a stool as if she weighed nothing. "Let me guess what you want to eat. Hmm, chili with cheese and sour cream, mixed green salad with some of my homemade avocado ranch dressing, hot blackberry cobbler with ice cream and a Pepsi—with an aspirin chaser. You are not to move until it all goes into that tiny tummy. We clear on that?"

The man knew she had the appetite of a dock worker. She'd have no trouble packing the food away. She laughed. "Sounds good. Bring it on. I'm starved."

He turned to move, then stopped. His facial expression turned serious. "You saved my guys' asses last night." Every citizen of Sanctuary was one of Scotty's people; the man's loyalty to the Maddox brothers and those who worked for them was bone deep.

She shrugged. "I just did what I could."

"Damn good work." He turned and began to prepare her food. "Just so you know, the Sheriff has cleared the shootings as self-defense. Your brother had no trouble documenting the less-than-stellar records of the bastards. Most of the a-holes had records miles long. Some of them had outstanding warrants. Ren is making sure you get the reward on those. A lot of cold cases were cleared with some of the deaths. Damn good work, little girl. But you don't need to be doing those sorts of things in the future. We protect our women here on Sanctuary."

Some of the tension from the previous night's battle dissipated now that she heard for a fact she wouldn't be charged with murder or manslaughter. She didn't need or want the reward and would tell Ren so. But she did need to clear up something. "Scotty?"

He walked to the island and put a salad and her soda in front of her. "What, princess?"

"I will defend myself—or anyone else belonging to SSI—if I need to." She touched the old salt's tattooed forearm, tracing the anchor and U.S. flag design. "I always try to avoid killing, but…"

Scotty's eyes filled with moisture as his lips twisted into a parody of a smile. "Yeah, I know, princess. I know. Some a-holes just ask for it." He turned his arm under hers then slid until he grasped her hand in his huge one. He squeezed her fingers gently. "Now eat up. I swear you've lost weight since you arrived here. You'll blow away in the wind if we don't put some meat on those bird bones."

She giggled. "Aye-aye, Scotty." She ate her way through the salad, two cups of chili, part of the dessert and three glasses of Pepsi. Leaning against the back of the counter stool, she sighed. "That was so good. Thanks. Now, I think I'll waddle off to find my brother."

"He was in the Bat Cave last I knew." Scotty washed some pots in the huge sink. His gaze fixed on something outside the large window over the sink. "Looks like Ren and the Sheriff are heading out to the scene of the battle. Don't expect we'll see the other guys until supper or so." He turned away from the view and captured her gaze with his stern one. "Since Ren isn't here to tell you, I will. Stay the hell away from Bannon and Jordan. They were asking about you at breakfast. One of the computer techs told them you were out with Ren and the guys—and they weren't happy."

Keely frowned. "Do you think they're the infiltrators? Or, are they just screw ups who lied to get a job in security?"

Early on she'd decided to trust Scotty. He'd been with SSI from the beginning and knew the Maddox brothers' father, having served with the elder Maddox in the Navy. Plus the gruff older man reminded her of her dad.

"Maybe. Probably. But one thing I do know, Bannon has a look in his eye when he watches you. Makes me want to kill him just for that alone."

"I know. He gives me the creeps." She shivered. "Well none of them have security access to get into the Bat Cave—and, even if they did, I have the techs and Tweetie down there with me. Safety in numbers."

"Take a weapon with you anyway." Scotty wiped his hands on his apron and pulled a sheathed battle knife from a drawer next to the sink. "Take this. I can't see that you're armed."

She walked to the older man and took the knife and hooked it on her belt. "I have a hold-out gun in an ankle holster. But this is good, too."

Scotty bent over and placed a fatherly kiss on her forehead. "Much cooler. You were feverish because you were running on empty. Now scoot. I'm making pot roast and all the fixin's for supper and I need to get started on the vegetables."

She hugged Scotty and left the room, mouth watering at the thought of pot roast. She loved red meat.

Wending her way through the back hallway, she stopped at the elevator to the sub-basement, entered her handprint and her retinal scan. The doors opened and she entered the elevator and pushed the close button. The trip to the sub-basement, a natural cave over which the Lodge was built, took less than thirty seconds. The doors opened to an oddly silent control center. Her holographic table was turned off. The computers and equipment ran 24/7 with back-up generators to handle the electrical needs during times when the public utilities were down. So while the electronic hum was present, a constant white noise, there were no voices and no evidence of people at all.

Something was wrong. At this time of the day at least one technician should be present monitoring communications, if nothing else. The hairs on the back of her neck stood as a frisson of awareness swept over her. "Tweetie?" She called as she stepped out of the elevator. The doors would remain open on this level until it was called from above.

She put a hand on the knife Scotty had given her, opening the sheath, and drawing the blade out. She clasped it in her right hand in a fight-ready grip. Moving slowly, she glanced from side to side, paying close attention to the shadows, watching for movement, listening for anything out of place. She headed for the far right corner of the room where her brother had his desk and monitoring station—and an intercom to the house. A dark shadow on the floor next to her brother's desk caught her eye. She hurried to it, concerned it was her brother. Her sigh of relief sounded abnormally loud in the silent room. The body was one of the technicians who worked with her brother.

She leaned down and felt for a pulse. Faint, but there.

Whoever had hit the tech was probably still in the room, had been allowed entrance by the hapless man, and was the reason her gut was sending warnings to her brain. Slowly, she turned in a circle. Someone was in the room—watching her. Waiting. She reached to activate the intercom and call for back up when movement in her peripheral vision had her turning, knife up and ready to defend.

It was Bannon. She looked around and saw no one else, but that didn't mean Jordan wasn't hiding somewhere, maybe holding her brother hostage. She had to get help. Tweeter could be somewhere in this room, hurt—or dead.

She moved so her back was protected by the rock wall behind Tweeter's desk. "You know, Bannon? I just promised Scotty I wouldn't kill anyone else today if I didn't have to—but at this point, I don't see how I can keep that vow." She watched his eyes. He had a habit of blinking when he made moves on her—or at least, he had the other times he'd attempted to grab her. She'd purposely forgotten to detail those other attacks to her brother and Scotty—probably a mistake, but she'd wanted to prove this asshole was a spy more than she wanted him kicked off Sanctuary for harassing her.

Of course, those other times he'd underestimated her skills—or overestimated his—because he'd lost each confrontation. She bet he wanted to hurt her badly at this point to prove his machismo. Men were stupid like that.

"Just you and me here, you beautiful little bitch." He moved forward, weaving side-to-side like a cobra attempting to mesmerize its prey.

Unfortunately for him, she wasn't beguiled. As he approached, she watched his eyes, only his eyes. There— the blink. She kicked his attacking hand, hitting the wrist, numbing it, causing him to drop his weapon. A quick glance showed it had been a knife. While he swore and attempted to grab her, she dashed by him, kicking the dropped knife under a desk, keeping her back to the wall and her front at an angle to his.

"Where the fuck did you learn your moves?" His voice held suppressed rage as he pulled another knife.

Lucky her, he was prepared better this time.

"Marines and SEAL Hell Week." She smiled at him, fluttering her lashes. His look of shocked disbelief was almost comical. Unfortunately, she didn't feel like laughing. "And in case you hadn't heard, I also attended Army Sniper School. Thus, all my confirmed kills last night. Any other questions?"

He snarled, swiping at her with the knife. She turned away from the thrust. He missed, but she didn't. With a backhanded move over his extended arm, she cut him from elbow to wrist. She danced away, using her leg in a vicious side kick to keep him back. That was the problem with knife-fighting, the attacker had to come in close enough to attack, thus opening himself up to being cut in return. This was why her Dad and brothers taught her defense movements against all kinds of potential attacks.

"Fucking bitch." Bannon switched the knife to his other hand as he held the bleeding arm against his torso. "Just wait until I have you on the ground under me. You're gonna beg me to kill you."

"Not gonna happen, asswipe." The ground or the begging. She taunted him with a grin as she moved in and out among the desks at the edge of the room. Her goal? The escape tunnel. Once inside she could seal him away from her and make her escape up the stairs into the Lodge's storage room off the kitchen. Only a few knew about the escape tunnel—and Bannon wouldn't be one of them. Not even the techs who worked in the Cave knew of it. Tweeter had shown her the day they arrived for a "just in case situation."

Bannon was hurt, but not enough to stop him. Even bleeding like a sacrificial pig and breathing harshly, he easily mirrored her moves, staying out of the range of her knife and legs. He swayed back and forth, thrusting his knife, playing with her, testing her, then retreating.

Keely was tiring, too many long days fighting Idaho weather and terrain with Tweeter and even longer restless nights without Ren to hold the nightmares at bay. She continued to parry his attacks, keeping him about three to four feet away from her at all times. She needed to reach the secret exit before she ran out of energy. He'd obviously learned something from their earlier encounters and had chosen to wear her down so he could eventually use his superior strength against her in one final, all-out attack. He wanted to hurt her; she wouldn't let him.

Finally she was close enough to the sliding panel to make it out; all she needed was a diversion to give her time to get through the door. It was then he decided to come at her. Using her free hand, she grabbed and threw a handy code book at him. He ducked and turned away. Taking advantage of his distraction, she slapped her hand on the hidden panel and squeezed through the opening while it was too small for a large man like Bannon to follow. Once through, she slapped the sensor to close the door and turned to defend the narrowing gap, slicing at his arm when he attempted to stop the door from closing. The panel shut firmly on his litany of swear words.

Breathing hard from exertion and adrenaline, she ran up the stairs and entered the storage area. "Scotty," she screamed as she ran into the kitchen. The old man came running along with Ren, Trey, Vanko, Price and a large man she didn't know.

"What the fuck happened?" Ren grabbed her arm, taking the bloody knife from her other hand and handing it to Scotty. He pulled her into his body for a bruising hug. "Are you hurt?" He held her away and scanned her, snarling when he noticed the blood spatter on her turtleneck sweater. "You're hurt." His tone was flat, lethal as he touched her everywhere looking for the source of the blood.

"No, no." She started to tremble from the aftermath of the fight. "It's Bannon's blood. He … he was in the Bat Cave … the tech … unconscious on the floor …

needs help. I, uh, I managed to get away." Gasping, she shrugged out of his deathlike grip and shoved him toward the hall and the elevator to the sub-basement. "Hurry … he'll get away. We need to find … Tweetie. He could be…"

"Sis?" She turned. Her brother had come in from outside. "What's going on?"

Keely ran to him and threw herself into his arms. She heard the other men leave. "Oh my God … you're safe. I went downstairs … Bannon was there. I was worried…"

"Did that bastard hurt you?" Her brother performed an identical scan to the one Ren had. "His blood, I hope?" He looked toward the elevator as it closed.

She nodded, panting from adrenaline overload. She'd have a heart attack if she kept stressing it like this.

"Tweeter, bring your sister over here," Scotty ordered. "She needs to sit. Ren and the others have the situation under control."

"Goddamnit, Keely. You're so white I can see the veins under your skin." He picked her up and carried her to a sunny window seat that was part of a small eat-in area. He sat and kept her on his lap as Scotty brought her a small glass of amber liquid.

"Drink this, little girl. Put some color back into

your face."

Keely sniffed it. Scotch. She took a sip and wrinkled her nose at the taste. Her brother pinched her thigh. "Drink it all down, fast."

She did and coughed. The potent liquor hit her already stressed system and made her lightheaded. "You trying to get me drunk?"

Her brother's denial was interrupted by a deep voice. "Give me my woman, Tweeter, and stop plying her with liquor." Ren had come into the room and moved to stand in front of them. Her brother held her out and Ren scooped her into his arms and turned toward the back entrance.

"Wait a minute," she said. "You got back upstairs too fast. What happened? Did you get Bannon?"

"Somehow he managed to get out while you found us. He's on the run with Jordan. Trey and the others are pursuing, using your nifty new security system. We put Vences under house arrest until we know how he figures into all this."

"Tweetie, we need to help coordinate the search from here…"

"No 'we' in this search, baby, just your brother and the others. You're going with me to my place and we're going to rest for awhile—or at least until my heart gets out of my throat."

"But Ren…" She looked into his eyes and shut up. She recognized the look as the man-had-reached-his limit look her dad would use when she and her brothers had pushed the boundaries he'd set for them. Ren wasn't going to budge on this issue. Fine. "Scotty is making pot roast for dinner and we are coming back here to eat it." She wouldn't be moved on that point. Normal life had to be established. She was tired of living from crisis to crisis.

Ren looked into her eyes. The corner of his mouth twitched, then stilled. "I can live with that—just as long you aren't out of my sight."

"Well, if I have to…" she trailed off as if she were making a huge concession, when she was quite happy to stay within his arms and sight for as long as he'd have her.

"You have to—or I might have a heart attack." He nuzzled her ear and whispered for her alone. "I almost lost you again, sweetheart. I just need to keep you close for awhile."

"Okay, big guy. It's fine—I'm fine." She breathed her assurances against his jaw line, then tasted it with her tongue. He shuddered, muttered a swear word, then kissed her. She sensed the lingering fear for her in the intensity of his taking. She gave herself up to the kiss, her arms around his neck, her fingers in his thick hair. She was safe—and desired. What more could a girl ask for?

Chapter Ten

"Crawl in bed, sweetheart." Ren gently shoved her toward his king-size platform bed. "I'll take a shower and join you in a bit."

Keely turned and placed her hands on his flannel shirt and began to unbutton it. "Want company in the shower?" Her voice was low, sultry—sexy—and it stoked his already over-active libido.

"Not this time." He kissed the tip of her nose. "I'll take a rain check, though." He brushed a silky curl out of her eye, his finger lingering to massage the creamy white skin above her eyebrow. "After last night and this morning, you have to be ready to drop in your tracks."

His shirt fully unbuttoned, she pulled it from his waistband, then began to attack the button-fly front of his jeans. Her hands were way too close to his hard-on. Shit, it wouldn't take much for him to shoot his wad. His cock was hard and throbbing for release just being in her company. His little brain knew what it wanted, and it wanted Keely. His big brain kept telling him how recently she'd been sexually traumatized in Boston, then attacked in Argentina by Trujo's mercs, and today by Bannon.

If those weren't enough reasons to leave her alone, she was a tiny, delicate pixie and he was a big, hard and far-too-experienced male. She needed a gradual introduction to his level of lovemaking; he'd go slow even if it killed him. They had their whole lives in front of them for hard, raunchy sex, but she'd only have one first time with him. He wanted it to be perfect.

So he'd take a shower and jack off. Then after a cuddling nap, he'd give her a couple of orgasms through heavy petting and some oral loving. Intercourse was not on the menu tonight and maybe not for awhile. *The truth was, he was afraid of hurting her. Yeah, he was a candy-assed coward.*

Keely's hands on his bared cock caused him to jerk out of his reverie. If she continued to stroke him he might not make it to the shower and self-relief. He'd take her on the hard wood floor—and wouldn't that be romantic?

"Sprite, don't start something we can't finish." He gently removed her hands from his pulsating dick and placing them by her side.

"Why can't we finish it?" Her green eyes glittered as she narrowed them. Her luscious, full mouth thinned.

Shit, she was pissed. "Keely … baby…" Fuck it, how could he explain his plans? He suspected whatever he said, she'd get more annoyed. Maybe she thought he was rejecting her. He wasn't. He couldn't. He wanted to make love to her more than anything he'd ever wanted in his whole life.

"Ren?" She sighed, a tone of resignation in her voice. "Did my Dad speak with you about me … about us?"

He nodded. She was too intuitive. His wary gaze never left her beautiful face, hoping he could interpret exactly what she was feeling, thinking. Problem was, she had a perfect poker face when she wanted. Probably learned it from her Dad. If Quinn ever did get around to teaching her poker, no one's money would be safe.

"Okay." She heaved a big sigh, her hands moving to his thermal undershirt. She drew random patterns on his chest with a finger. His nipples tightened, aching for her touch. "First, forget anything my Dad or brothers said." Her fiery green gaze captured his. "They aren't me—and they don't make my decisions. Understand?"

"Yeah, but…"

"No, yeah but…" She exhaled, a sound filled with frustration. "I think the real issue here is—I'm inexperienced and small and that scares you."

He opened his mouth to contradict her, but she covered his lips with her fingers, effectively silencing him. "Don't deny it, 'cause you'd be lying to both of us. I'm small and you're big, right?" She kept her fingers on his lips, so he nodded since she seemed to be waiting on some response from him. "However, I'll point out I'm slightly bigger than my mother."

He'd give her that point.

"You've seen my Dad. He's huge—big as you and maybe heavier."

Well, that was true.

"Mom survived the loss of her virginity at Dad's hands—and then birthed a set of twins, three other sons and then me. She told me sex with Dad was always good, even the first time. And I know for a fact that they still get it on today."

Whoa, way too much information.

He had to hand it to her—her logic was impeccable and irrefutable. But it still didn't make him feel any better. Her fingers dropped from his mouth. He choked back a laugh at the hot pink coloring Keely's cheeks. Imagining her parents having sex had thrown her for a loop, also.

Gamely, his little warrior continued. "I'm absolutely positive I'll survive losing my innocence to you. For chrissakes, Tweetie told me I don't even have a hymen anymore since that Argentinean doctor eliminated it with a too-big speculum. I'm pretty sure your penis will feel way better than a cold hunk of metal."

Shit. He hadn't needed the replay of the idiot doctor sticking a cold piece of metal in her sweet pussy. He still regretted not punching the stupid son of a bitch's lights out.

Keely ran agitated fingers through her curls. His fingers itched to stroke through the strands, calming them down. "And, really, Ren, at thirty-four years old, you should be experienced enough to make me feel really good. So… see … there's no problem." Her cheeks blazing red and her eyes downcast, she stroked his chest. "I want you—you want me. We should just do it."

Sounded really easy when she put it that way, but

it wasn't. He had mental images of her screaming in pain and bleeding all over the damn place. "Keely … baby…" He massaged her back, settling his hands at the top of her pert round butt. He could cup a cheek in each hand, she was so small. So tiny. So delicate. *Fuck.*

"Spit it out, Ren. What's the problem? I know you want me, 'cause this guy," she dropped one hand and stroked his randy cock, "has been as hard as a steel pike every time you're around me. So what's the issue other than you being afraid of hurting me?"

She was one hundred percent correct on each and every issue … but he wasn't ready to put his big cock in her tiny pussy. Call him a wuss, but that's the way things stood.

"Sweetheart, what am I going to do with you?"

"Make love to me?" Hope, and yeah, desire gleamed in her emerald gaze.

He shook his head as he pulled her hand away from his way-too-eager cock and placing it back on his chest where it was safe. "No intercourse for now. Let me court you."

Her lips thinned and then she opened her mouth— he assumed to offer more arguments. He forestalled any more of her excellent logic by nibbling at her cute lower lip as it jutted out. "Let me in, Keely." He nipped the pouty lip until she let him in. Angling his head, he moved a hand up to hold her head in place for his kiss. Then he ravaged her mouth, thrusting his tongue inside to claim every luscious millimeter. His other hand pulled her into his body so his hard-on could nestle against her firm lower belly. Once he had her where he wanted her, he changed his kiss. Now he fed. Sucking her tongue into his mouth, he slowly and thoroughly devoured her, absorbing her taste, imprinting his on her.

Her throaty moans shot his libido up another notch. He released her tongue to gently eat at her lips again, nibbling, licking, conquering and claiming. All the while, his hips thrust against her, his raging hard-on mindlessly seeking the hot, moist warmth lying under her clothing.

God, he had to slow this down or Keely would be under him before he could stop himself. His feisty sprite wasn't helping him any with his plan to court her slowly. She showed no fear of his sexual hunger— or his size. Instead she melted into him, accepting his body's urges. Her hands had crept under his undershirt and massaged his chest. When she found his nipples, he broke off the kiss. He groaned his pleasure into the curls on top of her head.

"Like that, huh?" She bit his pecs through the thin shirt, then began a journey of little stinging bites toward the nipples, which her fingers had so deftly brought to hard peaks. "I want you to do this to me."

Oh, hell, yeah. He wanted that too—later, after she had time to rest and he could jerk off first. He wouldn't budge on his decision—no intercourse until they had "dated" for awhile. She deserved, needed to be wooed.

But his little warrior had her own agenda, it seemed. She eyed him from between her lashes as she sucked on a nipple through his shirt, before gently teething then releasing it. She moved across his chest and did the same to its twin. His cock jerked and leaked pre-cum. His balls tightened, begging for release. "Jesus-fucking-Christ, you've got to stop." He gently disengaged her teeth from his chest.

"I want you to suck my breasts," she whispered against the nipple she'd gently abraded with her teeth, "and make me so hot I come. Then…" she sent him a look so filled with hunger he groaned, "I want you to do it all over again with your big hard cock in me."

"God, sweetheart, you have to slow down." He grunted when she teethed his nipple again. "Cannibalistic, are we?"

"No, I'm horny. You seem to have that effect on

me." She soothed the abused nipple by tonguing it through the shirt. His shirt was a soggy mess, and he really didn't give a flying good goddamn. His little warrior had a mean edge to her. He liked it. And God knew, she made him horny and had since she took out the bartender in Argentina.

Keely trailed kisses up his chest until she found the base of his throat. Between slow, licks of the skin lying over his rapidly beating pulse, she whispered, "I want your big cock in me … in my mouth … in my pussy. I want to be *experienced* by the time we eat pot roast. Got it?" She raked her teeth over his pulse. Her hand encircled his cock, stroking it firmly.

"Uh … careful, baby, the head is attached." God, he was weak; he needed to stop her before things got out of control.

She changed her caress, tighter and rougher on his shaft, then a light swipe over the head with her palm before moving more firmly down the shaft. "Better, big guy? And I do mean big. You are larger than all my brothers."

Ice cold water couldn't have deflated him any better. He let out a low snarl as he covered the hand on his cock, stilling its inciting movement. He tipped her chin up with his other hand. "You up close and personal with your brothers' cocks, Keely?" His voice was low and cold, his protective instincts rushing to the forefront of his brain. How the fuck had she seen her brothers' cocks? What had they done to her?

Her gaze watchful, she let go of his softening cock. "I lived in the same house. We were a family of eight with two bathrooms. Logistics alone say we'd cross paths to and from the shared bathroom." Her voice was soft, soothing as if she calmed a wild beast. She massaged his chest in a soothing circular motion. She read him well, knew his raging emotions were buried under an icy facade.

"And, face it," her lips quirked in a slight smile, "you guys are not all that shy about walking around in the nude with your dangly parts swaying in the breeze. So, yeah, I've seen my brothers' penises. But up close and personal?" She scrunched her nose. "Yuck. No." Standing on tiptoe, she kissed his chin. "Yours are the only dangly parts I want to be intimately acquainted with."

"Okay, that's good." He let out the breath he'd held. His body shuddered as he throttled back the anger that seemed to lie just under the surface where Keely's welfare was concerned. He'd known deep in his gut her brothers had never abused her, but sometimes appearances could be deceiving. The world was often a sick place.

"I know you want me, Keely." Cupping her face, he placed a light kiss on her lips, all rosy from his kisses. "And God knows, I want you so much I ache, but we're going to take this slow. No intercourse until we work our way through the vast array of foreplay first. You said it, I'm experienced and you're not. I don't want to hurt or scare you. I'm not a gentle lover, baby. I'm not sure I know how to be."

"I think you're worrying too much."

"And I think you've never had intercourse, so you don't really know how … rough it can get. Once I'm in your tight, sweet channel, I can't promise to go slow. I'd hurt you."

Keely's narrowed gaze examined his face. After several seconds of intense scrutiny, she sighed and leaned her forehead on his chest. "Go. Take your shower. Beat off if you need to."

He smiled at the disgruntled look he'd glimpsed on her face right before she buried it on his chest. It wasn't a sulky pout, but more the look of a kitten whose fur had been stroked the wrong way. He placed a kiss on the top of her curls. "Go on, baby. Take a nap. I'll join you once I take care of things in the bathroom."

She rubbed her cheek against him. "Okay, but I'm going on record that I wanted sex and you didn't. So don't blame me later for any consequences."

Thinking she alluded to the eternal hard-on he sported around her, he grinned. "Nope, not your problem. Just mine."

Ren took the fastest shower on record. The image of Keely's hand on his cock and the memory of her taste in his mouth—and of her lips and teeth on his nipples—had him so erect, it had taken only a few strokes of his cock for him to come—and come—and come. Unfortunately, the climax had only taken the edge off his arousal. He was already semi-erect just thinking about licking her pussy.

After drying off and with only a towel around his hips, he entered the bedroom. The bed was empty and Keely was nowhere in the room. "Keely," he called out as he entered the great room, figuring she might've gone to the kitchen for something to eat or drink. But she wasn't there either. He frowned. Had she gotten madder after he went into the bathroom? Had she left him? His stomach clenched at the thought, then he spied a note pad propped against a bowl of fruit on the kitchen island.

Picking up the pad, he read: *Ren—couldn't find*

what I needed here to take care of my itty-bitty vaginal opening and my needs, so I went over to the Lodge to hunt for the solution. Be back soon. Love, Keely.

Cursing, he threw on some clothes. All the while images of one of his men, face obscured, fucking her sweet body, taking what belonged to him, flashed in front of his eyes. Letting out a roar, he stopped dressing and hit the wall with his fist, making a dent in the dry wall. His chest heaving, he hit the wall again.

He shoved his bare feet into his boots and left his house without a coat. Running the fifty yards to the Lodge, he absently noted it was cold and blowing snow, but his rage kept him warm and moving. Who the fuck cared if he got pneumonia? Keely was letting some other man take care of her needs because he was too much of a fucking wimp to do it himself. God, he was a fucking idiot—and the man who accommodated her would be a dead one.

"Keely!" He shouted as soon as he entered the Lodge. Ten heads turned to look at him. A wide range of emotions crossed the faces of those in the room. He didn't care what they thought. He had to find Keely and stop her. Spying her brother, he stormed over and lifted him out of a chair. "Where is she?"

Tweeter shoved Ren's hands off him and stepped

back. "Jesus, Ren. She's in the kitchen. Why?"

"Kitchen?" She planned to lose her innocence in the kitchen? He looked toward the double doors. "Is she alone?"

"I think so. Why? Is she in danger?"

Ren shook his head. "Maybe. No. I don't know. What did she say when she came in?"

Scotty, standing behind the bar, smirked. "Asked me something about vegetables—and then asked if I had a tape measure."

"Vegetables? Tape measure?" A frown crossed Ren's face. "What the fuck does she need…? Ahh, shit!" She wouldn't—would she? Hell, yes, she would. Had she planned the note's wording to incite him? To have him come running over here like a crazy man? He'd bet on it. "Shit. Damn. Fuck." He shook his head. "I'm an idiot. I'm not gonna survive your sister." He shot Keely's brother an aggravated glare.

Tweeter punched him on the arm. "Welcome to the club. All of my brothers and I have felt the same way for years." He paused, a look of what could only be sympathy on his face. "Want my advice?"

"No … oh hell, yeah."

"Give her what she wants—or she'll just go behind your back and get it herself."

Ren shoved a shaky hand through his wet hair. "But what if what she wants will hurt her?"

Tweeter plopped back into his chair. "Just keep in mind, she's smart and won't do anything to cause those she loves unnecessary pain or worry. I can't ever recall her asking us to let her do something she hadn't examined from all angles."

"What the fuck kind of answer is that? She still could get hurt."

"Yeah, maybe. But she knows—and trusts—you'll protect her to the best of your ability. You'll learn, as we in her family have, to give in on those instances where the danger is mostly perceived and provide her back up and support when the danger is real." Tweeter smiled. "In my experience, I've found if the danger is real, Keely will be reasonable and actually step back and let me handle it. But she'll fight tooth and nail if I try to smother her just for the sake of establishing my male superiority. Understand?"

"Yeah. I'm an idiot." Ren rubbed a shaky hand over his jaw then took a deep breath, glancing toward the doors to the kitchen. "Keep everyone out of the kitchen for awhile. I need to clear up some things."

"Ren." A note in Tweeter's voice had him turning back.

"Yeah?"

"Don't underestimate her. She doesn't make idle statements. She may have already taken care of the, um, issue with the vegetable. Don't get mad or hurt her feelings, if she did. I'd hate to have to tromp you."

"I'll never hurt her. I love her."

"That's what I thought, but just wanted to clarify it for all present."

Ren groaned. His gaze swept the room and found smiling and interested faces. He was pretty damn sure they all knew what was going on with the vegetable scenario. God, Keely was gonna kill him. He could handle the ribbing this incident would create, but he didn't want her to be embarrassed. He glared at the room's inhabitants. "Not one word to her. If any of you tease her about this, I'll hand your asses to you."

"Well, hell, Ren, it's a little too late. The cat is out of that bag." Keely stood in the open doorway of the kitchen, her hands on her hips. She looked like Tinkerbell ready to take on Captain Hook and the pirates.

He walked toward her, slowly. His gaze scanned her for blood—or something. She looked fine. Tired, but fine. She also had her poker face on again.

"Keely … baby…" He stopped a couple of feet

from her. "I'm sorry. Come back to my place. We'll … discuss this misunderstanding." He held his arms open. "God, sweetheart, I love you. I didn't mean to make you unhappy."

She walked into his arms, her gaze never leaving his. "I know that, big guy. And please do take my brother's advice to heart. He hit it on the head—I won't do anything stupid to endanger myself. I love you too much to put you through that. But I do want some say in what happens to me. And you need to trust me on these kinds of, um, personal issues."

Ren couldn't speak. All he could think about was whether she'd shoved some obscene vegetable up her sweet little pussy and hurt herself because of him. God, he wanted to ask, but wouldn't—not until they had some privacy. Their sex life had had enough public exposure.

How long they stood staring into each other's eyes he wasn't sure. The room was so quiet you could hear a mouse scrabbling across the floor. Finally, a mischievous grin lit Keely's face, warning him she planned to say something outrageous. Before he could move to silence her, she said in a clear, carrying tone, "Scotty? I'm sorry to say that none of your vegetables measured up. I guess I'll have to settle for the real deal."

The room erupted with the sound of laughter.

Ren felt only relief and a resurgence of desire. The "real deal" stood at strict and stiff attention. Keely's heated gaze zeroed in on his cock's renewed interest, patently obvious in the sweat pants he'd hurriedly pulled on over his bare ass to chase after her.

She put her arms around his neck and jumped up and locked her legs around his waist. The motion rubbed her cleft against his hard-on. He almost groaned at the intense feeling.

Holding on with legs and one arm, she stroked a hand through the wet hair at the base of his neck. "You idiot. You left your house without a coat—and are still damp." In a lower voice only he could hear, "And no underwear either."

"Guess you'll have to warm me up—once we get back to our bedroom," he muttered against her ear. He kissed her temple. He secured her more firmly against him, holding her securely by the globes of her so-fine ass, and turned to head out of the Lodge.

"Scotty," Keely called out as they left the building.

"Yes, princess?" the old cook shouted back.

"Save me some frick-fracking pot roast!" she shouted as Ren trudged out the door and onto the porch.

He laughed. "Hungry, sweetheart?"

She caressed the nape of his neck. "Oh, yeah, but more for your meat than the beef kind."

"Me first, baby. I want to eat you up. I've had dreams about licking your pussy cream."

Her response was a low, breathy moan and a full-body shiver. Her legs tightened around his waist as she rubbed her sex against him. "I ache, Ren."

"God, baby, so do I." He reached his door, half-open from his hasty departure. He kicked it further open; he wasn't letting Keely out of his arms. No telling what she'd take it in her fool head to do. He snorted back a laugh. He still couldn't believe the little minx had intended to use a vegetable to stretch her vagina for him. "What kind of vegetable were you looking for?" He kicked the door shut and entered the alarm code one-handed as his other arm supported her total body weight.

"A cucumber was my top choice. But they're out of season." He choked back a laugh at the obvious disappointment in her voice. "So a zucchini squash was next on my list. But all of Scotty's zucchinis were too skinny." She leaned back and shot him a sexy smile. "Your penis is very, very thick. I can barely get my hand around it. I wanted the veggie to be as close to the real deal as possible. If I'd had my old vibrator I would have used it, but obviously Dad and the boys didn't pack it."

"You've used a vibrator?" He placed her on the bed and began to strip off his clothes. "No wonder your hymen was just a remnant. What was your vibrator like? Big? Skinny? Black? Soft? Hard?" He got hornier as his mind created images of Keely using a vibe.

"Well, um," she trailed off, blushing bright red. She was embarrassed now? After that little show in the Lodge? He choked back a laugh and lifted an eyebrow. She looked away and finally answered, "Um, my vibe was a six-inch, sort of skinny, purple glow-in-the-dark vibrator I named Vin."

He stopped stripping. He couldn't help it, he laughed. The image was just too funny.

She frowned. "Hey, don't laugh at old Vin. I had sexual urges just as any hormonal woman would. I was saving intercourse—for you, it seems—but there was no reason I couldn't get off, was there?"

"No, baby, you had every right to get off. God, if I'd known you'd already put Vin in your pussy, I might not have freaked so much over the thought of putting my nasty old cock in you." Still, he was bigger than the mechanical Vin, so some judicious stretching of her opening would be needed. A skinny glow-in-the-dark vibrator was a long way from his cock in full state of arousal. He climbed on the bed and lay on his side next to her, his hands going to the buttons on her flannel shirt. "You have way too many clothes on." He hadn't seen her fully naked since South America and he wanted to … very much.

Her gaze traveled down his nudity. Her eyes almost glowed. "God, you are so cut." She stroked a hand over the line of his hip, then traced his abs. His muscles clenched at her light touch. If possible, his cock hardened even more. "No fat—at all." She shrugged her flannel shirt off and then wiggled out of her jeans and long underwear with his help. "You aren't going to freak on me again, are you?"

"No. We're doing this." His way. Slow and steady. "My heart couldn't take another scare like I had when I found you'd gone." He kissed her shoulder then licked a path to her ear. "But if it hurts, I want you to let me know. We'll slow down … or something." He'd stop completely if she asked. It would kill him, but he'd do whatever she needed when she needed it.

"You won't hurt me. Plus it's like an injection, the quicker you stick it into the skin or vein, the better. So, when it's time to come into me, just do it. I'm betting I'll want you so much by then, I won't even notice any pain."

God, the little innocent was trying to reassure him when he was the one with all the experience. He shook his head, laughing silently at his stupid fears. Looking down to help her off with her undershirt, his gaze was captured by something extra on her perked nipples, showing clearly through the skintight white fabric.

"What are these?" He flicked a finger against one furled bud. "Nipple rings?" He whispered the words before he sucked the nipple through the shirt, teething the little ring. "When did you get them? You didn't have them in Argentina."

Before she could answer, he stripped her shirt over her head. He had to see the rings in her sexy little nips. His woman was full of surprises. "Fucking hot—gorgeous." He leaned over and took one little gold ring adorned with a green stone that matched her eyes between his teeth and tugged it gently. "Does that hurt?"

"No." She let out a sighing breath. "Feels good."

"When did you get these? On the way back from South America?"

He took the entire nipple in his mouth and tongued the little ring. Her hips moved in time with his tongue motion. He moved a hand to her golden-red, curl-covered mound and tested her wetness. She was soaked. As he played with her piercing, her pussy pulsed around his finger. He added a second finger and found she handled it easily. Old Vin must have done its job—she relaxed and accommodated insertion easily.

"Shit, baby, you are so fucking wet." She moaned as he added a third finger. Much tighter fit now. He expanded his fingers, stretching her slowly, letting her body adjust to the invasion. Her eyes, her body showed no signs of pain or discomfort. Good. He placed his thumb on her clit and firmly rubbed the tight little bundle of nerves while gently thrusting his fingers in and out of her opening, preparing her for his cock.

"Ren? Jesus, Ren, that is so-o-o good."

"Better than Vin the Vibrator?" He teased. He tugged her nipple ring with his teeth. Her eyes closed and she moaned. "Vin or me, baby?"

"Oh no comparison—you … Ren, if you keep doing that, I'll come." She blushed.

"That's the plan, sweetheart. To make you come and get you so hot that my cock will just slide right on in and find its new home." He trailed kisses up to her chin then sought her mouth, taking it with a tongue-tangling kiss.

Keely arched her back, shoving his fingers further

up her tight channel. "God, Ren, I'm coming." She grasped his head and screamed her pleasure into his mouth. To heighten and prolong her orgasm, he slid a fourth finger into her and pressed tightly on her clit, giving her the pressure she needed to ride her climax to the end.

After a minute or so of writhing, moaning and grinding against his hand, she relaxed into his body. Her vaginal walls continued to pulse around his fingers. He lightly stroked around her clit. She shuddered through a small after-climax, then released her grip on his head. She whispered against his lips, "God, that was … good … so good." She stroked his jaw with a limp hand.

He chuckled and peppered her face with tiny nibbling kisses. "That's just a taste, baby. Now, tell me about the nipple rings. How hard can I tug on them?"

Keely took another couple of deep breaths. Her eyes glowed with post-orgasmic satiation. "I've had them for about two years." She looked down at his tanned finger as he played with one ring. Her rosy bud tightened with each flick of his finger. "I took out the rings after … uh, Boston. They used them to … hurt me."

He cursed and started to pull his finger away. She covered his hand, pressing his finger on the ring. "It's fine now. You aren't hurting me. You never would." She turned her head, but not before he recognized remembered pain and fear in her eyes. He could kick his own ass for bringing up a bad memory.

"Fucking bastards," he muttered. He gently tongued the embellished ring. "Keely—may I … make new memories … to replace the bad ones?" He kissed and nuzzled her breast, inhaling her sweet, musky scent.

Her hand stroked his face, then tipped it up, away from his worship at her breast. She smiled. It was as if the sun had come out from behind a cloud. "You already did, big guy. But I wouldn't mind if you wanted to make some more."

Chapter Eleven

"It's my turn, I think." Keely placed a hand on his tanned chest and shoved him onto his back. Her goal was his penis, a work of art—thick, heavily veined, and pulsing with life. Her mouth watered. Before he could protest, her hand circled his shaft, holding it still for her tongue. She bathed his rigid length and purpled head with eager licks. She figured if she wasn't doing it right, he'd let her know.

"Keely … baby … ahh, fuck!" He threw his head back against the pillows and groaned. When she delicately cleaned off the pre-cum pooling on his glans, his head shot off the pillow, a heated look fixed on her.

"Stop, sweetheart. You really don't under…"

"I don't understand what? Am I doing it wrong? Don't you like it?" She leaned forward and took one long, very slow, very wet lick from the base of his penis to the tip. "I like this—a lot. Don't you?"

"I love it … but tonight was to be all about you."

"Then this is what *I* want to do. It makes me hot. I feel sexy … and like I am a participant and not just an object." She sent him a look from between her lashes. Okay, so she played him with the "object" comment. She liked him being in control, for the most part, but if she let him take the lead now, she'd never get to try out all the things she'd fantasized about because he'd jerk back on the reins, citing her inexperience. "You want me to be happy, right?"

"Uh, yeah."

He didn't look sure. She smiled. Poor baby, he expected a shy virgin and instead got her, a hungry one. "Then we're in agreement. Now lie back. Do you need another pillow? 'Cause I might be awhile here. There is so much to take in."

She firmed her grip on his shaft and cuddled his balls in her other hand. He couldn't go anywhere. She held him captive. Amazingly enough, it had been one of her brothers who'd told her, "Sis, if you control the balls, you control the man." Of course that had been in a demonstration of dirty street fighting techniques, but she figured the same general principle would apply here, except this time for pleasure and not defeat. Leaning over, she swirled her tongue over the head of Ren's cock. Once … twice … three times before she took him more fully into her mouth. His eyes closed and low shuddering groans shook his body as she sucked him in and out of her mouth using only the muscles of her cheeks and lips. Pausing, she held him in her mouth and hummed low in the back of her throat. The vibrations caused him to thrust his hips. His balls tightened in her other hand, readying to deliver semen to his shaft.

He grasped her head, trying to move her away. "Baby, you might want to let go. I'm gonna cum."

Well, that was the point. She couldn't allow him to dictate where he'd come and when. This was her time to please him—and dammit, he needed to let her. She firmly gripped the base of his cock, pulling upward and away from his balls which she held gently but securely in her other hand, stifling his need to come. He cursed, his fingers gripping her head tightly in reflex. She let his penis slide out of her mouth. "Move your hands."

"Jesus-fucking-Christ, Keely—where did you learn

that trick?"

"HBO Late Night. Some interesting shows on late at night." She breathed across the purpled head. "I'm not sucking this anymore until you move your hands. You can take control another time. I'm in charge this time." She slid her hand up and down his throbbing shaft.

He swore under his breath. She laughed silently at his dire promises of payback. She looked forward to it. "What did you say? I didn't quite catch it." She licked his glans once. His body shuddered and his penis jerked in her hand.

"Nothing."

"Good. Now drop them."

He pulled his hands away slowly, his fingers combing through her curls. She shivered at the gentle caress. He was hotter than hell and needed to come, but he still was gentle with her.

"Thank you." She kissed his lower abs just above his groin where the muscles quivered from the tension in his body. She placed a nibble-kiss to the top of his penis, then took him back into her mouth. His finger stroked her cheek as she suckled him. Silly man, he thought he could sneak his hand back in to take control. Stroking her face was allowed, for now. Tickling his shaft with her tongue as she moved up and down on his penis, she hummed once more. As she hummed louder, his hips arched to meet her mouth.

"Keely—you're heading into dangerous territory here." He grunted out the words, breathing heavily as if he'd just run a marathon.

Oh, yeah, she was—he just didn't know exactly what territory she sought.

She stopped her head motion with as much of his cock in her mouth as she could hold, then she suckled him using just her facial and mouth muscles, placing occasional licks under his cock head with her tongue. Again she sensed his impending climax in the tightening of his balls.

"Shit, baby. Fuck … fuck. Oh fucking hell." His back arched off the bed. His hand fell away from its light grasp of her face. He clutched the sheets.

Letting up, she kept the head of his cock in her mouth, then again halted his ejaculation by clamping down on the base of his penis.

Alternately cursing and praising her, his body collapsed onto the bed. He grabbed her shoulders and pulled her on top of him. *Finally. This had been her goal all along.* She smiled just as he pulled her lips to his and aggressively thrust his tongue into her mouth. His hips rubbed her lower body, seeking relief. His kiss was ravenous. Little nips to her lips, then soothing licks, then all thrusting tongue. Under her, his body was tense. His penis lay throbbing between them, hard and hot, and ready to blow.

As Ren held her to him with his lips and gentle but firm hands at her waist, she settled more fully on him, wiggling to get into the perfect position. His low groans into her mouth told her he liked the motion on top of him. *He wasn't getting away with mere frottage. She wanted all that lovely cock in her—and she'd get it whether he liked it or not.* She smiled as she kissed him deeply.

Before Ren could realize what she planned, she had the broad head of his penis positioned at her vaginal opening. Arching her back, she used one hand to nudge him inside, then she moved until his cock was lodged inside by at least two inches. His earlier loosening of her opening had done the trick. She held still, allowing her body to adjust to his breadth. It was a tight, pulsing fit—and she found she liked him inside her. It was like being mounted on a full-blooded stallion. All that power under her control was exciting.

Ren broke off the kiss. His hands held her still and tightly against him. "Fuck, baby. You okay?"

"You fit me perfectly. All that angst was for nothing." She smiled as she did a slight hip roll, taking another inch inside her. He threw his head back against the pillow, a low groan coming from the back of his throat. "Now, we're going to dance, you and me, and you're going to come inside me."

"I am?" His voice was low, husky, full of tension and lust.

"You are." She breathed the words against his lips before thrusting her tongue into his mouth. Her hips moved up and then back, seating him more fully inside her. She caressed one of his dusky nipples. His "fuck, baby" was swallowed as she kissed him. Sitting back, she braced her hands on his chest, kneading him like a cat. "Move me how it makes you feel good."

His slitted gaze captured hers, his eyes slate blue with passion. He whispered, "Hold on, baby. This might get rough. You worked me up good."

She just smiled and gripped his shoulders as he took control of her hip movements. He began slowly, moving her up and down, adding a clit-grinding rotation every third thrust.

"God, Ren that feels … amazing." She arched her back and picked up the rhythm he'd set. His hands relaxed now, merely guiding her.

"That's it, baby. God, sweetheart, you are so fucking beautiful." He glided his hands from her hips to her back, pulling her toward him. He lifted his head and captured one of her nipple rings with his teeth, gently tugging then sucking the nipple. His hips rose to meet her downward thrusts as she increased the pace.

She knew his climax was near when he released her nipple and threw his head back, his eyes closed, his mouth open, his breathing harsh and raspy mixed with low-throated groans. He slid his hands back to her hips, gripping them tightly. She let him take total control of his pleasure, because his pleasure was hers. The pace of hip meeting hip doubled. Ren's face set in the rictus of intense passion as the sounds coming from him became less human and more animalistic.

Then, "Fuck, baby … I'm coming."

She leaned over and kissed him. His groans filled her mouth as his seed spurt warmly inside her. It was one of the most wonderful, sexy feelings in the world, holding the man she loved in her arms as he gave her all that he was, trusting her to hold and keep him safe at his most vulnerable time.

As his body went totally lax under her, still connected, she snuggled her head on his damp chest, inhaling his citrus-musk scent. His harsh breathing caused her body to rise and fall on his chest; it was sort of like riding waves. She could stay like this forever.

Ren nuzzled the top of her head. He stroked her back and hips in soothing massage. "God that was … fucking wonderful."

She peeked at him and found his molten gaze on her. "I thought you might like it."

"Well, you'll fucking love this—and so will I." He shot her a wicked grin. Before she could ask what he meant, he rolled her over and had her pinned to the bed with his body. His lips took a leisurely path from her mouth, down her throat, to each nipple and finally followed a line down her torso to her soaking wet mound.

"Ren?" Her voice squeaked. "You can't mean to…"

One large hand rubbed her lower stomach in a gentle massage, holding her in place. "Oh, hell yeah, I mean to." He nuzzled the skin just above her curls. A slight frown creased his forehead. He looked up at her, his eyes concerned. "We didn't use anything, baby."

"I'm fine. So are you." She shot him a wicked grin. "I, uh, accessed your medical file."

"I wasn't worried about diseases, baby."

"Oh, that. I'm on the pill."

He smiled broadly, a sexy twinkle in his eyes.

"Good." He smacked his lips. "That way I can always eat you out after I come inside you."

"Jeez-Louise, Ren, do men really…"

"*Your* man does." He held her down with the hand on her tummy. "Now, just lie back and enjoy, sweetheart. 'Cause I'm going to eat you up."

Keely held her breath as the first swipe of his tongue made a lazy figure eight on her labia, almost sending her into orbit. Her clit was hyper-sensitive from his earlier ministrations and the grinding movement as she rode him. She shivered and her buttocks clenched. "Ren? I don't think this is a good idea. It's too … too…"

"Shh, baby, just let me use a little firmer pressure." He licked her more firmly, managing to miss her over-sensitized clit. She relaxed into the bed. "Better?" He nuzzled her inner thigh, then took a slow lick and a nip where her thigh met the outer mons.

"Yeah … uh, yeah." Her hips lifted to meet his tongue.

"Good." He resumed the firm tongue-stroking of her labia with an occasional dip into her vaginal opening. "Sweet and spicy." He took another dipping lick. "Want a taste?"

"Um…" She twisted and arched as a surge of pleasure had her gasping.

"No pressure, sweetheart. We can leave that for another time." He resumed licking her labia. His gentle tonguing reminded her—when she could actually process the sensations—of a cat grooming a kitten. He was very thorough.

She felt the impending orgasm, just out of reach. "Ren, I need … more." More what, she couldn't voice it, wasn't sure what *it* even was.

He murmured something into her mons and added her clit to his leisurely oral sensual torture.

She moaned, arching her back. The pressure was stronger now. This climb to orgasm was nothing like the other one he'd given her with his fingers. This one was work. She reached and reached for it, but it wouldn't come.

"Ren … it's there, but I can't…" She was frustrated, panicky.

"Shh, baby, just breathe. Trust me. I'll get you there."

And she did trust him, more than anyone she'd ever met. Letting out a sigh, she relaxed into the sensations he gave her.

He inserted a finger and stroked a spongy place inside her. Simultaneously, his teeth raked gently over her clit. "Oh my God!" Her back arched off the bed, her hips seeking the release that waited just out of her reach.

Ren lifted his head, his hand massaging her cramping stomach muscles. "Okay, baby?"

"Yes. More pressure. I need more…"

Continuing to stroke the highly sensitive spot inside her, he licked her labia and clit faster and with greater pressure. It was when his thumb or finger or whatever pressed hard on her clit that she screamed and climaxed. Her lover continued his firm tongue action and added more fingers to the one stroking the amazing spot, working her orgasm, giving her more pleasure than she'd ever known.

"Oh God that is so good … so good." She tossed her head from side-to-side and gripped Ren's hair to hold him tightly against her clit. "Ren, baby, that is soooo fricking good."

His amused snort against her sex threw her into another mini-peak. After what seemed like forever, she shuddered through one more mini-after-climax and relaxed into the mattress like a pile of over-cooked linguini.

"Keely? Sweetheart? You okay?" Ren kissed his way back up her body. He lay next to her and pulled her into his arms, surrounding her with his heat and strength.

She inhaled and sighed. She loved his smell—no, their smell. "It was perfect. Abso-frick-fracking-lutely perfect." She placed a kiss on his chest, right over his heart. "I love you. And I'm not moving for the next day or so. And you have to stay here and keep me company."

Ren chuckled. "What about the pot roast?"

She peered up at his relaxed and wholly contented gaze. "Do you think they'll deliver?"

She smiled as her lover threw his head back and laughed. This had to be the most perfect day of her life. She closed her eyes and snuggled into him and barely felt him covering them with the comforter they had kicked to the floor.

CHAPTER TWELVE

Two weeks later

"Tweetie?" Keely sat on the edge of her brother's workstation in the Bat Cave.

"Yeah?" He leaned back in his chair, rubbing a hand over tired-looking eyes.

He looked as exhausted as she felt, and she was so tired she'd been off her food for the last several days—and that only happened when she was burning the candle at both ends. They'd been working non-stop, tracing the identities of the mercs who'd died while attacking Sanctuary two weeks ago back to who'd paid them.

"I need to visit a town bigger than Grangeville or

Elk City."

"Why?" A frown creased his forehead. "Ren told us to stay on Sanctuary until we got a handle on exactly who tried to kill us."

"Duh, Trujo sent the two men who found me on the cliff and the larger group was sent by the DoD baddie. I thought we'd decided that."

"*We* had. Ren is still not convinced—and until he is, he isn't playing loose with your safety. He would also point out that we still have no fucking clue as to the identity of the DoD traitor. He wants that guy bad. Fuck, so do I—and so does the NSA and several other alphabet-soup agencies, not to mention the whole Walsh clan."

"I'm working on it." There was a distinctive snap in her voice. She waved a hand in the air. "Sorry, I'm not mad at you or Ren. God, I miss him. I wish we could've gone with him, to cover his ass."

Once she'd discovered information on the two men who'd attacked her on the cliff and that info tracked to a holding company in Florida owned under one of Trujo's aliases, Ren took a team and went to Miami to verify the connection. He was worried Trujo was now in the United States after they'd lost him in South America almost a month ago.

"He doesn't want Trujo on the same continent with you. That bastard wants you for spoiling his death trap and to fuck with Ren's mind. Ren would go apeshit if something happened to you." And a careless, grief-maddened Ren would be easier to kill.

"I know." Keely rotated her tired shoulders and neck then swept her unruly hair behind her ears. "Ren loves me, but I'm not a hot-house flower needing a lot of special care. I could help track Trujo's hiding place."

"You can do that here, on the computer. Plus, he has all the help he needs. Vanko, Price and Trey are with him. I'd bet on that team any day."

"Yeah, they're good. I just hate waiting." She looked around the room. "I need to get out of here. I feel like a mole, beginning to look like one, too."

He eyed her. "You look fine. Although now that you mention it, you are kind of pale."

"It's the clothing. It's all sweat-suit gray and doesn't fit. I need clothes, brother dear. I need a hair trim and a facial—and I need to see a doctor."

"Doctor!" He sat up. "What's wrong, Imp?" He looked over her again. "You sick?"

"No. I need to get a new prescription for birth control pills." She blushed. Until Ren had left two days ago to chase after Trujo, he'd made love to her several times a day. Once his fear of hurting her had passed, the man was a certified sex maniac—and she loved it. She'd been truthful that first time about being on the pill; she'd just neglected to mention that the last of her prescription had run out a week before they'd made love for the first time. Then she'd had her period and figured she was safe for a bit because of timing and the residual effect of having been on birth control. She needed a new round of pills for when Ren returned. Her man would want to pick up where he'd left off. And so would she. She really liked how he made love to her, all fiery heat and gentle touches.

"Oh, well, um…" He avoided her eyes, his face flushed. Her big brother was embarrassed. How sweet. "How about going to Coeur d'Alene? It's a bit closer than Boise. We could spend the night and you could do the girly things at the hotel spa. They have a small mall and a lot of shops for the tourists. Plus, Lacey goes to a doctor there for her female stuff."

"Maybe Quinn and Lacey would want to go with us?" She liked Lacey, Quinn's wife. She was a nurse and had a warm personality and a great sense of humor. She'd be fun to shop with.

"Ren left Quinn in charge, but I bet Lacey would like to go. While you two do the girly thing, I can get in some skiing."

Keely rounded the desk and kissed her brother on the cheek. "Thanks, Tweetie. I just need to get away. I love this place, but I'm going stir crazy."

"Yeah, well, we need to do this and get back before Ren finds out, or you'll see him go crazy and in a bad way."

"I'll just tell him it was this or no sex." She laughed at the darker red staining her brother's cheeks.

"Sis, I may know you're having, um, intimate relations with Ren, but please don't keep reminding me of it." He shook his head. "I still see you in footed, pink bunny pajamas, playing GI Joe and Barbie going to war."

She leaned over and kissed him again. "And you sat right down on that floor and played with me even when all the other brothers picked on you. I love you, Stuart Allen Walsh. You are the best brother in the whole universe."

"Love you, too, sis." He stroked a hand over her back. "Now go and ask Lacey. We can leave tonight. I'll get us a suite. It's too early for tourist season, so there should be rooms."

Thirty-six hours later

"SIS? WHERE'S LACEY? WE NEED to hit the road and get back before the storm hits."

Distracted, Keely ignored her brother's question as she watched him load the last of the packages into the back of the Hummer they'd driven to Coeur d'Alene. His skis were already strapped on top. She wondered if she'd ever wear half the clothes she'd just bought. In four months she'd need a maternity wardrobe.

She'd been shocked when the doctor informed her she was pregnant. It was routine to make sure a new patient wasn't pregnant before putting her on birth control pills. The pregnancy test showed positive. The doctor drew blood to be sure, but he wasn't betting against the results. Neither was she. Her nausea and lack of her usual hearty appetite had been early signs of her pregnancy. This morning she had full-blown morning sickness for the first time. She placed a hand over stomach where her and Ren's baby was even now growing. The doctor had given her a prescription for maternity vitamins, a book on what to expect from pregnancy, and an appointment for three months when she'd have an ultrasound.

"Yo, earth to Imp." Tweetie stood toe-to-toe, his

face so close she could count the pores on his nose. "What's wrong? You've been weird since last evening after your girls'-day-out."

Keely answered his earlier question, not sure she wanted to blurt out she was pregnant to her brother. Lacey knew, since she'd gone to the doctor's office with her, but Quinn's wife had promised not to say anything to anyone. God, she wanted her mama. She needed Ren, but she was scared about how he'd react.

"Lacey's coming. She went to get us all something to eat and drink for lunch on the road, so we wouldn't have to stop." She glanced at the small diner where her friend had disappeared. "She should be back any time."

"That's one answer. Now what's wrong with you? You look paler than ever, and were harder than normal to get out of bed this morning. I don't think shopping usually takes all that much out of you. You have more energy than that stupid fucking pink-battery bunny."

"I'm pregnant." *Well, hell.* She turned away from the shocked expression in her brother's eyes to watch Lacey cross the narrow street to the Hummer. She had several sacks and a drink carrier.

"You're what?" Tweeter grabbed her arm and turned her toward him.

"You heard me. Here's Lacey. She knows since

she was with me at the doctor's. I'd like to keep it just among us until I can get the nerve to tell Ren." She blinked away the tears gathering in her eyes. "Shit, he's going to be so mad."

Tweeter pulled her into his arms and rubbed her back. "Keely, he'll be ... well, I don't know what he'll be, but don't worry about it. You've got me—and the parents and the brothers, we'll help."

"I know." She blubbered into his ski jacket. "But he'll think I did it on purpose, and I didn't. How the heck did I know I was so frick-fracking fertile that a few missed days of pills and I'd get pregnant?"

"Shh, sis. I know you didn't plan this. Ren won't think it, either. And, if for some reason, he's mean about it, I'll kick his ass for you."

She snorted as she laughed. "I can kick his ass myself. I love you, Tweetie. Thanks. I'm just riding some hormonal roller coaster here. I'm already getting morning sickness. The doctor said he'd never seen the like."

"Then he hasn't met Mom. Remember what Dad said about her pregnancies? She was sick from day one and cried at the drop of a hat." Tweeter helped her into the front passenger seat. "Hey, Lacey, hand me those and hop in the back seat."

"Sure. She told you, huh?" Lacey glanced at her tear-stained face before handing Tweeter the food, which he placed on the console. He placed the drink carrier in Keely's lap then fastened her seat belt. "I'm glad she did. Ren will kick all our asses if anything happens to her. He threatened Quinn on that very topic and that was before the pregnancy."

Lacey got into the back seat and then leaned around Keely's seat. "I got you a turkey sandwich—mild and good for sensitive tummies—your Pepsi and some milk. You need to start to eat healthier for the baby. But I figured you needed the Pepsi for an emotional boost. Did you take your vitamin?"

"Yes." She looked at her brother as he settled into the driver's seat. "Tweetie, don't say anything to Ren or the guys, I need to tell him. It's bad enough I told you before him."

Before Tweeter could answer, Lacey patted her shoulder. "No, you needed to tell Tweeter. Ren would never get upset about that. He'd be more upset if you kept it a secret. Early pregnancy is full of potential problems, and we need to be ready to handle them. Thank God, we have a helicopter. Next trip to the doc we'll fly, it'll be better than the long drive. Now eat some of your food and then take a nap. Tweeter and I can handle the driving."

"Yeah, sis. You did your share on the way up. You do look whipped."

"I am. I didn't sleep much and then I was sick this morning." Really sick and that was with nothing in her stomach. She hoped she got over this fast, but after Tweeter's mention of the stories her Dad had shared about her Mom's experiences, she wasn't going to hold her breath. A call to her mama was definitely on her to-do list.

She found the packet marked turkey, removed half of the sandwich, and took a small bite, chewing it thoroughly. It landed okay, so she took another bite. With each bite, she felt better. By the time they hit the outskirts of Coeur d'Alene, she'd eaten half the sandwich and drunk the carton of milk.

Her brother shot her a smiling glance. "That's my girl. Now recline the seat and take a nap. I turned on the seat warmer so you won't get chilled. We'll be home before you know it."

"Ren and the others are home," Lacey said from the back seat. "Quinn just texted me. Ren is stomping around like a dyspeptic bull because we're gone. Quinn said he chilled him out. Didn't say how, but knowing my hubby he probably told Ren he was acting like an ass."

Keely choked on a sip of Pepsi. Coughing, she gasped. "Quinn really wouldn't say that, would he?"

"Oh hell yeah." Lacey chuckled. "Quinn has always gotten away with more than the other men, except maybe for Trey. Ren needs someonc to stand up to him and prove he isn't a god. Remember that, Keely. He'll respect you more—and won't take advantage of you. Don't let him make you feel guilty because you needed clothes and girl-time—and with the news from the doctor, he can't blame you for needing to seek medical attention."

"Yeah, sis, he'll blame me. He'll say I should've flown the doc to Sanctuary," Tweeter said around a mouthful of his sandwich.

"I won't let him pick on you, Tweetie," Keely said. "He can yell at me and then I'll probably cry and…"

Lacey laughed. "…and he'll beg your forgiveness on hands and knees, 'cause I can't see Ren handling your tears at all well. The more macho they are, the harder they fall, sweetie. Look at my Quinn. My two pregnancies had him apoplectic for nine months and he was flat on his back during my labor with empathy pains."

"I just hope Ren wants the baby." Keely shoved her

trash in the empty sack. "I do, but he's used to being alone and…"

"I told you the family would support you, sis." Tweeter reached over to stroke tears off her cheek. "Stop crying, Imp. You're killing me."

"Ren will be fine with it." Lacey sounded confident. "The days before he left to go after Trujo he was walking on air. He loves you, sweetie. Don't doubt that. And it's time for him to become a father. Remember, he has a few years on you. He sowed all his wild oats. He's due to settle down and start a family—with you."

As Lacey continued stating her opinions on what Ren might or might not do, Keely closed her eyes. She hoped Lacey was correct, but she was so emotional at the moment she couldn't think about any of this logically. She'd just have to wait and see what Ren said. Maybe she'd let him release some sexual tension first and then in the afterglow while they cuddled she could just slip it in.

As she nodded off to sleep, Tweeter said, "Shh, Lacey, she's asleep."

———

KEELY STARTLED AWAKE TO TWEETER'S cursing, Lacey's stifled screams and being tossed from side-to-side within her seat belt. She reached for the sissy bar and managed to croak out, "What's going on? Did we blow a tire?" She looked at her brother and was shocked to see a fierce, deadly look on his face.

"Someone is trying to run us off the road." Tweeter's voice was grim, and for good reason, there were thousand-foot drops off the roads in this area of the Bitterroots.

She turned in her seat and watched another large off-road vehicle approaching them from the rear at high speed. "He's coming fast, Tweetie."

"I see the fucker. Hold on." Tweeter took evasive maneuvers in an attempt to keep the attacker from getting a direct hit on them.

Keely felt under the seat and pulled out a semi-automatic machine pistol. She checked the magazine and found it fully loaded with armor-piercing rounds. *Ya-hoo.* Flicking off the safety, she lowered her window. "Where should I aim? Think the vehicle's armor-plated like ours?"

"No, it's a definitely maneuvering more like a street vehicle rather a military-equipped like this one. Go for the engine block, sis."

"Get me a shot, Tweetie. Stay down, Lacey. Once I start shooting, they'll shoot back and they might also have armor-piercing bullets. The seats will help stop those." A white-faced Lacey bent over in the back seat, lowering her profile.

"Fuck, sis, with the way you shoot, they'll be dying and frying and too busy to shoot back."

"Let's hope." Keely released her seat belt, braced herself against the wild movement of the Hummer as Tweeter continued to weave the vehicle, then turned in her seat. With her back on the dashboard and her feet planted against her seat back, she lowered the window to a cold blast of air. Her shot selection was limited; it all depended on Tweeter getting the assholes to come up on the passenger side and not the driver's. Plus, she'd have to take her shot right before the bastards attempted to ram them.

Keely waited as Tweeter used every defensive driving trick in the book. The pursuing vehicle attempted to counteract Tweeter's tactics, but failed. The pursued usually had the advantage in that they knew where they were going, the pursuer had to guess. It didn't take long for her to realize with the way the road curved, she had a better chance of shooting the bad guy's engine from the driver's side of the Hummer. She hit the window button and rolled her window up.

"Sis?" Tweeter kept his eyes on the road and the

mirrors. "What's up?"

"Driver's side will get me a kill shot. So once I'm set in the back seat, go right, left, right on my mark. I'm gonna take them out on one of the upcoming curves." She climbed into the back seat after tossing the gun over first, then assumed the same braced position on the rear driver side and lowered the window. She kept an eye on the curve of the road and when Tweeter had the best chance to hug the mountainside of the curve, she shouted, "Go for it."

As Lacey prayed next to her, Tweeter performed the series of swerves. The pursuers followed Tweeter's evasive actions, but there was enough of a lag time that she could see an opportunity for a shot. The other driver's slower reaction time and less-than-adequate equipment would kill him. "One more time, but sharper, Tweetie."

"Can you get them?"

"Yeah. Give me a few more patterns." The pursuing driver lost control in his attempt to follow them and struggled to regain it. The way the guy drove bothered her. Why hadn't he tried to ram them? He had several opportunities before Tweeter had turned up his level of evasion. That was odd. "Wonder who they're herding us to?" she muttered under her breath.

And bottom-line, who in the heck cared? The pursuit vehicle was the enemy and she had a "baby on board" to protect. She leaned out the window, bracing her body the best she could. She ignored all distractions and concentrated on her shot.

The less-stable street vehicle weaved crazily in the cold and wet conditions, not built for the kind of tactical maneuvering the driver was forcing upon it. In mere seconds, she imagined the shot in her head, plotting trajectories and planning where to hit the engine to do the most damage. If she could she would also take out the driver. Engine first though. Had to stop them.

"Last chance, sis, then we lose the S-curves." Her brother's voice was cool, controlled, his confidence in her made her smile. Any other man would have been screaming at her to shoot.

"Gotcha—go, go!"

Tweeter swerved right toward the edge of the road, to the point they were on the shoulder and shooting up gravel, road salt, ice and snow, then he jerked it to the left, then just as quickly back to the right. Keely took her shot as the pursuer attempted to follow to the right and failed. Her first blast of shots took out the engine. Smoke and steam billowed, but the driver didn't slow.

"Watch for it!" Her brother, accomplished driver and all around strategist, used his rear view mirror and positioned the Hummer to give her another shot.

The damaged vehicle still pursued, but not as fast as before. She switched to single shot and sighted down the barrel. For a split-second the steam coming out of the engine died down and she saw the raging gaze of the driver. With Tweeter holding the Hummer steady, she placed her shot in the middle of the driver's forehead. The pursuit vehicle—now without a driver to steer through the curve—crashed through the guard rail and disappeared over the side of the mountain. No one could survive the thousand-foot drop.

Keely let out the breath she'd held after that last shot and slumped on the floor behind the driver's seat. "Shut the windows, Tweetie. It's freezing in here." She could have done it herself, but her hand shook too much. "I think that has to go down as my best shots ever."

Lacey helped her into the seat behind the driver and fastened the seat belt. "God, that was amazing. I mean, I knew you were a good shot, all the guys said so, but from a swerving car at high speed. Jesus." The older woman took the gun Keely still cradled against her chest and placed it on the floor, then sat back in her own seat. "I texted an SOS to Sanctuary while I was bent over. Quinn texted back that the helicopter is coming to get us."

Tweeter pulled into a lay-about. He kept the engine running and turned to look at Keely. "Damn good shooting." He frowned and reached over the seat to stroke a finger down her cold, wet cheek. "You okay?"

Keely patted his hand with her trembling one. Adrenaline overload had her shaking like an aspen in a high wind. "Yeah. Fine. Let's avoid doing that again for awhile. My stomach can't take all that motion." She coughed and swallowed, fighting the nausea with sheer willpower. She reached through the split between the front seats for her Pepsi, still safely snuggled in the cup holder in the console and took a few sips. "God, I needed that." Picking up the gun Lacey had taken from her, she automatically checked the weapon, ejecting the partially filled magazine. She took the full one Tweeter handed her and shoved it home, then set the safety and put the gun next to her feet in case she needed it again. "Got any extra ammo? So I can reload that magazine?"

"Keely, you look green." Tweeter crawled over the console and got into the back seat with the two women. "Maybe you'd better lie down."

She shook her head. "Think, big bro. What were

those assholes really doing?"

Tweeter nodded. "I know what you're thinking. I agree. We need to get off this road."

Lacey looked from one to the other. "What? Weren't they going to drive us over the edge?"

"No, they could have done that at any time. They were herding us. Someone is waiting on us further up the road. Get back in the driver's seat, Tweetie—we need to go back the way we came. Lacey, get ready to give the chopper coordinates for the pick up." She looked out into the winter wonderland covering the rough terrain. It was snowing harder now, the wind picking up. Her stomach clenched at the worsening conditions. God, any later and she wouldn't have been able to make the shot. To add to her gut's discomfort, her neck itched like someone was watching them. *Well, hell.* "My gut and itchy neck say we need to get out of here now, Tweetie."

"Shit. Fuck. Damn. I never bet against your itchy neck." He pulled up the area map on the GPS. "We can take a small forest access road and meet the chopper at…" He read the coordinates off to Lacey who typed them into her phone connected to Sanctuary's communication systems by a satellite relay that only the NSA knew about. Keely was really glad she worked out the deal with the NSA: She'd find the DoD turncoat and SSI got to piggyback on the NSA satellites for communications in the middle-of-nowhere-Idaho. The fact that they also optioned her for other NSA work was just fine. She did most of her work on the computer and it would be something to do while she stayed at home and raised Ren's child.

"They're in the air and on their way." The tension in the older woman's voice was tighter than the skin on a movie star's butt.

"We're out of here." Tweeter put the car in gear and backtracked a mile or so to the ranger access road leading to a fire tower and the only flat land that could accommodate the jet helicopter. The Hummer handled the off-road drive easily.

"What will we do with the Hummer?" Lacey said.

"We won't all be going on the helo." Keely closed her eyes against the terrain moving up and down with the vehicle's rough motion. She was queasy and knew it was a combination of the pregnancy and the adrenaline overload. "You and I will be on the chopper, and Tweetie and some of the guys will go after whoever is waiting to ambush us between here and Sanctuary." She sighed. "If I weren't feeling so sick to my stomach and just frick-fracking tired, I'd argue with Ren about it."

"But you won't, Imp."

"No. I'm carrying his child, and the doctor warned me this pregnancy could have issues since I did get pregnant so quickly after going off the pill."

"You didn't fucking tell me that." Tweeter glared at her in the rearview mirror.

"I would've. But we had to get home, and I wasn't planning on the fun and games." She glared back. "You know what this means, don't you?"

"That Ren will hear about all this before he puts you on the helo?"

"No, but that will probably happen."

"No probably about it. If you don't tell him everything, I will. He needs to know."

She stuck her tongue out at him. He laughed. "And what I was getting at before you took a detour is that someone is still spying on us at Sanctuary." She looked out the window at the trees lining the narrow track leading to the fire tower. "Or someone is watching our comings and goings then following us. They could've followed us to Coeur d'Alene, then set this up for the return trip."

"Maybe we should've taken the helo?" Lacey suggested.

"Hell, they'd have just sabotaged the helicopter in Coeur d'Alene to keep us on the ground." Tweeter pulled into a parking area for the tower. There was just enough of a clearing to land the jet helicopter. "Lacey, tell them we're here."

Lacey, her lips thinned to the point of disappearing, entered the message. "They're five minutes out." She looked from Keely to Tweeter and back. "What do the bad guys want? To kill us? Or to capture Keely?"

Tweeter looked over the seat. "Depends on who was chasing us. In this instance, it looked like they wanted Keely; that was a herding maneuver. If we hadn't taken them out, we'd have found a roadblock with firepower down the road."

"So who's behind this latest attempt?" Lacey asked, her brow furrowing. "The traitor or Trujo?"

"I don't think this is the DoD traitor. He wants me dead." Keely rubbed a hand over her tired eyes. "I think this maneuver smells more like Trujo. He lured Ren out of Idaho by sacrificing those two men who attacked me, knowing we'd track them to Florida and him. Then his men waited for me to leave the security of Sanctuary. I'm just so pissed I fell for the money trail; in hindsight, it was too easy. Ren is gonna ream us all new assholes." She sighed and leaned her head back.

"I'll never get to leave Sanctuary again, not until after the baby is born."

Lacey sat up and gasped. "Who's that coming up the trail?"

Both Keely and Tweeter turned to look where Lacey pointed. "Shit. Shit. Shit," Tweeter said, "Get out of the car and inside the tower base."

Two vehicles followed them up the access road, their lights signaling their approach.

"Dad would kick our butts if we approached an enemy with lights running." Keely opened the rear driver's side door.

"Hey, let's be glad Dad didn't train these fuckers." Tweeter armed himself with a submachine gun he pulled out from under the driver's seat. "Lacey, take this." He handed Quinn's wife his sidearm, which he'd pulled from the holster under his jacket.

Keely was happy to see Lacey knew what to do with it. She picked up the submachine pistol and snagged the extra ammo for it Tweeter had under the seat.

"Let's get settled in and take these fuckers out." Tweeter retrieved a bag out of the back of the Hummer then led the way to the tower which had a cabin at the base for rangers to sleep over during fire season. He shot out the lock with another handgun he'd pulled from the bag, then ushered her and Lacey inside.

"Tweetie, I need to be the one to climb up." She knew he meant to get above the enemy and pick them off. "I'm the better shot. Hand me the sniper rifle you have in that bag."

Her brother frowned but quickly assembled the weapon he'd already begun pulling out. "There's not much protection up there. You'd be better off down here behind the mattress and the walls. No telling what they'll be shooting."

"They don't want me dead, if my guess as to who's behind this attack is correct." She was betting her life and theirs on it. "So, I imagine they'll try to wait us out." She headed for the interior stairs leading to the first exterior platform level. "Plus, the helicopter will be a sitting duck. I need to take as many of them out as I can. Demoralize them, maybe chase them off. I won't let them take pot shots at Ren and the guys."

He didn't argue against her conclusions. "Shit. Ren will kill me."

"Better than Ren being dead. Once he calms down, he'll admit I'm the better shot. You and Lacey can lay down cover fire for me."

Tweeter slammed his hand on a door jamb. "This sucks, sis." He handed her the sniper rifle.

"Ren thinks Tweeter's going up into the tower." Lacey smiled grimly, holding up her Blackberry. "I sort of lied."

"Thanks." Keely started to climb, the sniper rifle slung across her back, extra magazines zipped inside her fur vest.

"Hold it, sis." Tweeter slipped a headset on her, the receiver in her ear and the microphone hugging her cheek. "It's just us on this frequency—for now. Once the guys realize we have ears, they'll single out our frequency." Which meant Ren would know who was on the tower, shooting at the enemy. Well, it wasn't like they could keep it from him forever.

"Thanks. Wish me luck."

As she climbed, a voice shouted from the outside. "*Hola,* you in the cabin. You can't get away. We have your vehicle blocked. We want Keely Walsh. The rest can go free."

"Yeah, sure, right, and I believe in the frick-fracking tooth fairy." She muttered, cautiously sticking her head above the first level platform's floor. She slithered onto the metal decking and remained low.

This platform was about twenty feet in the air and should provide some good shots. Once again she blessed the men of SSI for having weapons with high-caliber bullets. She could take out an armored vehicle at eight hundred yards with the ammo in the sniper rifle. A few assholes would soon become kibbles and bits with the type of firepower she had. She'd take the vehicles out first. Trujo's men would regret picking on a pregnant, hormonal woman.

Her dark clothing allowed her to blend into the metallic structure of the fire tower. The platform had a railing that would allow her to shoot through the slats. She belly-crawled to the side where Trujo's men had parked their vehicles, blocking the trail out. Using the night vision device—or NVD as her Dad liked to call the scope—she zeroed in on the lead vehicle's engine, then found the second vehicle's engine. Looking down, the trajectory for the shot was an easy one hundred yards away. The wind had died down, so no trouble there.

Now to find the mercs. She peeked through the scope again, and found a group of them hovered around the back of the Sanctuary Hummer. The NVD's image enhancement was to military specifications and gave her an excellent view of what they were doing. "Frick-fracking hell."

"What's wrong, sis?" Tweeter's worried voice came over the headset.

"They're pawing through our things. My new lingerie! Perverted bastards."

Tweeter snorted back a laugh. "What's the head count?"

"Hold on a sec, Tweetie." Were all the bastards fingering her bras and thongs? Or had some stayed with the vehicles? She wanted to know where all the targets were before she started shooting. She swept the scope back to the enemy vehicles, soon to be hunks of worthless metal, when she gasped. "Trujo is here." She'd recognize his features, even though they were colored an eerie green due to the NVD. The bastard was just getting back into the lead vehicle.

"Well, shit." She heard Tweeter telling Lacey to inform their team. "The State Police are on their way. Ren called them. Also, a second Sanctuary chopper is on its way with heavier ordnance."

Keely knew that meant air-to-ground missiles. One way or another, Trujo wouldn't get off this mountain alive. She was going to make it sooner.

"I have eight human targets and two engine blocks to blow. I'm ready to take out the vehicles, no wait, I've got a guy sneaking up on the cabin." She aimed at the guy's head. He had to go before the vehicles and Trujo. The bastard was getting too close to Tweeter and Lacey's position. "Give me cover fire so they won't realize where the kill shots are coming from."

They'd figure it out eventually, but by then there wouldn't be as many left to shoot at her. She was a sitting duck; the only protection she had was the metal platform and some metal slats. Armor-piercing rounds would pass through the steel in this tower like a hot knife through butter. She could be wounded or worse.

"Covering your ass now." Tweeter's voice came across the headset.

As Lacey and Tweeter lay down cover fire, Keely took her head shot and got the guy making his way to the cabin before he could respond to the other gunfire. She got one other guy who made the mistake of zigging instead of zagging. "Six bad asses and two vehicles to go."

As her two allies continued to spray the area with bullets, Keely concentrated on the lead vehicle in which Trujo sat, protected, or so he thought. When she was satisfied she had a clear head shot, she took it. He fell from her sight. Then she took another guy out as he responded to the shot she'd put into Trujo. The drug lord could be wounded or dead, she couldn't worry about it. In the spirit of keeping all the bad guys on this mountain, she took out both the enemy's vehicles' engines. Steam billowed from the radiators. Their Hummer was blocked by the disabled vehicles and would be of no use to anyone trying to escape. "Four bad asses left. Vehicles are toast."

"Keely, stand down. Ren is preparing to buzz the area. Protect yourself, baby sis."

"Got it, big brother. You cover your and Lacey's asses."

Staying low, Keely moved away from the front of the platform and got behind the central iron staircase. Not much more protection, but she wasn't where she'd been and that was the best she could do. She needed to stay available in case the four baddies tried to take down the helicopter. Besides only a couple of stray shots had come to her level, so the people on the ground still didn't realize she was up here.

She lay on the cold metal platform, hugging it, and blended in as best she could. Absently she brushed at something warm and wet dripping down her face. Shit, she'd gotten hit by a stray bullet fragment, probably ricocheted off the tower's metal frame. Her face was so cold and numb, she hadn't even felt the fragment strike her. She took a careful inventory and also found a hole in the shoulder of her vest. It was also wet and just beginning to sting. Skinned. A further examination told her she was fine everywhere else. She snuck a hand under her body and rubbed her stomach. "It's okay, little one. You're in the safest place out here. And your daddy is on it."

The whup-whup-whup of the rotors and the buzzsaw noise of the jet helo's powerful engine echoed off the metal frame, vibrating it. Man, they'd come in quick; they were lining up for a strafing run. A few shots from the ground in the general direction of the helo were heard. The four bad asses left weren't giving up.

"Tweeter. Make sure Ren knows I'm up here. I'll cover the helicopter the best I can, but the enemy is mostly under cover now."

"Keely! Get the fuck off the platform and back into the cabin." The rescue team had obviously found the right frequency. Man, Ren sounded furious.

"Fine. Don't thank me for taking out four mercs out of eight plus the two vehicles. If I had a chopper, I would've had them all by now."

Someone laughed. She wasn't sure who, but knew it hadn't been Ren. He just snarled in that I-am-king-of-the jungle way. Yep, he was pissed his little woman hadn't stayed home tending the hearth. Tough.

Grumbling about ungrateful alpha-males, she

shimmied backwards until her feet met empty space where the ladder met the platform. She felt for and found the first step and then carefully lowered herself onto the metal ladder. She wasn't sure the wooden surround of the stairwell was any safer than the platform, but Ren was mumbling over the headset about "stupid fool women," "tying her ass to their bed so she wouldn't run off and get in trouble," and "coming to get her sweet ass down himself." The last threat scared her the most. She'd better move before he did something dumb and got shot.

"I'm climbing down, so stop your griping and watch your own frick-fracking ass." Ren's answer was just another growl. "Fine, be a smart ass. Whoa."

"Keely! What's wrong?" Ren's voice sounded really loud in her ears and made her head pound.

"Um, I'm…" The world began to swirl and fade in-and-out. She stopped and held onto the ladder for dear life. Then she experienced alternating hot and cold flashes and saw white lights flashing across her vision. "Oh, shit."

"Keely! What the fuck is wrong?" She heard panic in his tone, but she couldn't speak to save her life. She choked back bile and attempted to reorient as she held onto the stairs like a tick on a deer. She couldn't move for fear of falling and risking the new life in her womb.

"Sis? Are you sick again?" Tweeter's voice was soft and full of concern.

"Keely? Sick again. What sick? What again?" Ren could be heard telling whoever was flying to get the fucking helo on the ground for cleanup ASAP.

"Ren, I'm fine. Don't take a chance. The mercs have dug in." Nausea swept over her and she coughed and vomited to the side of the ladder. Breathing in shallow, slow breaths, she swallowed the next wave of sickness threatening to overtake her. She couldn't let it take her over, she'd fall off the ladder. She finally managed to speak over the background of Ren's ever-escalating curses. "Come get me, Tweetie. I can't see ... uh, not sure ... I can hold on much longer ... so sick."

"Keely, you hold on. Tweeter, you get your sister down, goddamnit." Ren's voice was hoarse and filled with worry.

"I'll get her, boss. Just watch your ass, she'll need you." Thank God for Tweeter's calm and commonsense. "I see your legs, sis, you're about half-way down." That was still ten feet to fall, though. She could hear her brother's feet on the metal rungs. The vibrations made her sicker. She hugged the ladder as if it were her new best friend.

Tweeter's warmth surrounded her legs, then her body as he shared her ladder rungs. "Shit, sis. You're bleeding."

"Bleeding. Keely! Trey, get those fuckers. I want to be on the ground two minutes ago." Ren was beyond furious as he ordered his brother and the rest of his team to take out the dug-in enemy.

Keely struggled to speak. "It's okay, big guy. Don't … don't do anything to get yourself killed—or arrested." She shuddered through another wave of nausea. "Just got skinned … tired … queasy … that's all." The explanation exhausted her even more, and her vision, what she had left, began to narrow. She couldn't succumb until she calmed Ren down.

"I've got her, Ren. Take your time. She's right, no need to come in all crazy-like." Tweeter placed his hands over hers. "Keely, just let your hands slide down the outside of the railing and let your legs fall free. I'll guide and support you; you won't fall."

"We're on the ground. We have control. Doing cleanup," Ren's voice announced. Double-taps could be heard in the background. "I'm coming in the cabin. Don't shoot me."

Sirens announced the State Police were on their way also. She could relax. Ren was safe. They were safe.

And if her aim had been true, Trujo was dead and one thorn in SSI's and her side was gone. His cartel was effectively shut down.

Keely sighed. "Tweetie, I can't hold on any longer."

"Let go then, sis. I've got you. We're almost down."

Tweeter's strong arm encircled her waist and clamped her body to his. The sensation of falling into a dark abyss was her last conscious thought.

CHAPTER THIRTEEN

Ren sat next to the hospital bed and held Keely's limp hand in his. He massaged her cold fingers while he waited to hear back from the doctor as to her x-rays. He frowned. Something was going on with that. Both Lacey and Tweeter had rushed the doctor and taken him aside. After a whispered conversation among the three, the doctor had shot him a quizzical glance, then nodded at the other two.

What weren't they telling him? Had Keely been sick while he'd been out chasing Trujo sightings? She had indicated as much over her headset. "Come on, baby," he whispered. "Wake up. I need to see those beautiful green eyes."

Keely didn't move. Just lay there.

God, he was scared. She looked so frail in the bed, so tiny, so mortal. She was as white as the sterile sheets. Even her lips were colorless. Dark circles under her eyes were more evidence that she either hadn't been sleeping well or had some illness that no one was telling him about.

After the nurse had left the room, he'd lifted the sheet to check on the wounds from her previous battles. No sign of infection there and some of the scars were even fading. Her current wound was just a gouge and nowhere near life-threatening—or a cause for her continued unconsciousness.

"This keeping things from me has got to stop." He cursed under his breath at the memories of her telling him she was fine each time he'd called from Florida. "You have to tell me when you're sick, baby. I would've come home. You're way more important than some bad guy." Who she'd taken out with one shot to the forehead.

His little love was stubborn and independent and thought she was an Amazon and not a fairy sprite. Must be from having all those alpha-males around her when she was growing up.

The door to the room opened. He jerked, reaching for his Glock, only releasing his grip when he saw the doctor come into the room. He grasped Keely's hand once more.

The doctor's face was a mask of calm. Ren snorted. Bet the guy practiced the expression in the mirror. "Mr. Maddox, everything looks fine. No concussion or skull fractures. The bullets in both instances just grazed her. No need for stitches. Your fiancée will be fine, maybe have a headache for a few days." He'd told the hospital he was Keely's intended so he wouldn't have to threaten the staff with his gun to remain with her. Tweeter had backed him up.

"Why did she faint? Why is she so pale? Why in the fuck is she still unconscious?" Ren's voice got louder with each question.

A murmur and low whimper from the bed had him turning away from the doctor and toward Keely. Her face was scrunched up as if she hurt. He raised the hand he held and kissed the back of her fingers. "Sorry, baby." His voice was a low croon. He switched his attention back to the doctor after soothing Keely. "What's wrong with her?"

The doctor smiled. "Nothing really. Just tired from the hormone overload and early morning sickness.

Don't imagine the adrenaline overload and getting shot helped much. She'll feel more like herself in a month or so once her hormone levels settle out."

"Hormone levels? Morning sickness?" Ren looked at Keely, his other hand going to cover her flat stomach. "She's pregnant?"

"Yes. Very early along. Less than a month, her brother told me, but the hormone levels are a little higher than average. Nothing to be worried about."

Fuck worried. He was terrified. He was elated. He wanted to shout it from the rooftop. He wanted to pull her into his arms, curl around her body, and shelter her and their unborn child.

God! He was going to be a daddy. His little warrior was going to be a mommy. At the thought of what she'd just survived, he wanted to vomit. Keely could've been shot in some place that needed more than a Band Aid. She could've fallen down the ladder from the fucking platform. Things were going to change. His little warrior was now grounded even if he had to chain her to the fucking bed.

Ren tuned back into the doctor's droning soliloquy. "Her brother told me their mother showed pregnancy symptoms earlier than most other women. So this is all genetic, Mr. Maddox. Really nothing to worry about."

Easy for him to say, he didn't know Keely.

"An ultrasound showed the fetus solidly attached in utero." The doctor coughed. "Although I'd suggest keeping her out of gun battles until after the birth. I was told she got dizzy on a ladder, and a fall could harm the baby."

Now that was more like it. He and the doctor were on the same page here. "No worries, doctor. Keely will follow all the rules until she gives birth. Can you recommend a book so I know what she should and shouldn't be doing?"

The doctor laughed. "Her brother said you'd ask something along those lines. He has the materials the OB/GYN in Coeur d'Alene provided Ms. Walsh. I take it she just found out earlier today. We're giving her the vitamins she needs in her IV. Her brother has her prescriptions and some samples for the vitamins the doctor prescribed. She'll do fine, Mr. Maddox. She really is a remarkably healthy young woman. After the morning sickness subsides she'll be back to her normal, energetic healthy self until she gets near the end when her mobility might need to be restricted."

"She'll be more careful period, doctor. I'll see to it personally." Ren gently massaged her abdomen.

"Well, yes, I'm sure you will. She can do the normal

things a woman and mother-to-be would do. Don't be surprised if she wants to paint rooms, clean out closets and the like. It's a nesting instinct."

Ren smiled at the image of her fixing up a nursery for the baby. Maybe she'd want to redo the master bedroom to be something other than the sterile monk's cell it was now. "She can do nesting things all she wants." He sobered and glanced at his hand on her seemingly frail body. "Um, what about sex?"

"Sex is fine. You can't hurt her or the baby." The doctor chuckled. "Some of the best sex my wife and I ever had was during each of her three pregnancies. It's the hormones."

Too much information. Ren didn't want to think of the ascetic-to-the-point-of-asexual doctor having wild monkey sex with his wife.

"When can I take her home? We'll be flying her in the helicopter that brought her here."

"I signed an order that she could be discharged once she wakes up."

Ren petted her belly once more then stood and walked toward the doctor. He held out his hand. "Thank you for everything. I'll go out with you. I need to talk to her brother about a few things."

The doctor shook the proffered hand. "I think

you'll find him and the other people who came with you in the cafeteria."

Ren followed the doctor out and then walked the short distance to the regional hospital's small cafeteria. Tweeter anchored a table along with Lacey, Quinn—who'd refused to stay at home while his wife was in danger—Trey, Vanko and Price. They'd left Scotty in charge of Sanctuary until they got back. Although the crusty old cook wanted to come and rescue the little princess, someone had to stay behind and keep an eye on the new recruits and the security of the base.

"She's pregnant." Ren looked around the table. Gasps and smiles all around. Not a single frown. Keely fit at Sanctuary. She fit him. He smiled. "Does anyone know how fast can we get married in Idaho?"

"You're not mad that Lacey and I knew before you did?" Tweeter asked.

"No. Did she know she was pregnant before she asked you to take her to see a doctor?" Ren was curious, not that it made a hill of beans difference. She was pregnant and she was his.

"No," Tweeter shook his head, "she needed to get a new prescription for birth control pills—and she needed a doctor in general since she planned to stay in Idaho."

Ren was relieved to hear she hadn't kept her pregnancy from him during all those phone calls. He was also relieved to hear she'd planned on staying with him *before* she found out.

Tweeter continued, "Lacey suggested the doctor she uses in Coeur d'Alene so we called ahead and got an appointment and a room."

"She also needed clothes, Ren," Lacey said. "She didn't have the right kind of clothing for a winter in Idaho."

"She had no clothing," Tweeter said. "The rat bastards back in Boston shredded all of her stuff. She was wearing borrowed sweats from Scotty and the few clothes she and Mom bought in Boise on our way here from South America."

"It's okay, guys," Ren said. "I see the need to go to Coeur d'Alene. I'm not blaming anyone for anything." Every eye at the table was on him. Shock was the mood. "Hey, I'm not an ogre."

His brother snorted. "Uh-huh, try Attila the Hun. I heard you tell Keely to stay put until we got back."

"I meant not to follow us to Florida." He was pissed when the others nodded their agreement with Trey's statement. "Of course, now that she's pregnant, she'll need to stay closer to home unless I'm with her to protect her. No more fighting for Keely."

"Oh, geez-fucking-Louise," muttered Tweeter. "That won't wash, Ren. You want to live in peace, you'd better let Keely make those decisions. Give her some credit for being smart enough to know what will and won't hurt her or the baby."

Ren skewered each person with a narrow-eyed glance. "She is not fighting anymore. Period. No guns. No knives. No hand-to-hand. Nothing. She can nest, as the doctor calls it, but that is the limit of her physical activity. I'm asking all of you to help me ride herd on her."

Lacey laughed and grabbed Quinn's hand. His third-in-command smiled and shook his head.

"What?" Ren couldn't help scowling. Quinn and his wife were laughing at him.

"Ren, women aren't helpless or weak when they're pregnant, especially women as strong and healthy as Keely." Lacey sent a teasing glance to her husband. "Ask Quinn. He tried the do-nothing approach when I was pregnant both times and failed…"

"Both times." Quinn chuckled and kissed Lacey on the mouth. "Yeah, take the advice of an old married man and father of two." He raised his wife's hand to his mouth for a gentle knuckle-nibble. "This woman even chopped wood. Rode horses. Did bench aerobics, yoga and weight-lifting. All of that plus rearranging the damn house four times."

The older man shook his head, his lips twisted into a wry grin. "Hell, the day she gave birth to our first, she was in labor for eight hours before she told me. She fucking played tennis—and won—then calmly came home and took a shower, during which her water broke. She got dressed, came out and got me up from a nap, and then announced we were having the baby. I went ballistic—she fucking ended up driving us both to the hospital."

"Keely will do what I tell her." Ren's heart was in his throat, where it had been since the doctor told him he was going to be a father. "She's tiny—and needs to be more careful."

"The doctor tell you that?" Trey asked, his eyes smiling.

"No, but…"

"Then I expect that Keely will do what she wants while she's carrying my niece or nephew," Trey said. "I also know she's smart enough to be careful and monitor her own activities without your help."

Vanko nodded, joining the chorus against him and his edicts. "My sister is much like Keely, and she cut back on her own during her pregnancies. She also did that to make her husband happy. I expect Keely will do so to make you happy, Ren. So don't worry about it. Women have been having babies for thousands of years and managing to survive."

"Yeah, look at our mother," Tweeter added. "Mom's smaller than Keely and had a set of twins and four others."

"Twins?" Ren gulped and reached for a glass of water, all of a sudden sick to his stomach. "No. She can't have twins. That would be too much."

"I'm not having twins, but if I were, you couldn't do much about it after the fact, big guy." Keely's soft voice came from behind him. He whirled around and pulled her to him, his face pressed to her stomach over where his child lay. He let her go only long enough to pull her onto his lap.

"Baby, you sure you should be up?" He looked around for a nurse. "Where's your fucking wheelchair? You shouldn't be walking around."

She snuggled her face into the crook of his neck and shoulder. "I escaped after the nurse took out the IV. She helped me get dressed. Then I waited and you didn't come back. So, I came to find you."

"Shit, Keely. You have to be careful. You fainted,

baby." He rubbed her back as he kissed her hair, her ear, her cheek. "We're getting married right away."

She raised her head and glared at him. "Why? Because I'm carrying your baby?"

"You're carrying *our* baby," he corrected. "I already had the ring and planned on courting you, but the timetable just got advanced a month or so."

"You have the ring?" Her face brightened. "Really?"

"Yep. It's back at Sanctuary—in the safe. Three-carat solitaire, princess cut for my warrior princess, set in platinum. I was going to give it to you after I softened you up to the idea."

"Consider me softened." She leaned into him and kissed his jaw, then snuggled her head back on his shoulder. "You happy about the baby?" She sounded meek, worried. He couldn't have that.

"Ecstatic—and scared. You?"

"The same." She rubbed a hand over his chest. "So, when?"

Everyone at the table watched and grinned. Ren could feel the love and support from his friends, his brother, and his soon-to-be brother-in-law. "That's what I was trying to find out from these yahoos before they started lecturing me on the care and feeding of pregnant warrior sprites."

"All you have to do is love me, Ren." Keely kissed his cheek and nuzzled him along his jaw. "The rest will fall in place."

"God knows, I love you, Keely Ann Walsh." He kissed her reverently on the lips; it was a promise, a pledge that he would love and care for her forevermore.

Keely opened to his kiss, setting his libido aflame. He pulled her into his body, taking control of the kiss from her, his tongue thrusting into her mouth, reclaiming what was his. His little warrior sucked on his tongue, tangling hers with his, and showed him right back that she also burned with the desire to reclaim what was hers.

"Yeah, we'd better get these two hitched and find them a room." Lacey laughed. "No waiting period or residency requirements in Idaho for a license. Just money for the fee and a birth certificate and a driver's license as identification."

"Good." Ren nuzzled the side of Keely's neck, inhaling her sweet musk. "We'll go to Grangeville and get the license after you rest up, baby."

"I'm fine. Just the morning sickness seems to come whenever it frick-fracking feels like."

Everyone laughed at her disgruntled tone.

"Like I said, we'll go when you *feel* up to it.

Shouldn't take long to do the paperwork." Ren pulled her even closer into his body. He was content. She was safe in his arms. "Do you want to be married in a church, sweetheart?"

"Not really." Keely stroked a hand over his chest. "When we get the license, let's see if a judge can marry us right then and there." She frowned and sighed. "Well, maybe not. Mama would kill me for eloping. She always wanted to see Daddy walk me down the aisle."

Ren squeezed her waist. "No problem, sweetheart. Call your family. We can fly them out here for a private ceremony at Sanctuary. We'll have a Christmas wedding; it's only a week away and you won't be leaving my side anyway. Besides I'd love to see you dressed up like the fairy princess you are."

"I love you." She smiled, a glorious smile that warmed him to his soul, then kissed him. She lay her head down on his shoulder and yawned. "Take me home, Ren."

"Just what I had in mind, baby."

Chapter Fourteen

Two and a half months later

Waking, Keely stretched, her foot sliding down the hairy calf of her lover—and husband of over two months. They'd gotten married on Christmas Eve, white dress and all. She smiled as sunlight reflecting off her rings caught her eye. She was married, pregnant, and finally free of the debilitating 24/7 morning sickness with a clean bill of health for her and the baby after an ultrasound the day before. Now all she needed was some hot and heavy sex with her man before she got to the waddling and swollen ankle stages of her pregnancy.

Ren had other ideas. While he wasn't going

without sex, he was being super-careful of her. Slow build-ups. Lots of petting and oral. Shallow thrusting in missionary style where he controlled all penetration. And while she always had mind-blowing orgasms, she wanted more. She wanted some deep thrusting, multiple orgasms and varying positions—the kind of sex her man had given her after she forced the issue with him the first time. The kind of sex that had gotten her pregnant. And she sure as heck wasn't waiting for it until after the baby was born.

Recalling the doctor visit that had assured both of them the baby and she were both fine, she smiled. Ren's awe-struck expression as he viewed their little jumping bean of a baby on the monitor had been priceless. He'd almost burst his buttons—and had shown the screen shots to about everyone at Sanctuary after they'd gotten home last night.

"Baby? You okay?" Ren's sleep-drowsy voice had her sex clenching and her nipples puckering. His big hand covering her stomach made her melt. He was so protective, so loving, and far too careful of her welfare since the pregnancy. She'd allowed him to get away with it because she'd had morning sickness. But that was gone—and she wanted her alpha male back.

"I'm … well…" she trailed off, all of a sudden

shy about asking for raunchy sex when the sex they'd been having had been wonderful—vanilla—but still probably better than a lot of other women ever had.

Ren leaned up. "What's wrong, Keely? You sick again?" His concerned gaze swept over her face as his hand massaged the place where their child grew.

"No," she turned into his body, her hand reaching for his cock lying hard and firm between them. "I'm horny. I want sex—and I want to be on top." She blushed, but managed to make eye contact.

His nostrils flared and his grey-blue eyes turned smoky grey with lust. "You want me to make love to you, baby? My pleasure."

He moved to pull her under him. She shoved his shoulder, tipping him onto his back. "No. I said I want to be on top this time. Then later tonight you can take me from behind. No more missionary unless I ask for it. I want the sex life we had before you found out I was pregnant."

"Keely … sweetheart…" His tone was the kind a parent used to reason with a recalcitrant two-year-old.

Cutting off his next words, she managed to contain her anger at the paternal attitude, but just barely. "No! I'm an adult." She climbed over his nude and highly aroused body, trapping his outer thighs between hers as she settled her butt on his tight quads. Then she pulled out her ace in the hole. "I called my mom last night. I asked her about deep, balls-to-the-wall sex during pregnancy. And she said go for it. Like you, my Dad was hesitant at first, but gave in, and Mom said he never regretted it. I'm asking you to give in to me."

His hands grabbed her hips and pulled her forward until her wet cleft snugged his throbbing cock. "I called your Dad—at your brother's suggestion." He threw her a sexy, but cheeky, grin. "Your Dad told me to stop being a candy-assed wuss and take you like the dominant male I am."

She threw back her head and laughed. "Neither one of us will ever be able to look my parents in the face again."

Ren pulled her down until her breasts touched his chest. "Kiss me. Take me, my little warrior."

Keely braced herself on one arm and tipped his chin with the other hand. "I love you." She nibbled at his lower lip until he let her into his mouth. Frenching him, she wiggled her ass until she felt his tip lodged at her opening. Breaking off the kiss, she said, "Put your cock in me."

His mouth tilted upward as his smoldering gaze captured hers. The sensual promises she read in his eyes had her shivering in anticipation. He reached between their bodies and nudged the head of his cock inside her very wet sex. "Like that?" His lips brushed hers in a sweet, tender kiss.

"Oh yeah. Just like that." She kissed him once more, a deep kiss of love and claiming. Her vaginal opening clenched and unclenched around the tip of his cock. The rhythm matched her ever-escalating heart rate. Letting go of his mouth, she sat up, arching her back, rising slightly to change the angle of penetration. She let his cock head slide out just a bit, then took him back in, settling ever more firmly upon his turgid length until he was seated completely.

"Oh fuck. You are so tight." His face was strained with passion. His breaths came heavy and fast. His body, rigid with the effort not to move. "Take me, love." He reached for her hips.

"No hands." She moved them to the side of his head. "I'm in charge here. Just lie back and enjoy while I do all the work for a change."

His gaze on her was intense. "What about your pleasure?"

"Oh, don't worry about that, big guy. I'm so close right now I'm worried I'll come before you."

"Sweetheart. Do it. I'm ready to burst."

She smiled. "Then we don't have an issue, do we?" Bracing her hands on his shoulders, she watched his face as she began to ride his cock. God, he was gorgeous in his passion. His ardent gaze never left her. She saw his pleasure reflected in his smoke-blue gaze. His sculpted cheeks flushed with his increasing arousal. His mobile lips opened as his breathing became harsh, erratic. She leaned over and took his mouth, letting him breathe for both of them.

As she increased her pace, his hips rose to meet her downward movements. Her clit rubbed against his pelvic bone and set her to quivering with each thrust. His groans punctuated her moans and gasps as they strove to reach the heights of passion together.

His impending climax transmitted itself to her as his body arched to meet her and his hands fisted by his head as if he could hold off his eruption until she came.

"Let go, big guy." She licked his lips, trailing her tongue to his ear. "When you come, I'll come. I promise."

Her whispered words did the trick. His roar as he climaxed echoed around the high-ceilinged bedroom. His hands grabbed her hips, holding her to him, taking control as he pounded into her from below. As his cum flooded her sex, she ground her pelvis against him, giving her clit the pressure she needed to soar. She screamed as she peaked then tipped over the edge. She rode him hard and fast—and deep, squeezing every iota of pleasure from their journey—and a fabulous journey it was. In that ultimate moment of connection, she had all of her man—heart, body and soul. It was an experience she wanted again and again for the rest of their lives.

As Ren's body relaxed into the bed, she continued to ride him, a sinuous rhythm and motion that brought them down, her body reluctant to give up his solid warmth. When his cock finally slipped from her, she trembled at the loss. Ren pulled her to him until she lay flat on top of him, her barely-there baby bump nestled between them, then gently shoved her head onto his shoulder. He stroked her from neck to bottom. "You okay, baby?" He kissed her sweaty forehead.

"Oh hell yeah." She nuzzled his neck. "We need to do that again—and really soon."

He laughed, his breath ruffling her hair. "Well, give me a chance to recover, and we'll discuss it. Plus, didn't you mention rear entry?"

She nodded, her hair catching in his morning beard growth. "Yeah. I figured over the back of the couch, so I can look out at the snow-covered mountains while you take me from behind. Let's give the moose and other wild animals a thrill."

He clutched her to him as he laughed. "It's a plan. Later, when it's dark and all the two-legged creatures are in bed. Right now, I need a shower and some food. How about you?"

"As long as we shower together, yeah. I still need some skin time, even if it is just bathing one another. Today for breakfast, I want one of Scotty's spicy chili omelets. I'm tired of the pap I've been eating because of all the morning sickness."

Ren lifted her off him. "Sounds good to me. Then what do you want to do today?"

She eyed him. "Go to the Bat Cave and help my brother track that frick-fracking traitor." She smoothed a hand over his bed-rumpled hair. "He's still out there, big guy. And you and other contract operators—and our U.S. Special Forces teams—aren't safe until his bad ass is caught."

"While the bastard's been lying low, we can't count on him not resuming business as usual. He was making too much fucking money to give it up for long. He needs to be taken out, if for no other reason than he has you in his sights. Bannon will have seen to that."

She frowned. "Do you think Bannon is even alive?

We haven't found a trace of him anywhere. The traitor either got Bannon a new ID or…"

"Killed him," finished Ren, "just like Bannon killed Jordan." Jordan's body had been found in a remote area of the Nez Perce Forest by a ranger. No signs of Bannon anywhere. Keely shivered. "Let's get that hot shower, baby. You're cooling off after that hot bout of sex." He grinned and kissed her. "Which I thank you very much for, by the way."

"You're very welcome." She didn't let him know her shivering wasn't because she was cold—it was more preternatural in nature. Her neck itched like crazy. Something bad was about to happen, and she didn't know what, when, where or who. She could only be vigilant.

Chapter Fifteen

"More bacon, Keely?"

She patted her tummy and shook her head. "No, thanks, Scotty. Junior and I are full."

Ren reached over and stroked her back. "Junior?"

"Yeah. When the baby was doing back flips in utero I saw two dangly things—the cord and a teeny-tiny penis. I thought you saw it, too."

"Ah, no." Ren pulled out the pictures the ultrasound tech had given them. He carried them in his wallet. He looked at them carefully and passed them to her brother who'd joined them for breakfast at the Lodge. "What do you think, Uncle Tweeter? Nephew or not?"

Tweeter studied the photos for a second or two. "Nephew."

"We're having a boy." Ren hugged her.

"Happy?" She leaned into his embrace.

"Elated." He kissed her ear. "How's the little mommy feeling?"

"Full—and not sick for a change, thank you Jesus." She took a drink of her juice. "Ready to do some work downstairs." She glanced at her brother who'd just shoved his plate away. "You ready to track some bad guys, Uncle Tweetie?"

Her brother shot her a grin. "Oh hell yeah. The program you created is ingenious, but it creates a lot of trails to follow. I could use some help fine-tuning the code to be more selective."

"Shouldn't be too hard." She turned to Ren. "I'll be down in the Bat Cave with my brother and three levels of security between me and the outside world. That do it for you?"

"That's an affirmative." He leaned over and kissed the tip of her nose. "I'll be out training with the men. Trey and Price want me to help weed out the recruits we aren't keeping on."

She frowned. "I've kept you from your work these past few months."

"Not an issue." He pulled her onto his lap and stroked her back. "I wouldn't have traded these past months for anything. Trey and the guys have handled things just fine. And now that we're taking on more operatives, I can stay out of the field even more. Do more recruiting, training, and operations planning."

"Will you miss the field?" She played with the hair at the nape of his neck.

He turned his head and kissed her neck. "No. I've got better things to do than to get my ass shot at. Face it, I'm getting old. It takes a lot more recovery time between jobs and injuries than it used to. Security work at this level is for younger guys. Plus now, I have a wife and a baby to keep me at home. I'm more than ready for that, sweetheart."

"Good." She kissed his jaw just under his ear. "I was worried I was cramping your style."

He whispered for her ears alone. "I'd rather wake up to what we had this morning than be sitting in some jungle for days waiting for my kill shot."

She laughed. "So glad I rate above sniping."

"You rate above it all, sweetheart." He kissed her once more, then lifted her off his lap, and tapped her butt. "Go to work. I'll see you at lunch."

"Yeah. I'm already thinking about chili with lots of

cheese—and dill pickle chasers."

Tweeter and Ren laughed as Scotty muttered, "Damn, got to make more chili before lunch. At this rate, I need to buy beef futures."

Ren left the Lodge and followed the cleared path to the barn they used for indoor training and workouts. It had snowed again overnight. At this time of the year, they always had two to three feet of snow on the ground. The pathways between the main buildings and lodgings now had packed snow walls along them. From the air, it looked like a snow maze. Maybe later he'd have the new recruits do some cat-and-mouse pursuits using the plowed paths. A few obstacles blocking the ends of some of the walkways and they could do some mock urban warfare.

More and more of their jobs for corporate clients involved rescuing kidnapped employees and executives in third-world cities. Usually, they mock-battled such rescues in the barn by constructing temporary walls; using the snow-lined paths would add the environment as an additional obstacle. Besides, they could always receive a job for a rescue in Siberia or somewhere equally as cold. It had been awhile since he had recruits do Arctic drills since a lot of their business was in the many jungles and deserts of third world countries, but that was no excuse to neglect cold-weather-warfare.

He shoved open the door to the barn. Trey had the ten recruits doing hand-to-hand combat. Today was Krav Maga, the Israeli special forces street fighting martial art. He preferred it and had been amazed when he'd found out that Keely had learned it from her twin brothers. It had probably saved her life in South America, that and her ability to knife fight.

His lips tilted into a slight smile. This morning's girl-on-top sex was all about his little warrior telling him she wasn't a fragile little female. Now that she wasn't throwing up two times a day—and hadn't that scared the shit out of him—she'd be back to her usual fighting weight and demand on being treated as a partner and not a helpless little woman.

He sighed. He was more than willing to resume a more active level of sex in their bed—and elsewhere—but fighting hand-to-hand and gun battles were still not on his list of "Things Keely Could Do." There would be hell to pay for him holding that opinion, but Keely would soon learn that he'd allow nothing and no one to harm her—not even herself. He didn't care how healthy she was and how safe the baby was in her womb, she was not a warrior. She was a mother-to-be and his woman. She could save all body contact sports for their bed. The jury was still out on sniping. She was the best damn sniper he'd ever seen, and he'd insist she keep her skills up. Even he knew that all his good intentions to keep her safe could go awry—and a gun was the best equalizer a woman had.

"Yo, Ren." Trey's fingers snapped in front of his face. "Wake up. Where's your head? Still in bed with that woman of yours?"

The men in the room all laughed.

Ren glared and the room went silent. He turned to his brother. "Let's leave Keely and our bed out of the training room."

Trey put up his hands. "Sorry. Touchy this morning. What's wrong? Is she sick again?"

His brother's voice held only concern, and Ren knew Trey had only been teasing. He needed to lighten up. Because of the no-women rule, the single men tended to tease the married ones. It was just Trey being one of the guys, and envious of Ren's good fortune.

"No, in fact, she ate more food than I've ever seen her eat. Your nephew is one hungry little baby."

"Nephew?" Trey's eyes lit up. "For real?"

Ren grinned. "Yeah, I didn't notice the little penis on the photos until it was pointed out to me. A son—

I'm having a son."

Trey slapped him on the back. "Way to go, daddy. Now how about helping me whip these sissies into shape?"

"Yeah." Ren stripped off his jacket. "Later we'll do some icy urban street mock warfare on the grounds. The snow walls along the walkways are high enough to provide cover now."

"Good idea," Trey said. "Never know when crazy Icelanders might start kidnapping corporate executives to make money for their bankrupt country."

Ren snorted and kicked his brother in the ass. "Fucking comedian, aren't you?"

"Yeah, asswipe. Let's show these guys some moves."

Trey threw a vicious punch which Ren blocked and the training began.

———

VANKO STOOD NEXT TO REN as they observed the activity on the grounds from the roof of the Lodge, the highest vantage point to give them an overview of the mock street battle taking place below them in the snow maze.

"Good idea, Ren." Vanko's gaze fixed on the two teams—black ski caps for baddies and white for good guys—playing out a running gun battle with simulated ammo that left red splats when the victim got hit. The ammo was similar to paint balls.

Ren eyed one guy on the white team. "What do you think about Risto Smith?" As Vanko watched the tall, dark-haired former Marine, Ren reviewed what he knew about the recruit. Of Finnish and Native American descent, Smith had been a LRRP in Afghanistan, the kind of guy that lived on the land for days and gathered intel for his Marine superiors. His military record showed two tours in Afghanistan and before that he'd seen his first duty as a regular grunt straight out of high school in Iraq. Smith had mustered out, gone back home to Upper Peninsula Michigan, and realized he couldn't hack civilian life or a civilian job. He applied to SSI and here he was.

Vanko finally replied. "Good man. Likes the cold. Told me he hated Iraq and loved being in Afghanistan at the higher altitudes and in the snow. Also told me his hometown gets over 200 inches of snow on the ground in a normal year. Makes me homesick for my home in the northern Ukraine."

"Sort of has an unfair advantage here." Ren chuckled. "Trey and Price both like him and he passed Keely's enhanced background check. We'll take him on. He stated on his application he'd like to work out of his U.P. home, but has no problem being stationed here, if required. Guess he has a private island in the Cisco Chain of Lakes area. We need someone in the Midwest."

"Good to have someone that close to central Canada and the border. Lots of drug running, smuggling of other kinds and potential for terrorists crossing into the U.S."

"Yeah, that there is." Ren made a note on his data pad. "We'll invite him to eat with us this evening. Talk money and equipment needs for that private island of his. We can negotiate it as a secondary SSI staging and training site."

"No need for electronic equipment from what I hear," Vanko said. "Risto's a geek like Tweeter and Keely. He was waxing poetic with Tweeter about some new server he built. Keely overheard and the three of them talked in a language none of the rest of us could understand."

"Keely spoke with him?" Ren turned to look at Vanko. "When was this?"

"A week or so ago. You were on a conference call." Vanko jabbed him in the gut. "She wasn't alone with him. She only sees you as a man, you know. The rest of us are brothers and buddies. Risto was really respectful. He'd even read some of her published papers."

He nodded. "Understood. I didn't realize she was interacting with the men so much. She's been so sick."

"Well, yeah." Vanko laughed. "She only sat there for about twenty minutes, then she turned green and ran for the bathroom. I'm glad she's over the sickness. I was beginning to get sympathy nausea."

"You and me both." He smiled and made another note to ask Keely what she thought about Risto on a personal level and not on the data she'd obtained. The sound of gunfire and breaking glass had him scanning the mock battleground. "That was live ammo. Where in the fuck did that shot come from? And what got broken?" A bullet whizzing by his cheek and hitting the wood of the door leading onto the roof had him ducking. "We're under attack!" He switched his headset on. "Trey, I just got shot at. Get those men weaponed up and secure the perimeter of the Lodge."

Trey's voice. "Roger that."

"The sniper is about five hundred yards east of here on a ridge. Permission to go nail his ass."

"Who's this?"

"Risto Smith, sir. I can get him."

"Risto, get live ammo and take someone to cover

your ass."

Price's voice. "I'm with Risto. I also saw where the shot came from. We're on it."

"Anybody have a sit rep on what window got hit?" Ren and Vanko made their way from the roof, down into the back of the Lodge.

"Great room window." Quinn's growling tones instantly recognizable. "Hit my damn scotch."

"Lock down the basement. I don't want Keely upstairs until this is over." Ren shoved his way into the house.

"Too late, big guy."

"Keely," Ren groaned. "Where the fuck are you, baby?"

"Patching up Quinn since Lacey isn't here to do it. He neglected to mention he was holding the scotch at the time."

"He okay?" Ren entered the back hallway at a jog and headed for the great room and Keely.

"Yes. Just a scratch." She muttered something he didn't catch. "Quinn is being very brave. He gets a sucker."

Quinn's amused snort came over the headset clearly. "I'll take that sucker as long as it is scotch-flavored and 120 proof. Now get your ass back downstairs, missy."

Ren crouched and duck-walked into the great room, the vast expanse of glass and one broken pane leaving anyone in the room open to being shot. "Where are you two?"

"Behind the bar," Keely said.

Reaching a control panel, Ren activated the metal blinds that would seal out anything but armor-piercing bullets or bombs. As the shield descended, several shots could be heard pinging off it. When the room was sealed off, he stood and moved swiftly to the bar. Keely held Quinn's head on her lap. Blood was everywhere. It had been more than a scratch.

"Shit. How bad?" He gestured for Keely to lift up the bloody towel she'd put on the wound in Quinn's shoulder. "Bullet still in there?"

"No," Quinn gritted through his teeth, "it's not. Where's Lacey?"

"I put out the alert. She should be underground with the other women, the techs and clerical staff." He looked at the two of them. "Which is where both of you are going now."

Vanko had come up and stood behind him. He'd gone to get weapons for them both and to clear out the upper floors and seal off the windows.

"Vanko, help me get them downstairs. Then we'll

go to war."

"I'll watch the holo-table and give you bogey positions." Keely helped him shift Quinn off her lap. "I came up to ask you if the hot spots I saw were the recruits or not, since we haven't given them I.D. with their own codes yet. Tweetie is feeding intel to Price and Trey on the unkowns."

Keely had improved the table so they could tell which signatures were the home team and which weren't. Every full-time operative, tech and woman on Sanctuary had a unique signature embedded in a card they carried at all times. The system should give them an advantage in the coming fight.

Vanko and Ren lifted Quinn off the floor and helped the wounded man to the elevator to the basement where the Sanctuary non-combatants would congregate.

"Keely, we got this. You go and help Tweeter in the Bat Cave," Ren said.

"We'll give you good intel, big guy." She stood on tiptoe and kissed him. "Watch your ass. I'm fond of it, you know."

He nodded. "But not as fond as I am of yours. Stay safe, baby."

Keely backtracked to the hall leading to the elevator for the Bat Cave. As she moved toward her goal, she got the sense she was being followed. Yeah, her neck itched. Shit. She touched her headset. "Ren, there's…" Her com device was ripped off her head before she could get the full warning out.

Two large arms wrapped around her middle and lifted her off the floor. "Got you, bitch."

"Bannon."

"Yeah. Meet my buddy." The man swung her around. Vences stood there, grinning like a loon. He had a coded card so Tweeter would not have seen him as a bogey. Bannon would have been a blip with a properly identified inhabitant.

"You had the naive act down pretty good, Vences. And your cover held up a lot better than Jordan's and Bannon's."

"Because it was all true." Vences leered at her. "Bannon recruited me after I came here, little *mamacita*."

"You preggers, bitch?" Bannon's hot breath blew past her ear. He roughly felt her stomach. "Ah, yeah, knocked up for sure. Never had me a pregnant woman before." Her skin wanted to shrivel up at his touch. The stink of his sweat brought back the nausea with a vengeance.

"And you aren't having one now." Ren would be here in a second and Bannon and company would be dead. They had no idea Ren was in the Lodge. Bannon dragged her uncooperative body toward the back entrance to the Lodge. She wondered how they'd gotten past Scotty—and where Ren and Vanko would make their moves.

"We're going for a ride. The big boss wants to ask you some questions. Seems your little cyber-programs have boxed out his jobs, cutting into his bottom-line. His bosses at DoD are looking at everyone, especially him, more closely now because of all your reports. He wants it stopped—and you dead. Sorry, baby. But I promise to make your last days memorable."

"Big boss? He's here? In Idaho?" She needed info and fast. She sensed Ren was close.

"Yeah. Makes you feel special, doesn't it?" Bannon bit her neck.

Because Ren was close and because the damn bite hurt, she screamed. Then she turned into Bannon, grabbing for his detestable hard-on and twisted it as she hooked a leg back and tripped the son of a bitch. She fell to the floor with him as he lost his balance. She managed to roll out from under his heavy weight, protecting her tummy with her arms. His hands were too busy cupping his tortured equipment to grab her. Vences headed for her, his arms reaching. She rolled away and managed to scramble to her knees to crawl toward the doorway.

Ren and Vanko slid around the edge, guns in hand. Bannon had his gun drawn but instead of aiming it at the two men, he had her in his sights. She hugged the floor, giving her man a shot. Three shots rang out simultaneously. She felt the whisper of Bannon's shot over her head as it hit the doorframe. She turned. The other shots took down Bannon and Vences.

"Make sure they're down," Ren ordered Vanko. He went to his knees and pulled her into his arms. "Baby, you okay? God, the fucker's shot just missed. Sweetheart, where are you hurt? You screamed." He patted her all over, brushing wood fragments from her hair, his thumb whisking across a bloody scrape from one piece of wood that had struck her forehead. "Jesus-fucking-Christ, that was too close. Status, Vanko?"

"Bannon's dead. Good shot, boss. Vences is wounded and will live, but not happily. I sort of aimed for his crotch."

Ren kept touching and scanning her for wounds. If she had the energy, she would have told him she was fine, but all she could do was let him care for her. She needed him to care for her. He rubbed her tummy as she shuddered and gasped for breath as the aftermath continued to hit her with a vengeance. He was right—it had been too damn close. If she hadn't hugged the floor … well, no use thinking about what might have happened.

"Fuck!" His piercing gaze had found the spot where Bannon had bitten her. He gently soothed the mark on her neck with a shaky thumb. "Goddamnit, baby, the fucking bastard bit you. You're white as the snow and shaky. You could be going into shock. We need to get you to a doctor."

"Shh, big guy. I'm fine. The baby's fine. Vences let him in, you know," she said in an attempt to distract him. "Vences' cover was good since it was real. His only lies were about his depth of military experience. He joined the other side here." And she was babbling. She took a breath and let it out, then took another. She had to calm down or Ren would lose it. He was really upset, probably more so than she was.

Ren gathered her into his arms and stood up. She could feel her big strong man tremble against her. "Lacey can look at the bite and clean it. You're fucking bleeding, Keely. We'll need to see your doctor as soon as possible to make sure you and the baby are really okay—and we need to ask about antibiotics for whatever germs the fucker left. No arguing, baby."

"Ren, sweetie," she stroked his beard-roughened face, "I'm okay ... really."

"I need to hear that from a doctor. Just humor me." He kissed the top of her head.

She sighed. He would do what he needed to do and she would let him. She loved him too much to let him worry. "Bannon told me the big boss is here in Idaho. The traitor wanted to interrogate me about what I'd done to shut down his business. I expect he wanted to figure out how to work around my programs now that NSA has them in place." She rubbed her cheek on his shoulder, inhaling his clean, unique scent to chase out the stink Bannon had left in her nostrils. "He was going to hurt me. Hurt our baby. I'd never have let him. You know that, right?"

"I know. But I'm glad it didn't get that far. God, baby, when you got cut off like that, I couldn't get back upstairs fast enough."

Vanko handed Vences off to Trey then paced them as Ren carried her through the great room. "Keelulya, I have never seen Ren in a berserker rage before. Made the ancient Vikings look like candy-assed pansies. I just stayed out of his way and covered his ass."

Keely smiled. "You're a good friend, Vanko. I knew you both would come. I only had to keep him talking and slow him down until you did."

Ren carried her along the plowed path to their cabin. She was pretty sure his goal was their bedroom and her taking a nap once her neck was treated. She wasn't going to argue with him over any of it. The baby made her sleepy at the oddest moments. She had a feeling naps were in her daily plans for the foreseeable future. "What about the big boss? He's somewhere close by." Keely yawned.

"He could be anywhere. Elk City. Grangeville," Ren said. "If we get one of the other attackers alive, we'll ask. But I suspect that only Bannon knew who he was."

At the sound of self-disgust in his voice, she looked at him. "Listen here, Renfrew Maddox. That man would've killed me—killed our baby—you had to kill him. We'll get the asshole who hired Bannon and the others. I promise. Besides, Bannon gave me two clues."

"I can guess the one—the traitor was not in D.C. but here. We can check out our prime suspects' whereabouts," Ren said. "But what's the other one?"

"That he's already under investigation by the

DoD." Keely snuggled her head onto his shoulder and sighed. "That means he's already under investigation *by me* because what the DoD knows, I know. NSA just hired me earlier today to look into five men. These are the only five men who could've sent you and other independent contractors into death traps. The only five men who could've had under-the-table business with Trujo at all. The only five men who could influence where U.S. Special Forces teams could go for black ops." She grabbed a fistful of his shirt. "I have them all in my sight, and I will uncover what they ate at their first birthday if I have to in order to find them. They'll rue the day they invaded my home and endangered my man and my baby."

"God, I love you, Keely Ann Walsh-Maddox." His kissed her forehead. "Not every man is lucky enough to have his own warrior sprite."

"Glad you finally realized that, big guy, 'cause I'm fighting at your side, not behind you from here on out. We'll protect what's ours." She yawned, ruining her position of strength statement and causing Ren and Vanko to chuckle. Well, let them laugh. She'd straighten them out—after her nap.

THE END

About The Author

Monette is a lawyer/arbitrator living with her retired pathologist husband in Carmel, Indiana. She also writes under the pen name Rae Morgan. You can visit her web site at http://www.monettemichaels.com.

Other Books by this Author

Writing as Monette Michaels:

DEATH BENEFITS

GREEN FIRE

THE VIRTUOUS VAMPIRE
A GOODEN AND KNIGHT MYSTERY, CASE FILE #1

THE DEADLY SÉANCE
A GOODEN AND KNIGHT MYSTERY, CASE FILE #2

COLD DAY IN HELL
BOOK 2 OF THE SECURITY SPECIALISTS INTERNATIONAL
(COMING 2012)

PRIME OBSESSION
BOOK 1 OF THE PRIME CHRONICLES

VESTED INTERESTS

Writing as Rae Morgan:

DESTINY'S MAGICK
BOOK 1, COVEN OF THE WOLF SERIES

MOON MAGICK
BOOK 2, COVEN OF THE WOLF SERIES

TREADING THE LABYRINTH
BOOK 3, COVEN OF THE WOLF SERIES

"NO SECRETS"
BOOK 4 IN COVEN OF THE WOLF,
IN THE ZODIAC: PISCES ANTHOLOGY

EARTH AWAKENED

A TERRAN REALM BOOK

ENCHANTRESS

"EVANESCENCE," IN THE EDGE OF NIGHT ANTHOLOGY

"ONCE UPON A PRINCESS," IN AIN'T YOUR MAMA'S
BEDTIME STORIES

Made in the USA
Lexington, KY
12 December 2011